POPULAR STORIES

ABOUT

GENII, FAIRIES, AND MAGICIANS.

FIRST APPEARANCE OF THE GENIE OF THE LAMP.

ALADDIN; OR, THE WONDERFUL LAMP.

CHAPTER I.

HOW ALADDIN MEETS WITH A WICKED AFRICAN MAGICIAN, WHO PRETENDS THAT HE IS HIS UNCLE, AND WHO INDUCES HIM TO ENTER AN ENCHANTED CAVE IN SEARCH OF THE WONDERFUL LAMP.

A GREAT many years ago, in the capital of one of the richest and most extensive kingdoms of Cathay, there lived a tailor, named Mustafa, who had no other distinction than that of his trade. This tailor was very poor, his profits barely producing enough for himself, his wife, and a son, with which Heaven had blessed him, to subsist upon.

Mustafa's son, whose name was Aladdin, had been brought up in a very negligent manner, and had been left so much to himself that he had contracted the most vicious habits of idleness and mischief, and had no reverence for the commands of his father or mother. Before he had passed the years of childhood his parents could no longer keep him in the house. He generally went out early in the morning, and spent the whole day in playing in the public streets with boys who were as idle as himself.

No. I.

When he was old enough to learn a trade, his father, being unable to have him taught any other than that he himself followed, took him to his shop, and began to show him how he should use his needle. But neither kindness nor the fear of punishment could restrain his mischievous and restless disposition. No sooner was Mustafa's back turned, than Aladdin was off, and returned no more during the whole day. His father continually chastised him, still Aladdin remained incorrigible; and Mustafa, to his great sorrow, was obliged to abandon him to his idle, vagabond kind of life. This conduct gave the father great pain, and the vexation of not being able to induce him to pursue a proper and reputable course of life, brought on so obstinate and fatal a disease, that after a few months it put an end to his existence.

As Aladdin's mother saw that her son never would follow the trade of his father, she shut up his shop, and converted all his stock and implements of trade into money, upon which, added to what she could earn by spinning cotton, she and her son subsisted.

Aladdin now, no longer restrained by the dread of his father, and regarding his mother so little that he even threatened her with violence whenever she attempted to remonstrate with him, gave himself completely up to a life of indolence and licentiousness. He continued to associate with persons of his own age, and was fonder than ever of entering into all their tricks and fun. He pursued this course till he was fifteen years old, without showing the least spark of feeling, and without making the least reflection on what was to be his future lot. He was in this state, when, as he was one day playing with his companions in one of the public places, as was his usual custom, a stranger, who was going by, stopped and looked at him.

This stranger was a noted and learned magician, called for distinction, the African magician. He was so styled from his being a native of Africa, having arrived from that part of the world only two days before.

Whether this magician, who was well skilled in physiognomy, had remarked in the countenance of Aladdin the signs of such a disposition as was best adapted to the purpose for which he had undertaken so long a journey, or not, is uncertain; but he very adroitly made himself acquainted with his family, discovered who he was, and the sort of character and disposition he possessed. He was no sooner informed of what he wished, than he went up to the young man; and, taking him apart from his companions, he asked him if his father's name was not Mustafa, and whether he was not a tailor by trade. "Yes, sir," replied Aladdin, "but he has been dead this long time."

At this speech the African magician threw his arms around Aladdin's neck, embraced and kept on kissing him, while the tears seemed to run down his cheeks, and his bosom to heave with sighs. Aladdin asked him what reason he had to weep. "Alas! my child," replied the magician, "how can I do otherwise? I am your uncle; your father was my most excellent brother. I have been several years upon my journey, and at the very instant of my arrival in this place, and when I was congratulating myself upon the hope of seeing him, and afford him pleasure by my return, you inform me of his death. Can I, then, be so unfeeling as not to evince my grief when I thus find myself deprived of my expected consolation? What, however, alleviates my affliction is, that, as far as my recollection carries me, I discover many traces of your father in your countenance, and that I have not been deceived in addressing myself to you."

He then asked Aladdin, putting at the same time his hand into his purse, where his mother lived; and as soon as he was told, the African magician gave him a handful of small money, and said to him, "My son, go to your mother, and make my respects to her; tell her that I will come and see her to-morrow, if I have an opportunity, in order to afford myself the pleasure of seeing the spot where my good brother lived so many years, and where he at last finished his career."

The African magician had no sooner quitted his new-created nephew, than Aladdin ran to his mother, highly delighted with the money his supposed uncle had given him. "Pray tell me, mother," he cried, the instant of his arrival, "whether I have not an uncle?" "No, my child," replied she, "you have no uncle, either on your poor father's side or mine." "I have just left a man, however," answered the boy, "who told me he was my father's brother, and my uncle. He even cried and embraced me, when I told him of my father's death. And to prove to you that he spoke the truth," added he, showing her the money which he had received, "see what he has given me. He bid me also give his kindest remembrances to you, and to say that he would, if he had time, come and see you to-morrow, as he was desirous of beholding the house where my father lived and died." "It is true, indeed, my son," replied Aladdin's mother, "that your father had a brother, but he has been dead a long time, and I never heard him mention any other." After this conversation, they said no more on the subject.

The next day the African magician again accosted Aladdin, while he was playing in another part of the city, with three other boys. He embraced him as before, and putting two pieces of gold into his hand, "Take this, my boy," said he, "and carry it to your mother. Tell her that I intend to sup with her this evening, and to purchase what is necessary for us to regale ourselves; but first inform me in what quarter of the city I shall find your house." Aladdin gave him the necessary information, and the magician departed.

Aladdin carried the two pieces of gold to his mother, and when he had told her of his supposed uncle's intentions, she went out and procured a supply of good provisions; and as she was unprovided with a sufficient quantity of china or earthenware, she borrowed what she might want from her neighbours. She was busily employed during the whole day, in preparing for night; and in the evening, when everything was ready, she desired Aladdin, as his uncle might not know where to find the house, to go into the street, and if he saw him to show him the way.

Although Aladdin had pointed out to the magician the exact situation of his mother's house, he was nevertheless ready to go; but at the very moment that he reached the door, he heard some person knock. Aladdin instantly opened it, and saw the African, bringing several bottles of wine and various sorts of fruits for them to regale with.

When he had put down the things that he had brought, he paid his respects to Aladdin's mother, and requested her to show him the place where his brother Mustafa was accustomed to sit upon the sofa. She had no sooner pointed it out than he prostrated himself before it, kissed the place several times, while the tears seemed to run in abundance from his eyes. " My poor brother," he exclaimed, " how unfortunate am I not to have arrived time enough to receive your embraces once more before you died !" The mother of Aladdin begged this pretended brother to sit in the place her husband used to occupy, but he would by no means hear of it. " No," he cried, " I will not do that : give me leave, however, to seat myself opposite ; that if I am deprived of the pleasure of seeing him here in person, sitting like the father of a family that is so dear to me, I may at least look at the spot as if he were present." Aladdin's mother pressed him no farther, but permitted him to take whatever seat he chose.

When the magician had taken the seat which he had chosen, he began to enter into a conversation with Aladdin's mother. " Do not be surprised, my good sister," he said, " at never having seen me during the whole of the time you have been married to my late brother, Mustafa. It is full forty years since I left this country, of which I am a native, as well as himself. In the course of this long period, I first travelled through India, Persia, Arabia, Syria, and Egypt ; and after passing a considerable time in all the finest and most remarkable cities in those countries, I went into Africa, where I resided for a great length of time. At last, as it is the natural disposition of man, how distant soever he may be from the place of his birth, never to forget his native country, nor lose the recollection of his family, his friends, and the companions of his youth, the desire of seeing mine, and of once more embracing my dear brother, took so powerful a hold of my mind, that I felt myself sufficiently strong, though in years as you perceive, again to undergo the fatigue of so long a journey. I therefore set about all the necessary preparations, and began my travels. It is useless to mention the length of time I was thus employed, the various obstacles I had to encounter, and all the fatigue I suffered, before I arrived at the end of my labours. Nothing, however, so much mortified me, or gave me so much pain, in all my travels, as the intelligence of the death of my poor brother, whom I so tenderly loved, and whose memory I must ever respect. I have traced almost every feature of his countenance in the face of my nephew ; and it was this that enabled me to distinguish him from the other young persons with whom he was. He can inform you in what manner I received the melancholy news that my brother no longer lived. We must, however, be thankful for those blessings we enjoy ; and I console myself in finding him again alive in his son."

The magician perceiving that Aladdin's mother was very much affected at this conversation about her husband, and that the recollection of him renewed her grief, changed the subject ; and turning towards Aladdin, he asked him his name. " I am called Aladdin," he answered. " Well, then, Aladdin," said the magician, " how do you employ yourself ? Are you acquainted with any trade ?"

At this speech Aladdin hung down his head, and was much disconcerted : but his mother answered for him. " Aladdin," said she, " is a very idle boy. His father did all he could to make him learn his business, but he could not accomplish it ; and since his death, in spite of everything I can say, he will learn nothing ; but leads the life of a vagabond, though I talk to him on the subject every day of my life. He spends all his time at play with other boys, as you saw him, without con-

sidering that he is no longer a child ; and if you cannot make him ashamed of himself, and profit by your advice, I shall utterly despair that he will ever be good for anything He knows very well that his father has left us nothing to live upon ; and sees that, though I pass the whole day in spinning cotton, I can hardly get bread for us to eat. In short, I am resolved soon to shut my doors against him, and make him seek his own livelihood."

Saying this, the good woman burst into tears. " This is not right, Aladdin," said the magician ; " you must think, nephew, of supporting yourself, and working for your bread. There is a variety of trades ; consider if there is not one you have an inclination for, in preference to another. Perhaps that which your father follow displeases you, and you would rather be brought up to some other ? Come, come, don't conceal your opinion ; give it freely, and I may perhaps assist you." As he found that Aladdin made him no answer, he went on thus : " If you have an objection to learning any trade, and yet wish to be a respectable and honest character, I will procure you a shop, and furnish it with rich stuffs, and fine sorts of linens ; you shall sell the goods, and with the money you make you shall buy other merchandise ; and in this manner your life will pass respectably. Consult your own inclinations, and tell me candidly what you think of the plan. You will always find me ready to perform my promise."

This offer flattered the vanity of Aladdin very much ; and he was the more averse to any manual occupation, because he knew well enough that the shops which contained goods of this sort were much frequented, and the merchants themselves well dressed and highly esteemed. He hinted, therefore, to the magician, whom he considered as his uncle, that he was much more inclined to the latter plan, and that he should all his life continue sensible of the obligation he was under to him. " Since, then, such an employment is agreeable to you," replied the magician, " I will take you with me to-morrow, and have you properly and handsomely dressed, as becomes one of the richest merchants of this city, and then we will procure a shop in the way I propose."

The mother of Aladdin, who had not hitherto been convinced that the magician was in fact the brother of her husband, no longer doubted it when he promised to do so much good for her son. She thanked him sincerely for his kind intentions, and after having charged Aladdin to conduct himself so as to prove worthy of the good fortune his uncle had led him to expect, she served up the supper. The conversation, during the whole time the supper lasted, turned on the same subject, and continued till the magician, who perceived that the night was far advanced, took leave of Aladdin and his mother and retired.

The magician did not fail to return the next morning to the widow of Mustafa, the tailor, as he had promised. He took Aladdin with him, and conducted him to a merchant's, where clothes, made of the finest stuffs, were sold. He made Aladdin try on such as seemed to fit him, and, after selecting those he liked best, " My nephew," said the magician, " choose such as you are most pleased with out of this number." Delighted with the liberality of his new uncle, Aladdin made choice of one. The magician bought it, together with everything that was necessary to complete the dress, and paid for the whole without asking the merchant to make any abatement.

When Aladdin saw himself thus magnificently dressed

from head to foot, he returned his uncle a thousand thanks; the magician, on his part, again promised never to forsake him, but to have him always with him. He then conducted Aladdin to the most frequented parts of the city, particularly where the shops of the most opulent merchants were; and when he was come to the street where the shops of stuffs and fine linens were, he said to Aladdin, "You will soon become a merchant such as one of these. It is proper that you should frequent this place, and become acquainted with them." After this, he took him to the largest and most noted mosques, to the khans, where all the foreign merchants lived, and through every part of the sultan's palace, where he had leave to enter. Having at length gone with him over every part of the city worth seeing, they came to the khan where the magician had hired apartments. They found several merchants, with whom he had made some slight acquaintance since his arrival, and whom he had now invited to partake of a repast, in order to introduce his pretended nephew to them.

The entertainment was not over till the evening. Aladdin then wished to take leave of his uncle, and go home; the magician, however, would not suffer him to go alone, but conducted him back to his mother's. When she saw her son so handsomely dressed, she was transported with joy; and bestowed a thousand blessings on the magician, who had been at so great an expense on her dear child's account, "Generous relation," she exclaimed, "I know not how to thank you enough for your great liberality. My son, I am aware, is not worthy of so much generosity; and he will be wicked indeed if he ever prove ungrateful to you, or does not conduct himself so as to deserve and be an ornament to the excellent situation you are about to place him in. For my part," added she, "I thank you with my whole soul! may you live many happy years, and witness my son's gratitude, who cannot prove his good intentions better than by following your advice."

"Aladdin," replied the magician, "is a good boy. He seems to pay attention to what I say. I have no doubt but we shall make him what we wish. I am sorry for one thing, and that is, that I am not able to perform all my promises to-morrow. It is Friday, and on that day the shops are shut; and it is impossible either to hire one, or furnish it with goods, because all the merchants are absent, and engaged in their several amusements. We will, however, settle this business on Saturday; and I will come here to-morrow to take Aladdin, and show him the public gardens, in which people of reputation constantly walk and amuse themselves. He has, probably, hitherto been ignorant of the way in which they pass their time there. He has associated only with boys, but he must now learn to live with men." The magician then took his leave and departed. In the mean time, Aladdin, who was delighted at seeing himself so well dressed, was still more pleased at the idea of going to the gardens in the environs of the city. He had never been outside of the gates, nor seen the neighbouring country, which was very beautiful.

The next morning, Aladdin got up and dressed himself very early, in order to be ready to set out the moment his uncle called for him. After waiting some time, which he thought an age, he became so impatient that he opened the door and stood on the outside to watch for his uncle. The moment he saw him coming he went and informed his mother of it, took leave of her, shut the door and ran to meet him.

The magician behaved in the most affectionate manner to Aladdin. "Come, my good boy," said he, with a smile, "I will to-day show you some very fine things." He conducted him out at a gate that led to some large and handsome houses, or rather magnificent palaces, each having a beautiful garden, in which they had the liberty of walking. At each palace they came to, he asked Aladdin if it were not very beautiful; while the latter often prevented this question by exclaiming, when a new one presented itself—"Oh, uncle, here is one much more beautiful than those we have before seen." In the meantime they kept going on into the country, and the cunning magician, who wanted to go still further, for the purpose of putting a design which he had in his head into execution, went into one of these gardens, and sat down by the side of a large basin of pure water, which received its supplies through the jaws of a bronze lion. He then pretended to be very tired, in order to give Aladdin an opportunity of resting. "My dear nephew," he said, "you must be fatigued as well as myself. Let us rest ourselves here a little while, and get fresh strength to pursue our walk."

When they were seated, the magician took out from a piece of linen cloth, which was attached to his girdle, various sorts of fruits, and some cakes, with which he had provided himself, and spread them on the bank before them. He divided a cake between himself and Aladdin, and gave him leave to eat whatever fruit he liked best. While they were eating, he gave his adopted nephew much good advice, desiring him to leave off playing with boys, and to associate with intelligent and prudent men: to pay every attention to them, and to profit from their conversation. "You will very soon," said he, "be a man yourself, and you cannot too soon accustom yourself to their manners and behaviour." When they had finished their slight repast, they got up, and pursued their way by the side of gardens, which were separated from each other by a small stream, that served chiefly to mark the limits of each, and not to prevent the communication between them; the honesty of the inhabitants of this city making it unnecessary for them to take other means of preventing any injury. The magician insensibly led Aladdin much further than the gardens extended: and they walked on through the country, till they came into the neighbourhood of the mountain.

Aladdin, who had never before taken so long a walk, felt himself very much tired. "Where are we going, my dear uncle?" said he. "We have got much further than the gardens, and I can see nothing but hills and mountains before us. And if we go any further, I know not whether I shall have strength enough to walk back to the city." "Take courage, nephew," replied his pretended uncle: "I wish to show you another garden, that far surpasses all you have hitherto seen. It is not far from hence; and after your arrival, you will readily own how sorry you would have been to have come thus near it, and not gone on to see." Aladdin was persuaded to proceed, and the magician led him on considerably further, amusing him all the time with entertaining stories, to beguile the way, and make it less fatiguing and unpleasant.

They at length came to a narrow valley, situated between two moderately sized mountains, of nearly the same height. This was the particular spot to which the magician wished to bring Aladdin, in order to put in execution the grand project that was the sole cause of his coming from the extremity of Africa to Cathay. "We shall now," said he to Aladdin, "go no farther; and I shall here unfold to your view some extraordinary things hitherto unknown to mortals; and which, when you shall have seen, you will thank me a thousand times for having made you an eye-witness of. They are indeed such wonders as no one beside yourself will ever have seen. I am now going to strike a light, and do you, in the meantime, collect all the dry sticks and leaves that you can find, in order to make a fire."

There were so many pieces of dry sticks scattered about, that Aladdin had collected more than was sufficient for his purpose by the time the magician had lighted his match. He then set them on fire; and as soon as they were in a blaze the magician threw a certain perfume, which he had ready in his hand, upon them. A thick and dense smoke immediately arose, which seemed to unfold itself in consequence of some mysterious words pronounced by the magician, and which Aladdin did not in the least comprehend. At the same instant the ground slightly shook, and opening in the spot where they stood, discovered a square stone about a foot and a half broad, placed horizontally, with a brass ring in the centre, for the purpose of lifting it up.

Aladdin was dreadfully alarmed at these things, and was about to run away, when the magician, to whom his presence in this mysterious affair was absolutely necessary, stopped him in an angry manner, and gave him at the same moment such a blow which not only beat him down, but nearly knocked some of his teeth out. Poor Aladdin, with tears in his eyes, and the blood streaming from his mouth, and trembling in every limb, got up. "My dear uncle," he cried, "what have I done to deserve such severity?" "I have my reasons for it," replied the magician; "I am your uncle, and consider myself as your father, and you ought not to make me any answer. Do not, however, my, boy," added he, in a milder tone of voice, "be at all afraid; I desire nothing of you, but that you obey me most implicitly: and this you must do, if you wish to render yourself worthy of the great advantages I mean to afford you." These fine speeches of the magician in some measure lessened the fright of Aladdin; and when the former saw him less alarmed, "You have observed," he said, "what I have done by virtue of my perfumes, and the words that I pronounced. You are now to be informed, that under the stone which you see here there is a concealed treasure destined for you; and which will one day render you richer than any of the most powerful potentates of the earth. It is, moreover, the fact, that no one in the world but you can be permitted to touch or lift up this stone, and go beneath it. Even I myself am not able to approach it, and to take possession of the treasure which is under it. And, in order to ensure your success, you must observe and execute in every respect, even to the minutest point, what I am now going to instruct you in. This is a matter of the greatest consequence both to you and myself."

Wrapped in astonishment at everything he had seen and heard, and full of the idea of this treasure, which the magician said was to make him for ever happy, Aladdin forgot everything else that had passed. "Well, my dear uncle," he exclaimed, as he got up, "what must I do? Tell me; I am ready to obey you in everything." "I heartily rejoice, my boy," replied the magician, "that you have made so good a resolu-

tion. Come to me; take hold of this ring, and lift up the stone." "I am not strong enough, uncle," said Aladdin; "you must help me." "No, no," answered the magician, "you have no occasion for my assistance; we shall neither of us do any good if I attempt to help you, you must lift it up entirely by yourself. Pronounce only the name of your father and your grandfather, take hold of the ring, and lift it: it will come without any difficulty." Aladdin did exactly as the magician told him; he raised the stone without any trouble, and laid it on one side.

When the stone was taken away, a small cavern was visible, between three and four feet deep, at the bottom of which there appeared a door, with steps to go down still lower. "You must now, my good boy," said the magician to Aladdin, "observe very exactly everything I am going to tell you. Go down into this cavern, and when you have come to the bottom of the steps which you see, you will perceive an open door, leading into a large vaulted space, divided into three successive halls. In each of these you will observe, on both sides of you, four bronze vases, as large as tubs, full of gold and silver; but you must take particular care not to touch any of it. When you get into the first hall, take up your robe and bind it round you. Then observe, and go on to the second without stopping, and thence, in the same manner, to the third. Above all, however, be very particular not to go near the walls, nor even to touch them with your robe; for if any part of your dress comes in contact with them, your instant death will be the inevitable consequence. This is the reason of my having desired you to fasten your robe closely round you. At the extremity of the third hall there is a door, leading to a garden planted with beautiful trees, all of which are full of fruit. Go on straight forward, and pursue a path which you will perceive, and which will bring you to the bottom of a flight of fifty steps, at the top of which is a terrace. When you shall have ascended the terrace, you will observe a niche before you, in which there is a lighted lamp. Take the lamp, and extinguish it. Then throw out the wick, and the liquid that is within, and put it in your bosom. When you have done this bring it to me. Do not be afraid of staining your dress, as what is within the lamp is not oil; and when you have thrown it out, the lamp will dry directly. If you should feel yourself very desirous of gathering any of the fruit in the garden, you may do so; and there is nothing to prevent your taking as much as you please."

When the Magician had given these directions to Aladdin, he took a ring from his finger, and gave it to his young companion; telling him, at the same time, that it was a preservative against every evil that might otherwise happen to him, and again bade him be mindful of everything he had said to him. "Go, my child," added he, "descend boldly; we shall now both of us become immensely rich for the rest of our lives."

CHAPTER II.

OF THE WONDERFUL THINGS ALADDIN SAW IN THE CAVE; THE TREACHEROUS CONDUCT OF THE MAGICIAN, WHO ENCLOSES HIM IN THE SUBTERRANEOUS VAULT; AND HOW HE WAS DELIVERED BY THE GENIE OF THE RING.

ALADDIN gave a spring, jumped into the opening with a willing mind, and went down to the bottom of the steps. He found the three halls, exactly answering the description the magician had given of them. He passed through them with the greatest precaution possible; as he was fearful he might be killed, if he did not most strictly observe all the directions he had received. He went on to the garden, and ascended to the terrace without stopping. He took the lamp, as it stood lighted in the niche, threw out its contents, and, observing that it was, as the magician had said, quite dry, he put it into his bosom. He then came down from the terrace, and stopped in the garden to examine the fruit, which he had only seen for an instant, as he passed along. The trees of this garden were all full of the most extraordinary fruit. Each tree bore a sort of different colour. Some were white, others sparkling and transparent, like crystal; some were red, and of different shades, others green, blue, violet; some of a yellowish hue—in short, of almost every colour. The white were pearls; the sparkling and transparent were diamonds; the deep red were rubies; the paler, a particular sort of ruby, called balass; the green, emeralds; the blue, turquoises; the violet, amethysts: those tinged with yellow, sapphires; in the same way, all the other coloured fruits were varieties of precious stones; and the whole of them were of the largest size, and more perfect than were ever seen in the world. Aladdin, who knew neither their beauty nor their value, was not at all struck with the appearance of them, which did not the least suit his taste, like the figs, grapes, and other excellent fruits, common in Cathay. As he was not yet of an age to be acquainted with their value, he thought they were all only pieces of coloured glass, and did not therefore attach any value to them. The variety, however, and contrast of so many beautiful colours, as well as the brilliancy and extraordinary size of each sort, nevertheless tempted him to gather some of each. And he took so many of every colour that he filled both his pockets, as well as his two new purses that the magician had bought for him at the time he made him a present of his new dress, that everything he wore might be equally new; and as his pockets, which were already full, could not hold his two purses, he fastened them on each side of his girdle, or sash, and also wrapped some in its folds, as it was of silk, and made very full. In this manner, he carried them so as they could not fall out. He did not even neglect to fill his bosom quite full, between his robe and shirt.

Laden in this manner, with an immense treasure, though ignorant of its value, Aladdin made haste through the three halls, in order that he might not make the magician wait too long. Having proceeded through them with the same caution as before, he began to ascend the steps he had come down, and presented himself at the entrance of the cave, where the magician was impatiently waiting for him. As soon as Aladdin had perceived him, he called out, "Give me your hand, uncle, to help me up." "You had better, my dear boy," replied the magician, "first give me the lamp, as that will only embarrass you." "It is not at all in my way," said Aladdin, "and I will give it to you when I am out." The magician still persevered in wishing to get the lamp, before he helped Aladdin out of the cave: but the latter had in fact so covered it with the fruit of the trees, that he absolutely refused to give it, till he had got out of the cave. The magician was in the greatest despair at the obstinate resistance the boy made; he put himself into the most violent rage; he threw a little

perfume upon the fire, which he had taken care to keep up, and he had hardly pronounced two magic words, before the stone, which served to shut up the entrance to the cavern, returned of its own accord to the place, with all the earth over it, exactly in the same state it was when the magician and Aladdin arrived there.

This African magician, as before stated, was not the brother of Mustafa, the tailor, and consequently not the uncle of Aladdin. He was a native of Africa, a country where magic is more studied than in any other; he had given himself up to it from his earliest youth; and after nearly forty years spent in enchantments, experiments in geomancy, fumigations, and reading books of magic, he had at length discovered that there was in the world a certain wonderful lamp, the possession of which would make him the most powerful monarch in the universe, if he were so fortunate as to obtain it.

By a late experiment in geomancy, he had discovered that this lamp was in a subterraneous place in the middle of Cathay, in the very spot, and under the very circumstances, that have just been detailed. Thoroughly persuaded of the truth of this discovery, he had come from the remotest part of Africa, and after a long and painful journey, had arrived in the city that was nearest this treasure. But though the lamp was certainly in the place which he had found out, he was nevertheless not permitted to take it away himself, nor to go in person to the very spot where it was. It was absolutely necessary that another person should go down to take it, and then put it into his hands. It was for this reason that he had addressed himself to Aladdin, who seemed to him to be an artless youth, and well adapted to perform the service he expected from him; and he had resolved, as soon as he had got the lamp from him, to raise the last fumigation, pronounce the two magic words, which produced the effect already seen, and sacrifice poor Aladdin to his avarice and wickedness, that he might not have an existing witness of his being in possession of the lamp. The blow he had given Aladdin, as well as the authority he exercised over him, were only for the purpose of accustoming him to fear him, and obey all his orders without hesitation; that when Aladdin had got possession of the wonderful lamp he might instantly deliver it to him. The reverse, however, of what he both wished and expected came to pass; for he was so much in a hurry to put an end to poor Aladdin, only because he was afraid that, while he was contesting the matter with him, some persons might come, and make that public which he wished to be kept secret, that he completely failed in his object.

When the magician found all his hopes and expectations frustrated, he had only one method to pursue, and that was to return to Africa, for which he departed the very same day. He pursued his journey along the most private roads, in order to avoid the city where he had met with Aladdin. He was also afraid to meet any person who might have seen him walk out with him, and come back without him.

To judge from all these circumstances, it might naturally be supposed that Aladdin was gone for ever; and indeed the magician himself, who thought he had thus destroyed him, had not paid any attention to the ring which he had placed on his finger, and which was now about to render Aladdin the most essential service, and be the means of saving him. Aladdin knew not the wonderful qualities either of that or the lamp; and it is indeed astonishing that the loss of both of them did not drive the magician to absolute despair: but persons of his profession are so accustomed to defeat, and so many events happen to them contrary to their wishes, that they never cease from endeavouring to conquer every misfortune, by charms, visions, and enchantments.

Aladdin, who did not expect this wicked treatment from his pretended uncle, after all the kindness and generosity which the latter had evinced towards him, experienced a degree of surprise and astonishment easier to conceive than explain. When he found himself as it were buried alive, he called aloud a thousand times to his uncle, telling him he was ready to give him the lamp. But all his cries were useless, and having no other means of making himself heard, he remained in perfect darkness. Giving, at length, a little cessation to his tears, he went down to the bottom of the flight of stairs, intending to look for the light in the garden where he had been before. But the walls, which had been opened by enchantment, were now shut by the same means. He felt all around him, to the right and left, several times, but could not discover the least opening. He then redoubled his cries and tears, sat down upon the step of his dungeon, without hoping ever again to see the light of day, and with the melancholy conviction, that he should only pass from the darkness which now encompassed him to the shades of an inevitable and speedy death.

Aladdin remained two days in this state, without either eating or drinking. On the third day, regarding his death as certain, he lifted up his hands, and joining them as in the act of prayer, he wholly resigned himself to the will of Heaven and uttered in a loud tone of voice, "There is no strength or power but in the high and great God." In this action of joining his hands, he happened to rub the ring which the African magician had put upon his finger, and of the virtue of which he was as yet ignorant. Upon its being thus rubbed, a genie of an enormous figure, and most horrid countenance, instantly appeared before him, coming down as it were from the vaulted roof, and he addressed these words to Aladdin: "What do you wish? I am ready to obey you as your slave; as the slave of him who has the ring on his finger; I and the other slaves of the ring!"

At any other moment, and on any other occasion, Aladdin, who was totally unaccustomed to such appearances, would have been so frightened at the sight of such a wonderful figure, he would have been unable to speak; but he was so entirely pre-occupied with the danger and peril of his situation, that he answered without the least hesitation, "Whoever you are, take me, if you are able, out of this place!" He had scarcely pronounced these words when the earth opened, and he found himself on the outside of the cave, and at the very spot to which the magician had brought him. It is easy to be conceived, that after having remained in complete darkness for so long a time, Aladdin had at first some difficulty in supporting the brightness of the open day. By degrees, however, his eyes became accustomed to the light, and on looking round him he was surprised to find not the least opening in the earth. He could not comprehend in what manner he had so suddenly come out of it. There was only the place where the fire had been made, which he recollected was close to the entrance of the cave. Looking round towards the city, he perceived it surrounded by the gardens, and thus knew the road he had come with the magician. He returned the same way, thanking God for having again permitted him to behold and revisit the face of the earth, which he had quite despaired of doing.

He arrived at the city, but it was with great difficulty that he got home. When he was within the door, the joy he experienced at again seeing his mother, added to the weak state he was in, from not having eaten anything for the space of three days, made him faint, and it was some time before he came to himself. His mother, who had already wept for him as lost or dead, seeing him in this state, did not omit anything that could tend to restore him. At length he recovered, and the first thing he said was, "Bring me something, my dear mother, to eat, before you do anything else. I have tasted nothing these three days!" His mother instantly set what she had before him. "My dear child," said she, "do not hurry yourself, it is dangerous; eat but little, and at your leisure: you must take great care how you indulge the pressing appetite you have. Do not even speak to me; you will have plenty of time to relate to me everything that has happened to you, when you shall have regained your strength. I am sufficiently satisfied at seeing you once more, after all the affliction I have suffered since Friday, and all the trouble I have also taken to learn what was become of you, when I found the night approach and you did not return home."

Aladdin followed his mother's advice; he ate but little and slowly, and drank sparingly. "I have great reason, my dear mother," said he when he had done, "to complain of you for putting me in the power of a man whose object was to destroy me, and who, at this very moment, supposes my death sure, or at least that I should not live another day. But you took him to be my uncle, and I was equally deceived. Indeed, how could we suppose him to be anything else, as he almost overwhelmed me with kindness and generosity, and made me so many promises of future advantage? But I must tell you, mother, that he was a traitor, a wicked man, a cheat! He was good and kind to me only that he might, after answering his own purpose, destroy me, as I have already told you, without either of us being able to know the reason. I can assure you I have not given him the least cause for the bad treatment I have received; and you will yourself be convinced of it by the faithful and true account I am going to give you of everything that has passed, from the moment that I left home till he put his wicked design in execution."

Aladdin then related to his mother everything that had happened to him and the magician, on the day when the latter came and took him away to see the palaces and gardens round the city; what had befallen him on the road, and at the place between the two mountains, where the magician worked such prodigies: how upon throwing the perfume into the fire and uttering some magical words, the earth instantly opened, and discovered the entrance to a cave, that led to most inestimable treasures. Neither did he forget the blow that the magician had given him, nor how, after having first coaxed him, he had persuaded him, by the means of the greatest promises, and by putting a ring upon his finger, to descend into the cave. He omitted no circumstance of what passed, or what he had seen in going backwards and forwards through the three halls, in the garden, or on the terrace whence he had taken the wonderful lamp. This he now drew from his bosom, and showed it to his mother, as well as the transparent and different coloured fruits that he had gathered as he returned through the garden, and the two purses, quite full, all of which he gave her; she, however, did not set much value upon them. The fruits were, in fact, precious stones; and the lustre which they threw round, by the aid of a lamp that was in the chamber, and which almost equalled the sun in brightness, ought to have informed her they were of the greatest value: but the mother of Aladdin had no more knowledge of their worth than her son. She had been brought up in a middle station of life, and her husband had never been rich enough to bestow any jewels upon her, nor had she ever seen any among her relations or neighbours; consequently it was not at all surprising that she considered them as things of no value, and only fit to please the eye by the variety of their colours. Aladdin, therefore, put them all behind one of the cushions of the sofa on which they were sitting.

He finished the recital of his adventure by telling her that when he came back and presented himself at the mouth of the cave to get out, upon refusing to give the lamp to the magician, the entrance to the cave was instantly closed, by means of the perfume thrown by the magician on the fire, which he had kept alight, and of some words that he pronounced. He could not then proceed any further without shedding tears, and representing the miserable state he found himself in, buried, as it were, alive in this fatal cave, till the moment he got out by the means of the ring, of which he did not even now know the virtues. When he had finished his account, he said to his mother, "I need not tell you more; the rest is known to you. This is the whole of my adventures, and full particulars of the danger I have been in since I left you."

Wonderful and surprising as this relation was, distressing too as it must have been for a mother, who, in spite of his defects, tenderly loved her son, she had the patience to hear it to the end, without giving him the least interruption. In the most affecting parts, however, particularly those that unfolded the wicked intentions of the African magician, she could not help showing by her actions how much she detested him, and how much he excited her indignation; and Aladdin had no sooner concluded, than she began to abuse the impostor in the strongest terms. She called him a traitor, a barbarian, a cheat, an assassin, a magician, the enemy and destroyer of the human race. "Yes, my child," she exclaimed, "he is a magician, and magicians are public evils. They hold communication with demons by means of their sorceries and enchantments. Thank our holy Prophet that he has not suffered the wickedness of this wretch to have its full effect upon you. You ought to return him many thanks for his kindness to you. Your death would have been inevitable, if he had not come to your assistance, and you had not implored his aid." She added many more things of the same sort, showing, at the same time, her complete detestation of the treachery with which the magician had treated her son; but as she was proceeding in this manner, she perceived that Aladdin, who had not slept for three days, wanted rest. She made him, therefore, retire to bed, and soon afterwards went thither herself.

CHAPTER III.

CONSTERNATION OF ALADDIN AND HIS MOTHER AT THE SUDDEN APPEARANCE OF THE GENIE OF THE LAMP.—HOW THE GENIE PROVIDES FOR THEIR DAILY WANTS.

As Aladdin had not been able to take any repose in the subterranean vault in which he had been, as it were, buried, with the idea of his certain destruction, it is no wonder that he passed the whole of that night in the most profound sleep, and that it was even late the next morning before he awoke. He at last got up, and the first thing he said to his mother was that he was very hungry, and told her she could not oblige him more than by giving him something for breakfast. "Alas! my child," replied his mother, "I have not a morsel of bread to give you. You ate last night all the trifling remains of food there was in the house. Have a little patience, however, and it shall not be long before I will bring you some. I have a little cotton of my own spinning, which I will go and sell, and purchase something for our dinner." "Keep your cotton, mother," said Aladdin, "for another time, and give me the lamp which I brought with me yesterday. I will go and sell that, and the money it will fetch will serve for breakfast and dinner too, and perhaps also for supper."

Aladdin's mother took the lamp from the place she had put it in. "Here it is," she said to her son; "but it is, I think, very dirty. If I were to clean it a little, perhaps it might sell for something more." She then took some water and a little fine sand to clean it with. But she had scarcely begun to rub the lamp, when instantly, and while her son was present, a hideous and gigantic genie rose out of the ground before her, and cried with a voice as loud as thunder, "What do you wish? I am ready to obey you as your slave, and the slave of those who have the lamp in their hands; I and the other slaves of the lamp." The mother of Aladdin was not in a condition to answer this address. She was unable to endure the sight of a figure so hideous and alarming as that of the genie; and her fears were so great, that she had no sooner begun to speak, than she fell down in a fainting fit.

As Aladdin had once before seen a similar appearance in the cavern, and did not either lose his presence of mind or his judgment, he instantly seized the lamp; and supplied his mother's place by answering for her in a firm tone of voice, "I am hungry, bring me something to eat." The genie disappeared, and returned in a moment with a large silver basin, which he carried on his head, and twelve covered dishes of the same material, filled with the choicest meat, properly arranged, and six loaves, as white as snow, upon as many plates; and having two bottles of excellent wine and two silver cups in his hand. He placed them all upon the sofa, and instantly vanished.

All this passed in so short a time, that Aladdin's mother had not recovered from fainting before the genie had disappeared the second time. Aladdin, who had thrown some water over her without any effect, again endeavoured to bring her to herself: but, whether her scattered senses returned of

THE GENIE BRINGING THE BRIDE AND BRIDEGROOM TO ALADDIN.

themselves, or that the smell of the dishes which the genie had brought produced the effect, she quite recovered. "My dear mother," cried Aladdin, "there is nothing the matter. Get up, and come and eat: here is what will put you in good spirits again, and at the same time satisfy my violent appetite. Come, do not let us suffer these good things to get cold before we begin."

His mother was extremely astonished when she beheld the large basin, the twelve dishes, the six loaves, the two bottles of wine and two cups, and perceived the delicious odour that exhaled from them. "My child," she said, "how came all this abundance here, and to whom are we obliged for such liberality? The sultan surely cannot have become acquainted with our poverty, and taken compassion on us?" "My good mother," replied Aladdin, "come and sit down, and begin to eat;

you are as much in want of something as I am. I will tell you of everything when we have broken our fast." They then sat down, and both of them ate with the greater appetite, as neither mother nor son had before ever seen a table so well covered.

During the repast, the mother of Aladdin could not help stopping frequently to look at and admire the basin and dishes; although she was not quite sure whether they were silver or any other material, so little was she accustomed to things of this sort; and, in fact, without regarding their value, of which she was ignorant, it was only the novelty of their appearance that attracted her admiration. Nor indeed was her son better informed than herself. Although they both merely intended to make a simple breakfast, yet they sat so long, that the hour of dining came before they had risen; the

2

dishes were so excellent, they almost increased their appetites; and as they were still hot, they thought it no bad plan to join the two meals together, and therefore they dined before they got up from breakfast. When they had made an end of their double repast, they found enough remaining, not only for supper, but even for two as good meals the next day.

When Aladdin's mother had taken away the things, and put aside what they had not consumed, she seated herself on the sofa, near her son. "I am waiting, my boy," she said, "for you to satisfy my impatient curiosity, and to hear the account you have promised me." Aladdin then related to her everything that had passed between him and the genie, from the time her alarm had made her faint, till she again came to herself. At this relation of her son, and the account of the appearance of the genie, his mother was in the greatest astonishment. "What do you tell me, child, about your genie? Never since I was born have I heard of any person of my acquaintance that has seen one. How comes it, then, that this villanous genie should have presented himself to me? Why did he not rather address himself to you, to whom he had before appeared in the cavern?"

"Mother," replied Aladdin, "the genie who appeared just now to you is not the same that appeared to me. In some things, indeed, they resemble each other, being both as large as giants; but they are very different both in their countenance and dress, and they belong to different masters. If you recollect, he whom I saw called himself the slave of the ring which I had on my finger; and the one who appeared to you was the slave of the lamp you had in your hand: but I believe you did not hear him, as you seemed to faint the instant he began to speak." "What," cried his mother, "is it, then, your lamp that was the reason why this cursed genie addressed himself to me, rather than to you? Ah! child, take the lamp out of my sight, and put it where you please, so that I never touch it again. Indeed, I would rather that you should throw it away or sell it, than I should run the risk of almost dying with fright by again touching it. And if you would also follow my advice, you would put away the ring as well. We ought to have no commerce with genii; they are demons, and our Prophet has told us so."

"With your permission, however, my dear mother," replied Aladdin, "I shall take care not to sell this lamp in a hurry, which has already been so useful to us both. I have, indeed, been once very near to it. Do you not see what it has procured us, and that it will also continue to furnish us with enough for our entire support? You may easily judge, as well as myself, that it was not for nothing my pretended wicked uncle gave himself so much trouble, and undertook so long and fatiguing a journey, since it was merely to get possession of this wonderful lamp, which he preferred to all the gold and silver which he knew was in the three halls, and which I myself saw, as he said I should. He was too well acquainted with the worth and qualities of this lamp to wish for any other part of that immense treasure. Since chance, then, has discovered its virtues to us, let us profit

by them; but in such a manner that we shall not make any bustle to draw down the envy and jealousy of our neighbours. I will take it, indeed, out of your sight, and put it where I shall be able to find it whenever I shall have occasion for it, since you are so much alarmed at the appearance of the genie. Neither can I resolve to throw the ring away. Without this ring you would have never seen me again; and even if I should now have been alive, it would have been almost the last moment of my existence. You must permit me, then, to keep it, and to wear it always carefully on my finger. Who can tell if some danger may not one day or other again happen to me, which neither you nor I can now foresee, and from which it may deliver me?" As the arguments of Aladdin appeared very just and reasonable, his mother had nothing to say in reply. "Do as you like, my son," she cried: "as for me, I wish to have nothing at all to do with genii; and I declare to you, that I entirely wash my hands of them, and will never mention them to you again."

After supper the next evening nothing remained of the good provisions which the genie had brought. The following morning, Aladdin, who did not like to wait till hunger approached, took one of the silver plates under his robe, and went out early, in order to sell it.

The Jew, who was both clever and cunning, took the plate and examined it. He had no sooner ascertained that it was good silver, than he desired to know how much he expected for it. Aladdin, who knew not its value, nor had ever had any dealings of the sort before, was satisfied with saying that he supposed the Jew knew what the plate was worth, and that he would depend upon his honour. Being uncertain whether Aladdin was acquainted with its real value or not, he took out of his purse a piece of gold equal to one seventy-second part of the value of the plate, and offered it to Aladdin. The latter eagerly took the money, and went away so quickly, that the Jew, not satisfied with the exorbitant profit he had made by this bargain, was very sorry he had not foreseen Aladdin's ignorance of the value of the plate, and offered him much less for it. He was upon the point of running after him, to get something back out of the piece of gold; but Aladdin himself ran very fast, and was already got so far, that he would have found it impossible to overtake him.

In his way home, Aladdin bought enough bread for his mother and himself, which he paid for out of his piece of gold. When he got back, he gave the change to his mother, who went to the market, and purchased as much provision as would last them for several days.

Thus they continued to live till Aladdin had sold the twelve dishes, one after the other, to the same Jew, exactly as he had done the first, when they found they wanted more money. The Jew having given him a piece of gold for the first, durst not offer him less for the other dishes, for fear of losing so good a bargain. He bought them all, therefore, at the same rate. When the money for the last plate was expended, Aladdin had recourse to the basin, which was at least ten times as heavy as any of the dishes. He wished to carry this to the same merchant, but its great weight prevented him; he was obliged, therefore, to bring the Jew to his mother's. After having ascertained the weight of the basin, the Jew counted out ten pieces of gold, with which Aladdin was satisfied.

While these ten pieces lasted, they were employed in the daily expenses of the house. In the meantime, Aladdin, thus accustomed to lead an idle life, abstained from going to play with boys of his own age from the time of his adventure with the African magician. He now passed his days in walking about, or conversing with such men as he got acquainted with. Sometimes he stopped in the shops belonging to large and extensive merchants, where he listened to the conversation of such people of distinction and education as came there, and who made these shops a sort of meeting-place. The information he thus acquired gave him a slight knowledge of the world.

When nothing remained of his ten pieces of gold, Aladdin had recourse to the lamp. He took it up, and looked for the particular spot that his mother had rubbed. As he easily perceived the place where the sand had touched it, he applied his hand to the same place, and the same genie, whom he had before seen, instantly appeared. But, as Aladdin had rubbed the lamp in a more gentle manner than his mother had done, the genie spoke to him also in a more softened tone. "What do you wish?" said he to him, in the same words as before: "I am ready to obey you, as your slave; and the slave of those who have the lamp in their hands; I and the other slaves of the lamp."

"I am hungry," cried Aladdin; "bring me something to eat." The genie disappeared, and in a short time returned, loaded with a similar service to that he had brought before, which he placed upon the sofa, and vanished in an instant.

As Aladdin's mother was aware of the intention of her son, she had gone out on some business, that she might not be in the house when the genie again made his appearance. She soon after came in, and saw the table and sideboard well set out; nor was she less surprised at the effect of the lamp this time than she had been the first. Aladdin and his mother immediately placed themselves at the table; and after they had finished their repast, there still remained sufficient food to last them two whole days.

When Aladdin again found that all his provisions were gone, and that he had no money to purchase any, he took one of the silver dishes, and went to look for the Jew, in order to sell it him. As he walked along, he happened to pass a goldsmith's shop, belonging to a respectable old man, whose probity and general honesty were unimpeachable. The goldsmith, who perceived him, called to him to come into the shop. "My son," said he, "I have often seen you pass, loaded as you are at present, and join a Jew; and then, in a short time, come back empty-handed. I have thought that you sold him what you carried. But perhaps you are ignorant that this Jew is a very great cheat; nay, that he will even deceive his own brethren, and that no one who knows him will have any dealings with him. Now, what I have more to say to you is only this—and I wish you to act exactly as you like in the matter: if you will show me what you are now carrying, and are going to sell it, I will faithfully give you what it is worth, if it be anything in my way of business; if not, I will introduce you to other merchants, who will not deceive you."

The hope of making a little more of his silver dish induced Aladdin to take it from under his robe, and show it to the goldsmith. The old man, who knew at first sight that the dish was of the finest silver, asked him if he had sold any like it to the Jew, and how much he had received. Aladdin ingenuously told him that he had sold twelve, and that the Jew had given him a piece of gold for each. "Ah! the thief!" cried the merchant: "but, my son, what is done cannot be undone, and let us, therefore, think of it no more; but, in letting you see what your dish, which is made of the finest silver we ever use in our shops, is really worth, we shall know to what extent the Jew has cheated you."

The goldsmith took his scales, weighed the dish, and after explaining to Aladdin how much a mark of silver was worth, and the different divisions of it, he said, that, according to the weight of the dish, it was worth seventy-two pieces of gold, which he immediately counted out to him. "This," said he, "is the exact value of your dish; if you doubt it, you may go to any one of our goldsmiths you please; and if you find that he will give you more for it, I promise to forfeit to you double the sum. All we get is by the fashion or workmanship of the goods we buy in this manner: and with this even the most equitable Jews are not satisfied." Aladdin thanked the goldsmith for the good advice he had given him, from which, too, he derived so much advantage. And for the future he carried his dishes to no one else. He took the basin also to his shop, and always received the value, according to its weight.

Although Aladdin and his mother had an inexhaustible source for money in their lamp, by which they could procure what they wished, they nevertheless continued to live with the same frugality as before, except that Aladdin put a little apart for some innocent amusements, and to procure some things that were necessary in the house. His mother took the care of her dress upon herself, and supplied it from the cotton she spun. From such a quiet mode of living, it is easy to conjecture how long the money arising from the sale of the twelve dishes and the basin, at the rate Aladdin had sold them at, must have lasted them. They lived in this manner for some years, with the profitable assistance which Aladdin occasionally procured from the lamp.

During this interval, Aladdin did not fail to resort frequently to the places where persons of distinction were to be met; such as the shops of the most considerable merchants in gold and silver, in silks, fine linens, and jewellery; and by sometimes taking a part in their conversation, he insensibly acquired the style and manners of the best company. It was at the jewellers' more particularly that he became undeceived in the idea he had formed, that the transparent fruits he had gathered in the garden which contained the lamp were only coloured glass, and that he learnt they were jewels of inestimable price. By observing all kinds of precious stones that were bought and sold in these shops, he acquired a knowledge of their value; and as he did not see any that could be compared with those he possessed, either in brilliancy or in size, he concluded that, instead of bits of common glass, which he had considered as trifles of no worth, he was in fact possessed of an invaluable treasure. He had, however, the prudence not to mention it to any one, not even to his mother, and there is no doubt that it was in consequence of his silence that he afterwards rose to the great good fortune to which we shall in the end see him elevated.

CHAPTER IV

HOW ALADDIN BEHELD THE PRINCESS BADROUL BOUDOUR ON HER WAY TO THE BATH, AND FELL DESPERATELY IN LOVE WITH HER; OF THE RESOLUTION HE FORMED IN CONSEQUENCE.

ONE day, as he was walking in the city, Aladdin heard a proclamation of the sultan, ordering all persons to shut up their shops, and retire into their houses, until the princess Badroul Boudour, his daughter, had passed to the bath, and returned.

This public order created in Aladdin a curiosity to see the princess unveiled; which, however, he could not accomplish but by going to some house where he was acquainted, and by looking through the lattices. Yet this by no means satisfied him, because the princess usually wore a veil as she went to the bath. He thought at last of a plan, which by its success completely gratified his curiosity. He went and placed himself behind the door of the bath, which was so constructed that he could not fail to see her face.

Aladdin did not wait long in his place of concealment before the princess made her appearance; and he saw her through a crevice perfectly well without being at all seen. A great crowd of females and eunuchs walked on each side of her, and others followed behind. When she had come within three or four paces of the door of the bath, she lifted up the veil, which not only concealed her face, but encumbered her, and thus gave Aladdin an opportunity of seeing her as she approached the door.

Till that moment Aladdin had never seen any other female without her veil, except his mother, who was rather old, and who even in her youth had not possessed any beauty; and he was, therefore, incapable of comparing the beauty of women. He had indeed heard that there were some females who were possessed of surprising beauty: but the expressions people use in commenting upon beauty never make the same impression which the examples themselves afford.

Aladdin had no sooner beheld the princess Badroul Boudour, than he forgot that he had ever supposed all women similar to his mother. His opinions were now very different, and he could not help surrendering his heart to the lovely being who had so charmed him. The princess was, in fact, the most beautiful brunette that ever was seen. Her eyes were large, well placed, and full of fire; yet the expression of her countenance was sweet and modest; her nose was properly proportioned, and pretty; her mouth small; her lips like vermilion, and beautifully formed; in short, every feature of her face was perfect and regular. It is, therefore, by no means wonderful that Aladdin was dazzled and almost out of his senses at beholding such a combination of charms, to which he had been hitherto a stranger. Besides all these perfections, the figure of the princess was elegant, and her air majestic; and merely the sight of her could attract the respect that was due to her rank.

Even after she had entered the bath, Aladdin stood for some time like one distracted, retracing and endeavouring to impress more strongly on his mind the image of her by whom he had been so charmed, and whose beauty had penetrated the inmost recesses of his heart. He at last came to himself, and recollecting that the princess had gone by, and that it would be perfectly useless for him to keep his station in order to see her return, as her back would then be towards him, and she would also be veiled, he determined to quit his post and retire.

When Aladdin reached home, he was unable to conceal his disquietude and distress from his mother. She was much surprised to see him appear so melancholy, and with such an unusually confused manner; and asked him if anything had happened to him, or if he were not well. He gave her, however, no answer whatever, and continued sitting on the sofa in a negligent manner, retracing in his imagination the lovely image of the princess Badroul Boudour. His mother, who was employed in preparing supper, forbore to trouble him. As soon as it was ready, she served it up close to him on the sofa, and sat down to table. But as she perceived that Aladdin was too much absorbed to attend to it, she invited him to partake of the cheer; but it was with great difficulty she could get him even to change his position. He at length ate, but in a much more sparing manner than usual; casting down his eyes all the time, and keeping such a profound silence that his mother could not obtain a single word in answer to all the questions she put to him, in order to learn the cause of so extraordinary a change.

After supper, she renewed the subject, and inquired the cause of his great melancholy; but she could get no intelligible information from him; and he determined to go to bed rather than afford his mother the least satisfaction.

It is not necessary to inquire how Aladdin passed the night, struck as he was with the beauty and charms of the princess Badroul Boudour; but the next morning, as he was sitting upon the sofa opposite his mother, who was spinning her cotton as usual, he addressed her as follows:—" Mother, I will now break the silence I have kept since my return from the city yesterday morning. I have perceived that it has pained you. I was not ill, as you seemed to think, nor is anything the matter with me now; yet I can assure you, that what I at this moment feel, and what I shall ever continue to feel, is much worse than any disease. I am myself ignorant of the nature of my feelings; but, doubtless, when I have explained myself, you will understand them.

"It was not known in this quarter of the city," continued Aladdin, "and therefore you of course are ignorant of it, that the princess Badroul Boudour, the daughter of our sultan, went, after dinner yesterday, to the bath: I learnt this intelligence during my walk in the city. An order was consequently published, that all the shops should be shut up, and every one keep at home, that due honour and respect might be paid to the princess; and that the streets through which she had to pass might be clear. As I was not far from the bath at the time, the desire I felt to see the princess unveiled made me take it into my head to place myself behind the door of the bath, supposing, as indeed it happened, that she might take off her veil just before she went into it. You recollect the situation of this door, and can therefore very well judge with what ease I could obtain a full sight of her, if what I conjectured should take place. She did, in fact, take off her veil in going in; and I had the happiness and supreme satisfaction of seeing this beautiful princess. This, my dear mother, is the true cause of the state you saw me in yesterday, and the reason of the silence I have hitherto kept. I feel such an ardent love for this princess, that I know no terms strong enough to express it; and I am convinced it can only be satisfied by the possession of the lovely princess Badroul Boudour, whom I have resolved to ask in marriage of the sultan."

Aladdin's mother listened with the greatest attention to the whole account of her son, till he came to the last sentence; but when she heard that it was his intention to demand the princess Badroul Boudour in marriage, she could not help interrupting him with a violent fit of laughter. Aladdin wished to resume his speech, but she prevented him. "Alas! my son," she cried, "what are you thinking of? You must surely have lost your senses to talk thus." "Mother," replied Aladdin, "I assure you I have not lost my senses; I am perfectly in my right mind. I foresaw that you would reproach me with folly and extravagance, even more than you have already done; but, whatever you may say, nothing will prevent me from again declaring to you, that my resolution to demand the princess Badroul Boudour of the sultan her father, in marriage, is unalterably fixed."

"Truly, my son," replied his mother, very seriously, "I cannot help telling you that you seem entirely to have forgotten who you are; and even if you are determined to put this resolution in practice, I do not know who will have the audacity to make this request to the sultan." "You yourself must," answered he, without the least hesitation. "I!" cried his mother, in a tone of the greatest surprise; "I go to the sultan! Not I, indeed; I will take care how I engage in such an enterprise. And pray, son, who do you suppose you are," she continued, "to have the impudence to aspire to the daughter of the sultan? Have you forgotten that you are the son of one of the poorest tailors in his capital, and that your mother's family cannot boast of anything better? Are you ignorant that sultans do not deign to bestow their daughters even upon the sons of other sultans unless they have some chance of coming to the throne?"

"My dear mother," replied Aladdin, "I have already told you that I perfectly foresaw everything you have said, and am aware of all that you can add further; but neither your reasons, nor your remonstrances, will in the least change my sentiments. I have told you that I would demand the princess Badroul Boudour in marriage, and that you must make the request. It is a favour which I require of you, and ask with all the respect I owe to you; and I entreat you not to refuse me, unless you would rather see me die than, by granting it, give me life, as it were, a second time."

Aladdin's mother was very much embarrassed when she saw with what obstinacy her son persisted in his mad design. "My dear son," she said, "I am your mother, and, like a good mother, I am ready to do anything that is reasonable and proper for your situation in life and my own. If this business were merely to ask the daughter of one of our neighbours, in a condition of life similar to yours, I would omit nothing, but willingly employ all my abilities in the cause. And to hope for success, even in such a case, you ought to possess some little fortune, or at least be master of some business. When poor people like us wish to marry, the first thing we ought to think about is how to live; while you, not to mention the lowness of your birth, and the little merit or fortune you have, at once aspire to the highest degree of fortune, and pretend to nothing less than to ask in marriage the daughter of your sovereign, who need only open his lips to blast all your designs, and destroy you at once.

"I will omit," continued Aladdin's mother, "what will be the consequence of this business to you, who ought to reflect upon that, if you have any reason left; and I will only consider what regards myself. How such an extraordinary design as that of wishing me to go and propose to the sultan that he would bestow the princess his daughter upon you came into your head, I cannot think. Now suppose that I have, I will not say the courage, but the impudence to go and present myself before his majesty, and to make such a mad request of him; to whom should I, in the first place, address myself for an introduction? Do you not suppose that the very first person I spoke to would treat me as a mad woman, and drive me back with all the indignity and abuse I should so justly merit? But even if I should overcome this difficulty, and procure an audience of the sultan—as indeed I know he readily grants it to all his subjects when they demand it of him for the purpose of obtaining justice —and that he even grants it with pleasure, when you have to ask a favour of him, if he thinks you are worthy of it; what should I do then? Are you in either of these situations? Do you think that you deserve the favour which you wish me to ask for you? Are you worthy of it? What have you done for your prince, or for your country? How have you ever distinguished yourself? If, then, you have done nothing to deserve so great a favour, and if, moreover, you are not worthy of it, with what face can I make the demand? How can I even open my lips to propose such a thing to the sultan? His illustrious presence, and the magnificence of his whole court, will instantly stop my mouth. How shall I, who trembled before your poor father, my husband, even attempt such a thing? But there is also another reason, my son, which you have not yet thought of, and that is, that no one ever appears before the sultan without offering him some present, when any favour is required. Presents have at least this advantage, that if, for any reason of their own, the persons solicited refuse your request, they listen to the demand that is made without any repugnance. But what present have you to offer? And even should you ever have anything that might be at all worthy the attention of so mighty a monarch, what proportion can your present possibly have with the demand you wish to make? Recollect yourself, and think that you aspire to a thing which it is impossible to obtain."

Aladdin listened with great patience to everything his mother said, in order to dissuade him from his purpose; and having reflected for some time upon every part of her remonstrance, he addressed her as follows: "I readily acknowledge, my dear mother, that it is a great piece of rashness in me to dare to carry my pretensions so high as I do; and that it must also appear very inconsiderate to request you, with so much earnestness and warmth, to propose this marriage to the sultan, without first having taken the proper means of procuring an audience and a favourable reception. I earnestly ask your pardon for doing so; but you must not wonder if the violence of the passion that possesses me has prevented me from thinking about everything that was necessary to procure me the gratification I seek. I love the princess Badroul Boudour far beyond what you can possibly conceive; or rather I adore her, and shall persevere in my wish and intention of marrying her. This is a matter on which my mind is irrevocably fixed. I am much obliged to you for the hints which you have thrown out in what you have said; and I look upon this beginning as an earnest of the complete success which I flatter myself will attend my proposals.

"You say that it is customary for him who seeks an audience of the sultan to bear a present in his hand, and that I have nothing worthy to offer him. I agree with you about the present, and also that I never once thought of it. But with regard to what you say about my having nothing worthy of his acceptance, that is a different matter. Do you not suppose, mother, that what I brought home with me on the day that I was saved in so wonderful a manner, as I have before told you, from an almost inevitable death, would be an acceptable present to the sultan?—I mean what I brought home in the two purses, in my sash, and in my vest, and which we have both hitherto taken for coloured glass; but I am now undeceived, and can inform you that they are precious stones of almost inestimable value, and exactly suitable to the state and dignity of a great sovereign. I became acquainted with their value by frequenting the shops of jewellers; and you may, I assure you, depend upon the truth of what I say. None of those which I have seen at our jewellers' are to be compared with those we have, either for size or beauty; and yet the dealers set a very high price upon them. In fact, we are

both of us ignorant of the value of ours: although that is the case, however, as far as I can judge from the little experience I have had, I am persuaded the present cannot but be very agreeable to the sultan. You have a porcelain dish sufficiently large, and of a very good shape, for holding them. Bring it here, and let us see the effect it will produce when we have arranged them according to their different colours."

Aladdin's mother brought the dish, and he took the precious stones out of the two purses and arranged them. The effect they produced in broad daylight, by the variety of their colours, by their lustre and brilliancy, was so great, that both mother and son were absolutely dazzled, and were in the greatest astonishment, they having previously seen them only by the light of a lamp. It is true that Aladdin had seen them on the trees, hanging like fruit, when they afforded a most brilliant sight; but as he was then, as it were, a child, he looked upon these jewels only as things proper to play with.

After having for some time admired their beauty, "You cannot now," said Aladdin, resuming the conversation, "excuse yourself any longer from presenting yourself to the sultan, under the pretence that you have nothing to offer him. Here is a present which, in my opinion, will procure for you the most favourable reception."

Although the mother of Aladdin, notwithstanding its great beauty and brilliancy, did not think this present near so valuable as her son did, yet she nevertheless supposed it would be very acceptable; and had, therefore, nothing to answer on that point. She then recurred to the nature of the request which Aladdin wished her to make to the sultan: this was a constant source of disquietude to her. "I cannot, my son," she said, "possibly conceive that this present will produce the effect you wish, or that the sultan will look upon you with a favourable eye. And it becomes necessary for me to acquit myself with propriety in the business you wish me to undertake. I feel convinced I shall not have courage enough to carry me through, but be struck quite dumb; and thus not only lose all my labour, but the present also, which, according to what you say, is most uncommonly rich and valuable. If I should fail in this manner, how painful will it be for me to come back and inform you of the destruction of all your hopes and expectations! I have thus told you what I know will happen, and you ought to believe it. But," added she, "if I should act so contrary to my opinion as to submit to your wishes, and shall have sufficient courage to make the request you desire, be assured that the sultan will either ridicule me, and send me back as a mad woman, or that he will be in such a passion, and with reason too, that both you and I shall most infallibly become the victims of his anger."

Aladdin's mother continued to give her son many other reasons, in order to prevail upon him to change his mind; but the charms of the princess Badroul Boudour had made too strong an impression upon the heart of Aladdin to suffer his intentions to be altered. He persisted in requiring his mother to perform her part of what he had resolved upon; and the regard she had for him, as well as the dread lest he should give himself up to some horrid excess, at length conquered her repugnance, and she acceded to his wishes.

As it was now very late, and the time of going to the palace to be presented to the sultan was past for that day, they let the matter rest ti l the next. Aladdin and his mother talked of nothing else during the rest of the day, and he said all he could think of to confirm her resolution of presenting herself to the sultan. But notwithstanding all that he could say, his mother could not be persuaded that she should ever succeed in this affair: and indeed she had every reason to be doubtful of it. "My dear child," said she, "even should the sultan receive me as favourably as my regard for you would lead me to wish, and should listen with the greatest patience to the proposal you request me to make, will he not inquire what property you possess, and where your estates are?—for he will of course, in the first instance, rather ask about this matter than about your personal appearance. If, I say, he should ask me this question, what answer do you wish me to make?"

"Do not, mother, let us distress ourselves," replied Aladdin, "about a thing that may never happen. Let us first see how the sultan will receive you, and what answer he will give to your request. If he should wish to be informed of what you mention, I will find out some answer to make him. I put the greatest confidence in my lamp, by means of which we have been able for some years past to live in the manner we have done. It will not desert me when I have most need of it."

His mother had not a word to say to this speech of Aladdin. She might naturally suppose that the lamp would be able to perform much more astonishing things than simply to procure them the means of subsistence. This satisfied her, and at the same time smoothed all the difficulties which seemed to oppose themselves to the business she had promised to undertake for her son. Aladdin, who easily penetrated his mother's thoughts, said to her: "Above all things keep this matter secret; for upon that depends all the success we may either of us expect." They then retired for the night: but love, joined to the great schemes of aggrandisement which the son had in view, prevented him from passing the night so tranquilly as he wished. He got up at daybreak, and went immediately to call his mother. He was anxious that she should dress herself as soon as possible, in order that she might repair to the gate of the sultan's palace, and enter at the same time that the grand vizier, the subordinate viziers, and the other officers of state, went into the divan, or hall of audience, where the sultan always held his council in person.

CHAPTER V.

ALADDIN'S MOTHER SOLICITS THE HAND OF THE PRINCESS BADROUL BOUDOUR FOR HER SON.— HER GRACIOUS RECEPTION BY THE SULTAN, AND THE PROMISE HE MADE TO HER.

ALADDIN'S mother did everything as her son wished. She took the porcelain dish in which the jewels were deposited, and folded it up in a very fine and white linen cloth. She then took another cloth, which was not so fine, and tied the four corners of it together, that she might carry it with less trouble. She afterwards set out, to the great joy of Aladdin, towards the palace of the sultan. The grand vizier, accompanied by the other viziers and the proper officers of the court, had already gone in before she arrived at the gate. The crowd of persons who had business at the divan was very great. The doors were opened, and the mother of Aladdin went into the divan with the rest. It was a beautiful saloon, very spacious, and with a magnificent entrance. She placed herself opposite to the throne of the sultan, near the grand vizier, and other officers who formed the council on both sides. The different parties who had suits to press were called up one after the other, according to the order in which their petitions had been presented; and their affairs were heard, pleaded, and determined, till the usual hour of breaking up the council. The sultan then rose, took leave of the members, and went back to his apartment, into which he was followed by the grand vizier. The other viziers and officers who formed the council then went away; as also did all those whose private business had brought them there, some being delighted at having gained their cause, while others were but ill satisfied with the decisions pronounced against them: in addition to whom was a third party, they who were anxious to have their business come on as early as possible.

Aladdin's mother, who saw the sultan arise and retire, rightly imagined that he would not appear any more that day, as she observed that every one was going away: she therefore determined to return home. When Aladdin saw her come back with the present in her hand, he knew not at first what to think of the success of her journey. He could hardly open his mouth to inquire what intelligence she had brought him, from the fear that she had something unfortunate to announce. The good woman, who had never before set her foot within the walls of a palace, and of course knew not in the least the customs of the place, very soon relieved her son from his anxiety by saying, with an air of gaiety, "I have seen the sultan, my son, and I am persuaded he has seen me also. I placed myself directly opposite him; and there was no person in the way to prevent his seeing me: but he was so much engaged in speaking with those on each side of him, that I really felt compassion to see the trouble he had, and the patience with which he listened to them. This lasted so long, that I believe at length he was quite worn out; for he got up before any one expected it, and retired suddenly, without staying to hear a great many others, who were ranged in readiness to address him in their turn: and, indeed, this gave me great pleasure, for I began to lose all patience, and was extremely tired with standing so long. There was, however, no other restraint; and I will not fail to return to-morrow: the sultan will not then, perhaps, be so much engaged."

However desperate Aladdin's passion was, he was obliged to be satisfied with this excuse, and to summon up all his patience. He had, at least, the satisfaction of knowing that his mother had got over the most difficult part of the business, which was to obtain an interview with the sultan; and therefore hoped that, like those who had spoken to him in her presence, she would not hesitate to acquit herself of the commission with which she was entrusted, when the favourable moment of addressing him should arrive.

The next morning, quite as early as on the preceding day, Aladdin's mother set out for the sultan's palace with the present of jewels; but her journey was useless. She found the gate of the divan shut, and learned that the council never sat two days together, but alternately, and that she must come again on the following morning. She went back with this intelligence to her son, who was again obliged to exert his patience. She returned again to the palace six different times on the appointed days, always placing herself opposite to the sultan; but she was every time as unsuccessful as at first, and would probably have gone a hundred times as uselessly, if the sultan, who constantly saw her standing opposite to him every day the divan sat, had not taken notice of her. This is the more probable, as it was only those who had petitions to present, or causes to be heard, that approached the sultan, each in his turn pleading his cause according to his rank; and Aladdin's mother was not in this situation.

One day, however, when the council was broken up, and the sultan had retired to his apartment, he said to the grand vizier, "For some time past, I have observed a woman who has come regularly every day I hold my council, and who carries something in her hand, wrapped up in a linen cloth. She remains standing, from the beginning of the audience till it is concluded, and always takes care to place herself opposite to me. Do you know what she wants?"

The grand vizier, who did not wish to appear ignorant of the matter, though in fact he knew no more about it than the sultan himself, replied: "Your majesty, sire, is not ignorant that women often make complaints upon the most trivial subjects; she appears to have come to your majesty with some complaint, that they have sold her some bad meat, or something else of equal insignificance." This answer, however, did not satisfy the sultan. "The very next day the council sits," said he to the grand vizier, "if this woman returns, do not fail to call her, that I may hear what she has to say." The grand vizier only answered by kissing his hand, and placing it on his head, to show that he would rather lose it than fail in his duty.

The mother of Aladdin had already been so much in the habit of going to the palace on the days the council met, that she now thought it no trouble, provided she by these means proved to her son that she neglected nothing that depended upon her, and that he had, therefore, no reason to complain of her. She consequently returned to the palace the next day the council met, and placed herself near the entrance of the divan, opposite to the sultan, as had been her usual practice.

The grand vizier had not made his report of any business, before the sultan perceived Aladdin's mother. Touched with compassion at the excessive patience she had shown, "In the first place," said he to the grand vizier, "and for fear you should forget it, do you not observe the woman whom I mentioned to you? Order her to come here, and we will begin by hearing what she has to say, and expedite her business." The grand vizier immediately pointed out the woman to the chief of the ushers, who was standing near him, ready to receive his orders, and desired him to bring her before the sultan. The officer went directly to the mother of Aladdin, and having made a sign to her, she followed him to the foot of the throne, where he left her, and went back to his place near the grand vizier.

Aladdin's mother, following the example that so many others, whom she had seen approach the sultan, had set her, prostrated herself, with her face towards the carpet which covered the steps of the throne; and she remained in that situation till the sultan commanded her to rise. She did so, and the sultan then addressed her in these words: "For a long time past, my good woman, I have seen you regularly attend my divan, and remain near the entrance, from the time it assembled till it broke up. What is the business that brings you here?" On hearing this, she prostrated herself a second time, and on rising, thus answered: "High monarch, mightier than all the monarchs of the world, before I inform your majesty of the extraordinary and almost incredible cause that compels me to appear before your sublime throne, I entreat you to pardon the boldness—nay, I might say the impudence—of the request I am going to make to you. It is of so uncommon a nature, that I tremble, and feel almost overcome with shame to propose it to my sultan." In order, however, that she might have full liberty to explain herself, the sultan commanded every one to leave the divan, and remained with only his grand vizier in attendance: he then told her that she might speak, and make known everything without fear.

The goodness of the sultan, however, did not perfectly satisfy Aladdin's mother, although he had thus prevented her from being obliged to explain her wishes before the whole assembly. She was still anxious to screen herself from the indignation which she could not but dread that the proposal she had to make to him would excite, and from which she could not otherwise defend herself. "Sire," said she, again addressing the sultan, "I once more entreat your majesty to assure me of your pardon beforehand, in case you should think my request at all injurious or offensive." "Whatever it may be," replied the sultan, "I pardon you; no harm shall happen to you from anything you may say: speak, therefore, with confidence."

When Aladdin's mother had thus taken every precaution against the possible anger of the sultan at the very delicate proposal she was about to make to him, she faithfully related by what means Aladdin had seen the Princess Badroul Boudour, and with what a violent passion the fatal sight had inspired him;—the declaration that he had made concerning her, and the mission with which he had charged his mother, together with all the remonstrances the latter had urged, in order to avert his thoughts from this passion. "A passion," added she, "as

ALADDIN'S MOTHER OFFERING HER SON'S PRESENT TO THE SULTAN.

injurious to your majesty as it is to the princess your daughter; but my son would not profit by anything I could say, nor would he acknowledge his temerity; he obstinately persevered and threatened to commit some rash action in his despair, if I refused to come and demand of your majesty the princess in marriage. I have been obliged, therefore, to comply with his wishes, although this compliance was very much against my will. And once more, I entreat your majesty to pardon not only me for making such a request, but also my son Aladdin, for having conceived the rash and daring design of aspiring to so illustrious an alliance."

The sultan listened to this speech with the greatest patience and good humour, and showed not the least mark of either anger or indignation at the request; nor did he even turn it into ridicule. Before he returned any answer to the good

woman, he asked her what she had got tied up in a cloth. Upon this she immediately took up the porcelain dish, which she had at first set down at the foot of the throne, and having uncovered it, she presented it to the sultan.

It is impossible to express the surprise and astonishment which the monarch felt when he saw such a quantity of the most precious, perfect, and brilliant jewels, the size of every one of which was greater than any he had before seen. His admiration for some time was so great, that it rendered him absolutely motionless. When, however, he began to recollect himself, he took the present from the hand of Aladdin's mother, and exclaimed in a transport of joy, "Ah! how very beautiful, how extremely rich!" And then having admired them all one after another, and, put each again in the same place, he turned to his grand vizier, and showing him the dish, asked him if it was not also his opinion that he had never before seen any jewels so perfect and valuable. The vizier was himself delighted with them. "Well," added the sultan, "what do you say to such a present? Is not the donor worthy of the princess my daughter? and must I not give her to him who comes and demands her at such a price?"

This speech of the sultan very much alarmed the grand vizier; because the former had, some time before, given him to understand that he had an intention of bestowing the hand of the princess upon his only son. He was afraid, therefore, and his fears were not without foundation, that the sultan would be dazzled by so rich and extraordinary a present and alter his mind. He approached the sultan, and, whispering in his ear, "Sire," said he, "every one must allow that this present is not unworthy of the princess; but I entreat you to grant me three months before you determine absolutely. I hope that long before that time my son, for whom you have had the condescension to express that you feel a great regard, will be able to offer you a much more considerable present than that of Aladdin, whom your majesty does not know." Although the sultan was quite persuaded that it was impossible for his grand vizier to enable his son to make so valuable a present to the princess, he nevertheless granted him this favour. He, therefore, turned towards Aladdin's mother, and said to her, "Go, my good woman, return home, and tell your son that I agree to the proposal he has made through you, but that I cannot bestow the princess my daughter in marriage until I have ordered and prepared a variety of furniture and ornaments, which will not be ready for three months. At the end of that time come hither again."

The mother of Aladdin went back, and felt the greater joy because she had, in the first place, conceived even access to the sultan for a person of her condition as absolutely impossible; and because, also, she had received so favourable an answer, when she had expected a rebuke that would have overwhelmed her with confusion. When Aladdin saw his mother enter the house, there were two circumstances that led him to suppose she brought him good news: one was, that she had returned that morning much sooner than usual; and the other, that her countenance expressed pleasure and good humour. "Well, mother," said Aladdin, "what have I to hope? Am I doomed to die with despair?" When she had taken off her veil, and sat down on the sofa by his side, "My son," she said, "that I may not hold you any longer in suspense, I will, in the first place, tell you that so far from thinking of dying, you have every reason to he satisfied." She then went on with her narrative, and told him that she had obtained an audience before every other person, which was the reason that she had come back so soon; the precautions she had taken to make her request to the sultan in such a way that he should not be offended when he came to know that it was to demand of him the princess Badroul Boudour in marriage for her son; and the very favourable answer the sultan had given her from his own lips. She then added,

that, as far as she could judge from every thing the sultan did, it was the present that had had such a powerful effect upon his mind as to induce him to return so favourable an answer. "At least, I think so," added she; "because before the sultan returned me any answer at all, the grand vizier whispered something in his ear, and I was afraid that it would tend to lessen the good intentions he seemed to have towards you."

When Aladdin heard this, he thought himself the happiest of mortals. He thanked his mother for all the pains she had taken in the transaction, and for the happy success which was so important to his repose. So impatient was he, however, to possess the object of his affection, that three months seemed to him to be an age; he nevertheless endeavoured to wait with patience, considering the word of the sultan as irrevocable. In the meantime, he not only reckoned the hours, the days, and the weeks, but even every moment, till the period should elapse.

It happened one evening, when about two months of the time were passed, that as Aladdin's mother was going to light her lamp she found she had no oil in the house. She therefore went out to buy some, and on going into the city she found that there was some festivity going forward. All the shops were ornamented with branches and decorations, and every preparation making for an illumination, each person endeavouring to excel his neighbour in splendour and magnificence, in order to show his zeal. Every one was giving marks of his pleasure and rejoicing. The streets were crowded with officers in their dresses of ceremony, mounted upon horses most richly caparisoned, and surrounded with a great number of attendants and domestics on foot, who were traversing the city in every direction. Upon seeing all this, she asked the merchant of whom she bought the oil what it all meant. "Where do you come from, my good woman," said he, "not to know that the son of the grand vizier is this evening to be married to the princess Badroul Boudour, the daughter of our sultan? She is just now coming from the bath, and the officers whom you see have assembled here in order to escort her back to the palace, where the ceremony is to be performed."

Aladdin's mother did not wait to hear any more. She returned home with all possible speed, and arrived quite out of breath. Her son was not in the least prepared for the bad news she brought him. "Every thing, my son," she exclaimed, "is lost. You depended upon the fair promises of the sultan, and it will come to nothing." Aladdin was alarmed at these words, and instantly inquired, "On what account, mother; will not the sultan keep his word? How do you know anything about it?" "This very evening," answered she, "the son of the grand vizier is to marry the princess Badroul Boudour at the palace." She then related to him in what way she had learned the news, and informed him of all the circumstances which prevented her from having the least doubt of its truth.

Aladdin received this intelligence like a thunderstroke. Any person but himself would have been quite overwhelmed by it: but a sort of secret jealousy prevented him from remaining long in this state. The lamp came instantly to his recollection—that lamp which had hitherto been so useful to him; and then, without venting his rage in vain reproaches against the sultan, or the grand vizier, or the son of that officer, he only said, "This minister's son, mother, shall not be so happy to-night as he expects: while I am gone for a few moments into my chamber, do you prepare supper."

His mother easily comprehended that Aladdin intended to make use of the lamp, in order, if possible, to prevent the marriage of the grand vizier's son with the princess Badroul Boudour from being completed. Nor did she deceive herself, for he was no sooner in his own room, than he took the wonderful lamp, which he kept there, that his mother might never again be alarmed at it, as she had been when the genie had put her into so great a fright. He had no sooner taken the lamp, and rubbed it in the usual place, than the genie instantly appeared before him. "What do you wish?" said he to Aladdin. "I am ready to obey you as your slave, and the slave of those who have the lamp in their hands; I, and the other slaves of the lamp." "Attend to me, then," answered Aladdin. "You have hitherto brought me only what I wanted to eat and drink. I have now a business for you of more importance. I have demanded of the sultan the princess Badroul Boudour, his daughter, in marriage. He promised her to me, and only requested a delay of three months. Instead, however, of keeping his word, he has this very evening, before that period has elapsed, given his daughter in marriage to the son of his grand vizier. I have just now been informed of it, and the thing is certain. What, therefore, I have to order you to do is this: as soon as the bride and bridegroom shall be placed by each other's side, take them up, and bring them both instantly here in their bed." "Master," replied the genie, "I will obey you. Have you anything else to command?" "Nothing at present," added Aladdin. The genie instantly disappeared.

Aladdin then went back to his mother, and supped with her in the same tranquil manner as usual. After supper he entered into conversation with her for some time respecting the marriage of the princess, as of a thing that did not in the least embarrass him. He afterwards returned to his chamber, and left his mother to repose whenever she pleased. He, of course, did not retire to rest, but waited in expectation for the return of the genie, and the execution of the orders he had given him.

CHAPTER VI.

THE MARRIAGE OF THE PRINCESS BADROUL BOU-
DOUR WITH THE SON OF THE GRAND VIZIER.—
THE DISAGREEABLE CIRCUMSTANCES THAT FOL-
LOWED THEIR UNION.

IN the meantime everything was prepared in the sultan's palace to celebrate the nuptials of the princess, and the time was spent in ceremonies and rejoicings till the night was far advanced. When all this was concluded, the son of the grand vizier, at a sign that the chief of the eunuchs belonging to the princess privately gave him, retired unperceived; and this officer then introduced him into the apartment belonging to the princess, his wife, and conducted him to the chamber where the nuptial couch was prepared. He retired to bed first; and in a short time after, the sultana, accompanied by her own women and those of her daughter, brought the bride into the room; and, after she had embraced her and wished her a good night, she retired with all the other females.

Scarcely had this taken place, before the genie, like a faithful slave of the lamp, took up the bed in which were the bride and the bridegroom, and, to the great astonishment of both, transported them in an instant to Aladdin's chamber, where he set them down.

Aladdin, who was waiting for this event with the greatest impatience, did not long suffer the son of the grand vizier to remain in bed with the princess. "Take this bridegroom," said he to the genie, "and shut him up in the closet above the sewer, and return again in the morning, just at daybreak." The genie instantly took the grand vizier's son out of bed, and transported him to the place Aladdin had commanded, where he left him, having first breathed upon him in such a way that the effects of it in every limb were felt in a lassitude that prevented him from stirring from his place.

How violent soever the passion was which Aladdin felt for the princess, he did not enter into any long conversation with her, when he was with her alone. "Fear nothing, most adorable princess," he exclaimed, with an impassioned air, "you are here in safety; and however violent the love which I feel for you may be, with whatever ardour I adore your beauty, be assured that I will never exceed the limits of the profound respect I have for you. If I have been forced," he added, "to proceed to this extremity, it has not been with the intention of offending you, but to prevent an unjust rival from possessing you, contrary to the promise which the sultan your father had made in my favour."

The princess, who knew nothing of all these particulars, paid very little attention to what Aladdin said. She was indeed no longer in a condition to answer him. The alarm and astonishment into which this surprising and unexpected adventure had thrown her, had such an effect upon her that Aladdin could not get a single word from her. He did not, however, remain long in this state, but immediately laid down in the place of the grand vizier's son, with his back turned towards the princess, having first taken the precaution to place a sabre between the princess and himself.

Aladdin was satisfied with having thus deprived his rival of the happiness, with the enjoyment of which he had this night flattered himself, and slept very tranquilly. But how different was the case with the princess!—never in her whole life did she pass so unpleasant and disagreeable a night. And it is only necessary to reflect for an instant on the place and situation in which the genie had left the son of the grand vizier, to judge that the bridegroom spent the hours of darkness in a still more afflicting manner.

Aladdin had no occasion to rub his lamp the next morning to call the genie. He returned at the appointed hour, and while Aladdin was dressing himself. "Here I am," said he to Aladdin; "what commands have you for me?" "Go," answered Aladdin, "and bring back the son of the grand vizier from the place where you have put him, place him again in his bed, and transport it back to the palace of the sultan, whence you brought it." The genie instantly went to relieve the grand vizier's son from his post, and as soon as he appeared Aladdin took away his sabre. He placed the bridegroom by the side of the princess, and in a moment replaced the bed in the very same chamber of the sultan's palace whence he had before taken it.

It is necessary to remark, that during all these transactions the genie was invisible to the princess and the son of the grand vizier: the sight of his hideous form would have killed them with fright. They did not even hear a single word of the conversation that passed between Aladdin and him, and perceived only the agitation of the bed, and transporting of it from one place to another: and indeed it is easy to imagine that this frightened them quite enough.

The genie had no sooner put the nuptial couch in its place, than the sultan entered the chamber and wished the princess a good morning. The son of the grand vizier, half dead with the cold he had suffered all night, jumped out of bed as soon as he heard some person opening the door, and went into the dressing-room where he had undressed himself in the evening.

The sultan came up to the bed-side of the princess, and kissed her between her eyes, as is the usual custom in wishing any one good morning. He asked her, with a smile upon his face, how she had passed the night; but when he lifted up her head and looked at her with greater attention, he was extremely surprised to observe her in the most dejected and melancholy state. She cast upon him the most sorrowful looks, and showed, by her whole manner, that she laboured either under the most severe affliction or the greatest degree of discontent. The sultan again spoke to her, but as he found he was unable to get a word from her, he retired. He could not, however, but suspect from her continued silence that something very extraordinary had happened. He went immediately to the apartment of the sultana, to whom he mentioned the state in which he had found the princess, and the reception she had given him.

As soon as the sultana was dressed she went to the apartment of the princess, who was not yet risen. She approached the bed, and wishing her a good morning, embraced her; but her surprise was excessive when she found that the princess was not only silent, but was in the greatest distress. She therefore concluded that something which she could not yet comprehend had happened to her. "My dear daughter," said the sultana to her, "what is the reason that you so ill repay the caresses I bestow upon you? You ought not to act thus towards your mother. Something surely has occurred which I do not understand. Tell me, then, candidly, and do not suffer me to remain so long in

an uncertainty that distresses me beyond measure."

At length, fetching a deep sigh, the princess Badroul Boudour broke silence. "Alas! my most honoured mother," she cried, "pardon me if I have failed in any respect that is due to you. My mind is so entirely absorbed by the strange and extraordinary things that have happened to me this night, that I have not yet recovered from my astonishment and fears, and have some difficulty to collect myself." She then related how, the instant after she and her husband were retired, the bed had been taken up and transported into an ill-furnished and dismal chamber, where she found herself quite alone, without in the least knowing what was become of her husband; and that she found in this apartment a young man, who after having addressed a few words to her, which her terror prevented her from understanding, lay down in her husband's place, having first put his sabre between them; and that when morning approached, her husband was restored to her, and the bed again brought back in an instant of time. "The whole of this transaction," she added, "was but just completed when the sultan my father came into my chamber. I was then so absorbed in grief and distress, that I could not answer him a single word, and I am afraid that he was very angry at the manner in which I received the honour he did me. I hope, however, that he will pardon me, when he shall have become acquainted with my melancholy adventure, and the lamentable state in which I even now find myself."

The sultana listened with great attention to everything the princess had to relate, but she could not give full credit to the account. "You have done well, my child," she said to the princess, "not to inform the sultan your father of this matter. Take care that you mention it to no one, unless you wish to be taken for one who has lost her reason, which will certainly be the case if you should talk in this way to any other person." "Madam," replied the princess, "I assure that I am in my right senses, and know what I say: you may ask my husband, and he will tell you the same thing." "I will take care and inform myself of it," answered the sultana; "but even if he gives me the same account you have done, I shall not be more persuaded of the truth of it: in the meantime, however, arise, and drive this phantasy from your mind. It would be indeed a curious thing to see you under such a delusion during the feasts that have been ordered on account of your nuptials, and which will last for many days, not only in the palace, but all over the kingdom. Do you not already hear the trumpets, cymbals, and other instruments? All this ought to inspire you with joy and pleasure, and make you forget the fanciful dream which you have related to me." The sultana then called her women; and after she had made her get up, and seen her at her toilet, she went to the sultan's apartment, and told him that a strange fancy possessed his daughter, but that it was a mere trifle. She then ordered the son of the grand vizier to be called, in order to inquire of him about what the princess had told her. But he felt himself so highly honoured by his alliance with the sultan, that he determined to feign ignorance of everything. "Tell me, son-in-law," said the sultana, "have you got the same strange ideas in your head as your wife?" "Madam," he replied, "may I be permitted to ask you for what reason you put this question to me?" "That is sufficient," answered the sultana; "I do not wish to know more; you have more sense than she has."

The festivities in the palace continued throughout the day, and the sultan forgot nothing that he thought might inspire the princess with joy. He endeavoured to make her partake of the diversions and various exhibitions that were going on; but the recollection of what had passed on the preceding night made such a strong impression on her mind, that it was very evident something occupied her whole attention. The son of the grand vizier was not less afflicted at the wretched night he had passed; but his ambitious views made him dissemble; and therefore, if any persons had judged from his appearance, they would have thought him the happiest bridegroom in the world.

Aladdin, who was well informed of everything that passed in the palace, did not doubt but that the newly-married pair would again sleep together, notwithstanding the distressing adventure that had happened to them the night before. He did not choose, however, to let them repose in quiet. A short time before night came on, he again had recourse to his lamp. The genie instantly appeared, and addressed Aladdin with the accustomed speech in offering his services. "The grand vizier's son and the princess Badroul Boudour," replied he, "are again to sleep together this night. Go, and as soon as they have lain down, bring the bed hither as you did yesternight."

The genie obeyed Aladdin with punctuality, as on the night before; and the vizier's son passed this night in as cold and unpleasant a situation as he did the former; while the princess had the mortification of having Aladdin for her bedfellow, with the sabre, as before, placed between them. In the morning the genie came according to Aladdin's orders, replaced the bridegroom in the bed, and took it back to the chamber of the palace whence he had taken it.

After the extraordinary reception which the princess Badroul Boudour had given the sultan on the preceding morning, he was very anxious to learn how she passed the second night, and whether she would again receive him in the manner she had before done. He went, therefore, to her apartment early in the morning, that he might satisfy himself. The grand vizier's son, still more mortified and distressed at his bad treatment the second night than he had been on the first, no sooner heard the sultan than he got up as fast as possible, and ran into the dressing-room. The sultan came to her bed-side, and wished the princess a good morning, after having caressed her in the same manner as he had done the day before. "Well, my daughter," he said, "are you in as bad humour this morning as you were yesterday? Tell me how you have passed the night." The princess preserved the same silence, and the sultan perceived that she was still more dejected and distressed than she had been the morning before. He could, therefore, but infer that something very extraordinary

had happened to her. Irritated at the mystery she made of it to him, "Daughter," said he, in an angry tone, and at the same time drawing his sabre, "either tell me what you thus conceal, or I will instantly strike off your head."

The princess, terrified at the manner in which the sultan menaced her, and at the sight of the drawn sabre, at length broke silence. "My dear father," she exclaimed, with tears in her eyes, "if I have offended your majesty, I earnestly entreat your pardon. From your known goodness and clemency, I trust I shall change your anger into compassion when I shall have related, in a full and faithful manner, the occasion of the distressing and melancholy situation in which I have been placed both last night and the night before." This preamble appeased and softened the sultan. She then related at length what had happened to her on both these horrible nights, and in a manner so affecting that he was penetrated with grief for the suffering of his beloved daughter. She thus concluded her narrative: "If your majesty has the least doubt of any part of what I have said, you can easily inquire of the husband you have bestowed upon me; I am very well persuaded he will prove to you the truth of everything I have related."

The sultan entered very fully into the distressing feelings this surprising adventure must have excited in his daughter's mind. "My child," said he, "you were wrong not to explain to me yesterday the strange business which you have just related, and in which I am not less interested than yourself. I have not bestowed you in marriage with the view to render you unhappy, but, on the contrary, to increase your happiness, and to afford you every enjoyment you so well deserve. Drive away, then, from your memory the melancholy ideas of what you have been relating to me. I will take care that you shall experience no more nights so disagreeable, nay, so insupportable, as those which you have now suffered."

When the sultan got back to his apartment he immediately sent for the grand vizier. "Have you seen your son," he asked him, "and has he mentioned anything in particular to you?" When the latter replied that he had not seen him, the sultan reported to him everything he had heard from the princess Badroul Boudour. He then added, "I have no doubt but that my daughter has told me the truth. I wish, nevertheless, to have this matter confirmed by the testimony of your son. Go, therefore, and ask him what has happened to him."

The grand vizier instantly went to his son: he informed him of what the sultan had said, and commanded him not to disguise the truth, and to tell him everything that had passed. "I will conceal nothing from you, my father," replied his son, "and everything the princess has told the sultan is true: but she was unable to give an account of the bad treatment which I in particular have experienced. Since my marriage I have spent two of the most dreadful nights you can possibly conceive; and I cannot describe to you all the various evils I have gone through. I do not mention the fright I was in at finding myself lifted up in my bed four different times, without being able to see any one; and being transported from one place to another without being able to conceive in what way it was brought about. But you can yourself judge of the dreadful state I was in, when I tell you that I passed both nights standing upright in a narrow and loathsome closet, without having the power of moving from the spot where I was placed, although there seemed to be no obstacle whatever to prevent me. After having said this, I have no occasion to enter into a greater detail of my sufferings. Let me, however, add, that all this has by no means lessened my respect and affection for the princess my wife; though I confess to you most sincerely, that with all the honour and splendour that I derive from having the daughter of my sovereign for my wife, I would much sooner die than enjoy this high alliance if I must continue to undergo the severe and horrible treatment I have already suffered. I am sure the princess must be of the same opinion as myself, and there is no doubt but that our separation is as necessary for her comfort as for my own. I entreat you, therefore, my dear father, by all the affection which led you to obtain this great honour for me, to induce the sultan to decree our marriage null and void."

However great might be the ambition of the grand vizier to have his son so nearly allied to the sultan, yet the fixed resolution which he found he had formed of dissolving his marriage with the princess, made him think it necessary to request his son to have patience for a few days before it was finally settled, in order to see whether this unpleasant business might not have an end. He then left his son, and returned to the sultan, to whom he acknowledged that everything was true, as he had himself learned from his son. And then, without waiting till the sultan himself spoke to him about annulling the marriage, to which he observed that the latter was very much inclined, he requested permission for his son to leave the palace and return to him, under the pretext that it was not just that the princess should be exposed an instant longer to so terrible a persecution through regard for his son.

The grand vizier had no difficulty in obtaining his request. The sultan, who had already determined on the matter in his own mind, immediately gave orders for the rejoicings to be put a stop to, not only in his own palace, but in the city, and throughout the whole extent of his dominions; and in a short time every mark of public joy and festivity within the kingdom ceased. This sudden and unexpected change gave rise to a variety of different conjectures. Every one was inquiring why these contrary orders were issued, and all affirmed that the grand vizier had been seen to come out of the palace, and go towards his own house, accompanied by his son; and that they both seemed very much dejected. Aladdin was the only person who was acquainted with the actual reason; and he rejoiced most sincerely at the happy success arising from the use of the lamp. And having now learnt for a certainty that his rival had left the palace, and that the marriage between the princess and him was annulled, he had no further occasion to rub his lamp, and have recourse to the

genie, in order to prevent his rival's happiness. What, however, was most singular, was, that neither the sultan, nor the grand vizier, who had completely forgotten Aladdin and the request he had made, entertained the least idea that he had any part in the enchantment which had been the occasion of the dissolution of the marriage of the princess.

CHAPTER VII.

ALADDIN AGAIN DEMANDS THE HAND OF THE PRINCESS.—THE NEW CONDITIONS IMPOSED BY THE SULTAN.

ALADDIN suffered the three months which the sultan wished to elapse before the marriage of the princess Badroul Boudour and himself to pass without making any application. He kept, however, an exact account of every day; and when the period was expired, he sent his mother on the very next morning to the palace to remind the sultan of his promise. She went to the palace, and stood at her usual place, near the entrance of the divan. The sultan no sooner cast his eyes that way, than he recollected her, and she instantly brought to his mind the request she had made, and the exact time to which he had deferred it. As the grand vizier approached, to make some report to him, the sultan stopped him by saying, "I perceive that good woman who presented us with the beautiful collection of jewels, some time since; order her to come forward, and you can make your report after I have heard what she has to say." The grand vizier immediately called to the chief of the ushers, and pointing her out to him, desired him to bring her forward.

Aladdin's mother advanced to the foot of the throne, where she prostrated herself in the usual manner. After she had risen, the sultan asked her what she wished. "Sire," she replied, "I again present myself before the throne of your majesty, to represent to you, in the name of my son Aladdin, that the three months which you had desired him to wait, in consequence of the request I had to make to your majesty, are expired; and to entreat you to have the goodness to recall the circumstance to your remembrance."

When the sultan had desired a delay of three months before he answered the request of this good woman the first time he saw her, he thought he should hear no more of a marriage which, from the apparent poverty and low situation of Aladdin's mother, who always presented herself before him in a very coarse and common dress, appeared so little suited to the princess, his daughter. The application, therefore, which she now made to him to keep his word, embarrassed him very much, and he did not think it prudent to give her, at the moment, a direct answer. He consulted his grand vizier, and told him the repugnance he felt at concluding a marriage between the princess and an unknown person, whom fortune, he conjectured, had not raised much above the condition of a common subject.

"Sire," replied the vizier, "it seems to me that there is a very easy and yet certain method to avoid this unequal marriage, and of which this

Aladdin, even if he were known to your majesty, could not complain; it is, to set so high a price upon the princess, your daughter, that all his riches, however great they may be, cannot amount to the value. This will be a way to make him desist from so bold, not to say arrogant an attempt, and which he certainly does not seem to have considered well before he engaged in it."

The sultan approved of the advice of his grand vizier, and after some little reflection, he said to Aladdin's mother, "Sultans, my good woman, ought always to keep their word; and I am ready to adhere to mine, and render your son happy by marrying him to the princess my daughter; but as I cannot bestow her in marriage till I am better acquainted how she will be provided for, tell your son that I will fulfil my promise as soon as he shall send me forty large basins of massive gold, quite full of the same kind of jewels which you have already presented to me from him, brought by an equal number of black slaves, each of whom shall be conducted by a white slave, young, well-made, of good appearance, and richly dressed. These are the conditions upon which I am ready to bestow upon him the princess, my daughter. Go, my good woman; and I will wait till you bring me his answer."

Aladdin's mother again prostrated herself at the foot of the throne, and retired. In her way home, she smiled within herself at the foolish thoughts of her son. "Where, indeed," said she, "is he to find so many golden basins, and such a great quantity of coloured glass to fill them? Will he attempt to go back to the subterraneous cabin, the entrance of which is shut up, in order to gather them off the trees? And where can he procure all these handsome slaves which the sultan demands? He is far enough from having his pretensions fulfilled; and I believe he will not be very well satisfied with my embassy." When she entered the house, with her mind occupied by these thoughts, from which she judged Aladdin had nothing more to hope, "My son," said she, "I advise you to think no more of your marriage with the princess Badroul Boudour. The sultan, indeed, received me with great kindness, and I believe that he was well inclined towards you; the grand vizier, however, if I am not mistaken, made him alter his opinion, as you will yourself think when you have heard the account I am going to give you. After I had represented to his majesty that the three months were expired, and requested him, as from you, to recollect his promise, I observed that he did not answer me until he had spoken for some time in a low tone of voice to the grand vizier." Aladdin's mother then gave him an exact detail of everything the sultan had said, and of the conditions upon which he consented to the marriage of the princess his daughter. "He is even now, my son," added she, "waiting for your answer; but, between ourselves," she continued, with a smile, "he may wait long enough." "Not so long as you may think, mother," replied Aladdin; "and the sultan deceives himself if he supposes, by such exorbitant demands, to prevent me thinking any more of the princess Badroul Boudour. I expected to have much greater difficulties to surmount, and

that he would have put a much higher price upon my incomparable princess. But I am now very well satisfied, and what he requires of me is trifling in comparison to what I would give him to possess such a treasure. While I am considering how to comply with his demands, do you go and see about something for dinner, and leave me to myself."

As soon as his mother was gone out to purchase some provisions, Aladdin took the lamp, and having rubbed it, the genie instantly appeared, and demanded of him, in the usual terms, what it was that he wanted, for he was ready to obey him. "The sultan agrees to give me the princess, his daughter, in marriage," said Aladdin; "but he first demands of me forty large heavy basins of massive gold, filled to the very top with the various fruits of the garden from which I took the lamp, of which you are the slave. He requires, also, that these forty basins should be carried by as many black slaves, preceded by an equal number of young, handsome, and elegant white slaves, very richly dressed. Go, and procure me this present as soon as possible, that I may send it to the sultan before the sitting of the divan is over." The genie merely said that his commands should be instantly executed, and disappeared.

In a very short time the genie returned with forty black slaves, each carrying upon his head a large golden basin of great weight, full of pearls, diamonds, rubies, and emeralds, equally valuable for their brilliancy and size with those which had already been presented to the sultan. Each basin was covered with a cloth of silver, embroidered with flowers of gold. All these slaves, with their golden basins, together with the white ones, entirely filled the house, which was but small, as well as the court in front, and a garden behind it. The genie asked Aladdin if he were contented, and whether he had any further commands for him; and, on being told he had not, he immediately disappeared.

Aladdin's mother was in the greatest surprise on coming home to see so many persons and so much riches. When she had set down the provisions which she had brought with her, she was going to take off her veil, but Aladdin prevented her. "My dear mother," he cried, "there is no time to lose. It is of consequence that you should return to the palace before the divan breaks up, and should immediately conduct there the present and dowry which the sultan demands for the princess Badroul Boudour, that he may judge, from my diligence and exactness, of the ardent and sincere zeal I have to procure for myself the honour of an alliance with him."

Without waiting for his mother's answer, Aladdin opened the door that led into the street, and ordered all the slaves to go out, one after the other. He then placed a white slave before each of the black ones, who carried the golden basins on their heads. When his mother, who followed the last black slave, was gone out, he shut the door, and remained quietly in his chamber, with the full expectation that the sultan, after receiving such a present as he had required, would now readily consent to accept him for a son-in-law.

The first white slave that went out of Aladdin's

house occasioned every one who was going past to stop; and before all the eighty slaves, alternately a black and a white one, had finished going out, the street was filled with a great crowd of people, who collected from all parts, to see so grand and extraordinary a sight. The dress of each slave was made of a rich stuff, and so studded with precious stones, that persons who thought themselves the best judges reckoned each of them of inestimable value. Each dress was also very appropriate, and well adapted to the wearer. The graceful manner, elegant form, and great similarity of each slave, together with their marching at regular distances from each other, and the dazzling lustre constantly shed by the different jewels that were set in their girdles of massive gold, added to the branches of precious stones, fastened to their head-dresses, which were all of a particular make, produced in the multitude of spectators who were assembled such excessive admiration that they could not take their eyes from them so long as any one of them remained in sight. But all the streets were so thronged with people, that every one was obliged to remain in the spot where he happened to be.

As it was necessary to pass through several streets before they could arrive at the palace, the procession went through a great part of the city; and most of the inhabitants, of every rank and quality, were witnesses to this splendid spectacle. As soon as the porters at the gate of the first court of the palace perceived this astonishing procession approaching, they made the greatest haste to open it, as they took the first for a king, so richly and magnificently was he dressed. They were advancing to kiss the hem of his robe, when the slave, instructed by the genie, stopped them, and, in a grave tone of voice, said, "Our master will appear, when the time shall be proper!"

The first slave, followed by all the rest, advanced as far as the second court, which was very spacious, and contained the apartments inhabited by the sultan when the divan sat. The officers, who were at the head of the sultan's guards, were very handsomely clothed, but they were completely eclipsed by the eighty slaves who were the bearers of Aladdin's present, and who themselves formed part of it. Nothing, in short, throughout the sultan's whole palace appeared so beautiful and brilliant; and however magnificently dressed the different nobles of the court might be, they dwindled to nothing in comparison with what was now to be seen.

As the sultan had been informed of the march and arrival of these slaves, he had given orders to have them admitted. As soon, therefore, as they presented themselves before the door of the divan they found it open. They entered in regular order, one part going to the right, and the other to the left. After they were all within the hall, and had formed a large semi-circle before the throne of the sultan, each of the black slaves placed the basin which he carried upon the carpet. They then all prostrated themselves so low that their foreheads touched the ground. The white slaves also, at the same time, performed the same ceremony. They then all got up, and in doing so, the black slaves skilfully uncovered the basins, which were before

them, and then remained standing, with their hands crossed upon their breast, in a very modest attitude.

The mother of Aladdin, who had in the meantime advanced to the foot of the throne, having first prostrated herself, thus addressed the sultan: "My son Aladdin, sire, is not ignorant that this present which he has sent your majesty is very much beneath the inestimable worth of the princess Badroul Boudour. He nevertheless hopes that your majesty will favourably accept it, and that you will endeavour to make his alliance agreeable to the princess. He has the greater reliance that his expectations will be fulfilled, because he has tried to conform himself to the conditions which it pleased you to point out."

The sultan was unable to pay the least attention to the complimentary address of Aladdin's mother. The very first look he cast upon the forty golden basins, heaped up with jewels of the most brilliant lustre, finest water, and greatest value he had ever seen, as well as the eighty slaves, who seemed like so many kings, both from the magnificence of their dress and their fine appearance, made such an impression upon him that he could not restrain his admiration. Instead, therefore, of making any answer to the compliments of Aladdin's mother, he addressed himself to the grand vizier, who could not himself conceive where such an immense profusion of riches could possibly come from. "Well, vizier," he exclaimed in the hearing of all, "what do you think of the person, whoever he may be, who has now sent me so rich and wonderful a present; a person of whom neither I nor you have the least knowledge? Do you not think that he is worthy of the princess, my daughter?"

Whatever jealousy or pain the grand vizier might feel at thus seeing an unknown person become the son-in-law of the sultan in preference to his own son, he was nevertheless afraid to dissemble his real opinion on the present occasion. It was very evident that Aladdin had by these means become, in the eyes of the sultan, deserving of being honoured with so high an alliance. He therefore answered the sultan in these terms: "Far be it from me, sire, to suppose that he who makes your majesty so handsome a present should himself be undeserving the honour you wish to bestow upon him. I would even say that he deserved still more, if indeed all the treasures of the universe could be put in competition with the princess your daughter." All the nobles who attended and formed the divan showed, by their applause, that their opinion was the same as that of the grand vizier.

The sultan hesitated no longer. He did not even think of informing himself whether Aladdin possessed any other qualification that would render him worthy of aspiring to the honour of becoming his son-in-law. The sight alone of such immense riches, and the wonderful celerity with which Aladdin had fulfilled his request, without making the least difficulty about the conditions, however exorbitant, and for which he had stipulated, easily persuaded him that Aladdin would not be deficient in anything that could render him as accomplished and deserving as he could wish. That he might, therefore, send back Aladdin's mother as well

ALADDIN VIEWING THE ENCHANTED PALACE

satisfied as she could possibly expect, he said to her, "Go, my good woman, and tell your son that I am waiting with open arms to receive and embrace him; and that the greater diligence he makes to come and receive from my hands the gift I am ready to bestow upon him in the princess my daughter, the greater pleasure he will afford me."

CHAPTER VIII.

THE JOY OF ALADDIN ON RECEIVING THE MESSAGE OF THE SULTAN.—HE MAKES MAGNIFICENT PREPARATIONS FOR HIS NUPTIALS WITH THE PRINCESS.

ALADDIN's mother had no sooner departed, as happy as a woman of her condition could be, in seeing her son exalted to a situation beyond her greatest expectations, than the sultan put an end

to the audience; and coming down from his throne he ordered the eunuchs belonging to the princess to be called, and to take up the basins, and carry them to the apartment of their mistress, where he himself went, in order to examine them with her at their leisure.

The eighty slaves were not forgotten; they were conducted into the interior of the palace, and when, some time after, he was speaking of their splendour to the princess, he ordered them to come opposite to her apartment, that she might see them through the lattices, and be convinced that, so far from having given an exaggerated account of them, he said much less than they deserved.

In the meantime Aladdin's mother reached home, and instantly showed by her manner that she was the bearer of most excellent news. "You have every reason, my dear son," she said, " to be satisfied. You have accomplished your wishes, contrary to my expectations and what I have hitherto declared. But not to keep you any longer in suspense, I must inform you that the sultan, with the applause of his whole court, has announced that you are worthy to possess the princess Badroul Boudour; and he is now waiting to embrace you, and to conclude the marriage. It is, therefore, time for you to think of making some preparations for this interview, that you may endeavour to equal the high opinion he has formed of your person. After what I have seen of the wonders you have brought about, however, I am sure you will not fail in anything. I ought not, moreover, to forget to tell you that the sultan waits for you with the greatest impatience; and, therefore, that you must lose no time in making your appearance before him."

Aladdin was so delighted with this intelligence, and so taken up with the thoughts of the enchanting object of his love, that he hardly answered his mother, but instantly retired to his chamber. He then took up the lamp that had thus far been so friendly to him, by supplying all his wants and fulfilling all his wishes, and had no sooner rubbed it than the genie again showed his ready obedience to its power, by instantly appearing to execute his commands. "Genie," said Aladdin to him, "I have called you to take me immediately to a bath: and when I shall have finished bathing, I wish you to have in readiness for me a richer, and, if possible, more magnificent dress than was ever worn by any monarch." Aladdin had no sooner concluded his speech than the genie rendered him invisible, like himself, took him in his arms, and transported him to a bath formed of the finest marble of the most beautiful and diversified colours. Without being able to see any one who waited upon him, Aladdin was undressed in a large and handsome saloon. From thence he was conducted into the bath, moderately heated, and was here washed and rubbed with various sorts of perfumed waters. After having passed through the different chambers by which the various degrees of heat in the bath were regulated, he went out; but quite a different person, as it were, from what he was before. His skin was white and fresh, his countenance blooming, and his whole body felt lighter and more active. He then went back to the saloon, where, instead of the dress he had left, he found the one he had desired the genie to procure. By his assistance he dressed himself, showing the greatest admiration at every part of it as he put it on; and the whole of it was far beyond what he could possibly have conceived. This business was no sooner over, than the genie transported him back into the same chamber of his own house whence he had brought him. He then inquired if he had any other commands. "Yes," replied Aladdin, "I am waiting till you bring me a horse, as quickly as possible, which shall surpass in beauty and excellence the most valuable horse in the sultan's stables; the housings, saddle, bridle, and other furniture of which shall be worth more than a million of money. I also order you to get me, at the same time, twenty slaves, as well and richly clothed as

those who carried the present, to attend on each side and behind my person, and twenty more to march in two ranks before me. You must also procure six female slaves to attend upon my mother, all as well and richly clothed as those of the princess Badroul Boudour, each of whom must carry a complete dress, fit in point of splendour and magnificence for any sultana. I want also ten thousand pieces of gold, in ten separate purses. These are all my commands at present. Go, and be diligent."

Aladdin had no sooner given his orders to the genie, than he disappeared, and in a moment after returned with the horse, the forty slaves, ten of whom each had a purse with ten thousand pieces of gold in every one, and the six female slaves, each carrying a different dress for Aladdin's mother, wrapped in silver tissue, and presented the whole to him.

Aladdin took only four of the purses, and presented them to his mother for any purpose, as he said, for which she might want them. He left the other six in the hands of the slaves who carried them, desiring them to throw them out by handfuls to the populace as they went along the streets in the way to the palace of the sultan. He ordered them also to march before him with the others, three on one side and three on the other. He then presented the six female slaves to his mother; telling her that they would for the future consider her as their mistress; and that the dresses they had in their hands were for her use.

When Aladdin had arranged everything as he wished, he told the genie that he would call him when he had any further occasion for his service. The latter instantly vanished. Aladdin then hastened to fulfil the wish the sultan had expressed to see him as soon as possible. He sent one of the forty slaves—whom it is useless to call the best made or most handsome, for they were all equally so—to the palace, directing him to address himself to the chief of the ushers, and inquire when his master, Aladdin, might have the honour of throwing himself at the feet of the sultan. The slave was not long in performing his errand; and brought word back that the sultan was waiting for him with the greatest impatience.

Aladdin instantly mounted his horse, and began his march in the order that has been mentioned. Although he had never been on horseback in his life, he nevertheless appeared perfectly at ease, and the best judges of horsemanship would never have taken him for a novice. The streets through which he passed were in an instant filled with crowds of people, who made the air resound with their acclamations and their shouts of admiration, particularly when the six slaves who carried the purses threw handfuls of gold on all sides. Not only they who remembered to have seen him playing about the streets like a vagabond could not now recognise him, but even those who had seen and known him very lately had great difficulty to recollect him, so much were his features and appearance changed. This all arose from the power possessed by the wonderful lamp, of acquiring for those who had it in their keeping every perfection adapted to the situation which such persons arrived at, by making a good and proper use of its virtues. More attention was, therefore, paid by every one to the person of Aladdin than to the magnificence with which he was surrounded, and which most of them had before seen, when the slaves who carried, and those who accompanied the present, went to the palace. The horse, also, was much admired by those who were judges, and able to appreciate its beauty and excellence, without being dazzled by the richness and brilliancy of the diamonds and other precious stones with which it was covered. When the report spread about that the sultan had bestowed upon Aladdin the hand of the princess Badroul Boudour—and this was soon universally known—no one ever thought about his birth, or even envied him his good fortune, because he appeared so well to deserve it.

He at length arrived at the palace, where everything was ready for his reception. When he came to the second gate, he wished to alight, agreeably to the custom observed by the grand vizier, the generals of the army, and the governors of the superior provinces; but the chief of the ushers, who attended him by the sultan's orders, prevented him, and accompanied him to the hall of audience, where he assisted him in dismounting from his horse, though Aladdin opposed it as much as possible, not wishing to receive such a distinction: all his efforts were, however, vain. In the meantime, all the ushers formed a double row at the entrance into the hall: and their chief, placing Aladdin on his right, went up through the midst of them, and conducted him quite to the foot of the throne.

As soon as the sultan perceived Aladdin, he was not more surprised at seeing him more richly and magnificently clothed than himself, than he was astonished at the propriety of his manner, his noble figure, and a certain air of grandeur, very far removed from the degraded state in which his mother had appeared in his presence. His astonishment, however, did not prevent him from rising, and quickly descending two or three steps of his throne, in order to prevent Aladdin from throwing himself at his feet, and embracing him with the most evident marks of friendship and affection. After this civility, Aladdin again endeavoured to cast himself at the sultan's feet; but he held his hand, and compelled him to ascend and sit between him and his grand vizier.

Aladdin then addressed the sultan in these words: "I receive the honours which your majesty has the goodness to bestow upon me, because it is your pleasure; but you must permit me to say, that I have not forgotten that I was born your slave, that I am well aware of the greatness of your power, and that I am not ignorant how much my birth places me beneath the splendour and brilliancy of that superior rank to which you are elevated. If there can be the shadow of reason," he continued, "from which I can in the least merit so favourable a reception, I candidly avow that I am indebted for it to a boldness which chance alone brought about, and, in consequence of which I have raised my eyes, my thoughts, and my desires, to the divine princess who is the sole object of my wishes. I request your majesty's pardon for my rashness, but I cannot dissemble that grief would occasion my death should I lose the hope of seeing my desires accomplished."

"My son," replied the sultan, again embracing him, "you would do me injustice to doubt, even for an instant, the sincerity of my word; your life is too dear to me not to endeavour to preserve it by presenting you with the princess my daughter. I prefer the pleasure I derive from seeing and hearing you to all our united treasures."

As he concluded this speech the sultan made a sign, and the air was immediately filled with the sound of trumpets, hautbois, and cymbals; and the sultan then conducted Aladdin into a magnificent saloon, where a great feast was served up. The sultan and Aladdin ate by themselves; the grand vizier and the nobles of the court, each according to their dignity and rank, waited upon them during their repast. The sultan fixed his eyes constantly upon Aladdin, so great was the pleasure he derived from seeing him. They entered into conversation on a variety of topics; and, whatever the subject of their discourse happened to be, Aladdin spoke with so much information and knowledge, that he completely confirmed the sultan in the good opinion which he had at first formed of him.

When the repast was over, the sultan ordered the grand judge of his capital to attend, and commanded him instantly to prepare a contract of marriage between the princess Badroul Boudour and Aladdin. While this was doing, the sultan conversed with Aladdin upon different subjects, in the presence of the grand vizier and the nobles of the court, who all equally admired the solidity of his understanding, the great facility and fluency of his language, and the purity and delicacy of his metaphors.

When the judge had drawn up the contract with all the requisite forms, the sultan asked Aladdin whether he wished to remain in the palace and conclude all the ceremonies that day? "Sire," he replied, "however impatient I may be to have entire possession of all your majesty's bounties, I request you to permit me to defer my happiness until I have built a palace for the reception of the princess that shall be worthy of her merit and dignity. And for this purpose, I request that you will have the goodness to point out a suitable situation near your own palace, that I may always be able to pay my court to your majesty. I will then neglect nothing to get it finished with all possible diligence." "My son," answered the sultan, "take whatever spot you think proper. There is a large open space before my palace, and I have thought for some time about filling it up; but remember, that to have my happiness complete, I cannot too soon see you united to my daughter." Having said this, he again embraced Aladdin, who took leave in as polished a manner as if he had been brought up and spent all his life at court.

Aladdin then mounted his horse, and returned home with his suite in the same order in which they came, going back through the same crowd, and receiving similar acclamations from the people, who wished him all happiness and prosperity. As soon as he had entered the court and alighted from his horse, he retired to his own chamber. He instantly rubbed the lamp, and called the genie as usual. He had not to wait; the genie appeared directly, and offered his services. "Genie," said Aladdin to him, "I have hitherto had every reason to praise the precision and promptitude with which you have executed whatever I have required of you, by means of the power of your mistress, this lamp. You must now, through your regard for her, appear, if possible, more zealous, and make greater dispatch than you have yet done. I command you, therefore, to build me a palace, in as short a time as you possibly can, opposite to that belonging to the sultan, and at a proper distance; and let this palace be every way worthy to receive the princess Badroul Boudour, my bride. I leave the choice of the materials to yourself, that is to say, whether it shall be of porphyry, of jasper, of agate, of lapis lazuli, or of the finest marble; and also the form of the palace: I only expect, that at the top there shall be erected a large saloon, with a dome in the centre, and four equal sides, the walls of which shall be formed of massive gold and silver, in alternate layers, with twenty four windows, six on each side; that the lattices of each window, except one, which is to be purposely left unfinished, shall be enriched with diamonds, rubies, and emeralds, set with the greatest taste and symmetry, and in such a style that nothing in the whole world can equal it. I also wish this palace to have a large court in front, another behind, and a garden. But, above everything else, be sure that there is a place, which you will point out to me, well supplied with money, both in gold and silver. There must also be kitchens, offices, magazines, receptacles for rich and valuable furniture, suited to the different seasons, and all appropriate to the magnificence of such a palace. And also stables filled with the most beautiful horses, with the grooms and attendants for the kitchen and offices, and female slaves for the service of the princess. In short, you understand what I mean. Go, and return as soon as it is completed."

The sun had retired into the west by the time Aladdin had finished giving his orders to the genie respecting the construction of the palace. The very next morning, when the day first broke, Aladdin, whose love for the princess prevented him from sleeping in tranquillity, had scarcely risen before the genie presented himself. "Sire," said he, "your palace is finished; come and see if it be according to your wish." Aladdin signified his assent, and the genie transported him to it in an instant. He found it to exceed his utmost expectation, and he could not sufficiently admire it. The genie conducted him through every part of it, and he everywhere found the greatest riches, applied with the utmost propriety. There were, also, the proper officers and slaves, all dressed according to their rank, and suited to their different employments. Amongst other things, he did not omit to show him the treasury, the door of which was opened by a treasurer, of whose fidelity the genie assured him. He here observed large vases, filled to the very top with purses of different sizes, according to the sums they contained, and so nicely

arranged, that it was quite a pleasure to behold them. The genie then carried Aladdin to the stables, in which were the most beautiful horses in the world, with all the officers and grooms busily employed about them. He then led him into the different magazines filled with everything necessary for them, both useful and ornamental, as well as for their support.

When Aladdin had examined the whole palace, without omitting a single part, from the top to the bottom, and more particularly the saloon with the four-and-twenty windows, and had seen all the riches and magnificence it contained, as well as every other thing even in greater abundance and with greater propriety than he had ordered, "Genie," said he, "no one can possibly be better satisfied than I am. There is one thing only which I did not mention to you, because it escaped my recollection: it is, to have a carpet of the finest velvet laid from the gate of the sultan's palace to the door of the apartment in this palace which is to be appropriated to the princess, that she may walk upon it when she leaves the sultan's palace." "I will return in an instant," replied the genie; and he had not been gone a moment before Aladdin saw his wish accomplished. The genie again made his appearance, and carried Aladdin back to his own house just as the gates of the sultan's palace were about to be opened.

The porters who came to open the gates, and who were accustomed to see an open space where Aladdin's palace now stood, were much astonished at observing it filled up, and at seeing a velvet carpet, which came from that part directly opposite to the gate of the palace. They could not at first make out what it was; but their astonishment increased when they beheld the superb palace of Aladdin. The news of this wonderful event soon spread throughout the palace, and the grand vizier, who had arrived just as the gates were open, was not less astonished than the rest. He instantly went to the sultan, and sought to make the whole business pass for enchantment. "Why do you endeavour, vizier," said the sultan, "to make this appear the work of enchantment? You know, as well as I do, that this is the palace of Aladdin, which I, in your presence yesterday, gave him the permission to build for the reception of the princess my daughter. After the immense display of riches we have seen, can you think it so very extraordinary that he should be able to build a palace in so short a time? He wished, no doubt, to surprise us, and we every day see what miracles riches can perform. Confess that it is through motives of jealousy you wish to make this appear an enchantment." The hour for entering the council-hall prevented the continuance of this conversation.

When Aladdin had returned, and dismissed the genie, he found that his mother was up, and had put on one of the dresses which he had ordered for her the day before. About the time the sultan left the council, Aladdin requested his mother to go to the palace, attended by the female slaves that the genie had procured for her use. He desired her also, if she saw the sultan, to inform him, that she came for the purpose of having the honour of accompanying the princess in the evening, when it was proper for her to go to her own palace. She then set out; but although she and her slaves were dressed as richly as any sultanas, there was much less crowd to see them, as they were veiled, and the richness and magnificence of their habits were hidden by a sort of cloak that quite covered them. Aladdin himself mounted his horse, and left his paternal house, never more to return; but did not forget his wonderful lamp, whose assistance had been so highly advantageous to him, and had in fact been the cause of all his happiness. He went to his own palace in the same public manner, and surrounded with all the pomp, with which he had presented himself to the sultan on the preceding day.

As soon as the porters of the sultan's palace perceived the mother of Aladdin, they gave notice of it through the proper officer to the sultan himself. He immediately sent orders to the bands, who played upon trumpets, cymbals, tabors, fifes, and hautbois, and who were already placed in different parts of the terrace, and in a moment the air echoed with their joyful sounds, exciting pleasure throughout the city. The merchants began to dress out their shops with rich carpets and seats, adorned with foliage, and to prepare illuminations for the night. The artificers quitted their work, and all the people thronged to the great square that still was left between the palaces of the sultan and Aladdin. That of the latter first attracted their admiration, not merely because they had been accustomed to see only the sultan's, which could not be put in comparison with Aladdin's; but their great surprise arose from their not being able to comprehend by what unheard-of means they beheld so magnificent a palace in a spot where the day before there were neither materials brought nor foundations laid.

Aladdin's mother met with the most honourable reception, and was introduced by the chief of the eunuchs into the apartment of the princess Badroul Boudour. As soon as the latter perceived her, she ran and embraced her, and made her take a place upon her own sofa. And while her women were dressing her, and adorning her person with the most valuable of the jewels with which Aladdin had presented her, she entertained her with a magnificent collation. The sultan, who wished to be as much as possible with the princess his daughter before she left him to go to the palace of Aladdin, paid great honour and respect to his mother. She had very often seen the sultan in public, but he had never yet seen her without her veil, as she then was. And although she was of rather an advanced age, there were still to be observed some traces from which it might be concluded she had in her youth been handsome. The sultan, too, had always seen her very plainly, and indeed indifferently, dressed; and he was, therefore, the more struck at finding her now as magnificent as the princess his daughter.

When the evening approached, the princess took leave of the sultan her father. Their parting was tender, and accompanied by tears, and they embraced each other several times, without uttering a word. The princess at last left her apartment and proceeded towards her new residence, with Aladdin's mother on her left hand, followed by a hundred female slaves magnificently dressed. All the bands of instruments, which had been incessantly heard since the arrival of Aladdin's mother, united at once, and marched with them. These were followed by a hundred slaves, an equal number of black eunuchs in two rows, with their proper officers at their head; and four hundred young pages belonging to the sultan, marched in two troops on each sides, with flambeaux in their hands. The brilliancy of these, joined to the illuminations in both palaces, made the loss of day unnoticed.

In this order did the princess proceed, walking upon the carpet which was spread from Aladdin's palace to that of the sultan. And as she continued to advance, the musicians, who were at the head of the procession, went on, and mixed with those who were placed on the terrace of Aladdin's palace, thus forming a concert, which confused and extraordinary as it was, augmented the general joy, not only amongst those in the open square, but in the two palaces, in all the city, and even to a considerable distance around.

The princess at length arrived at the new palace, and Aladdin ran with every expression of joy to the entrance of the apartments appropriated to her, in order to welcome her. His mother had taken care to point out to the princess her son in the midst of the officers and attendants who surrounded him; and when she perceived him, her joy at finding him so handsome was excessive. "Adorable princess," cried Aladdin, accosting her in the most respectful manner, "if I should have the misfortune to have displeased you by the temerity with which I have aspired to possess so amiable a person, and the daughter of my sultan, I must confess that it was to your beautiful eyes and to your charms alone that you must attribute it, and not to myself." "Prince,—for it is thus that I must now call you," replied the princess,— "I obey the will of the sultan my father; and it is enough to have seen you to own that I obey him without reluctance."

Aladdin was delighted at so satisfactory and charming an answer, and did not suffer the princess to remain long standing, after having walked so far, which she was not in the habit of doing. He took her by the hand, which he kissed with the greatest demonstrations of joy, and conducted her into a large saloon, illuminated by an immense number of tapers, where, through the attention of the genie, there was a table spread with everything that was rare and excellent. The dishes were of massive gold, and filled with the most delicious viands. The vases, the basins, and the goblets, with which the sideboard was amply furnished, were also of gold, and of the most exquisite workmanship. The other ornaments which embellished the saloon, exactly corresponded with the richness of the other parts. The princess, enchanted at the sight of such an assemblage of riches in one place, said to Aladdin, "Nothing, I thought, prince, in the whole world was more beautiful than the palace of the sultan my father; but the sight of this saloon alone tells me I was deceived." " My princess," replied Aladdin, placing her at the table in the seat he had destined for her, " I am very sensible of your politeness, but at the same time know how to appropriate the compliment."

The princess Badroul Boudour, Aladdin, and his mother sat down, and instantly a band of the most harmonious instruments, played upon by females of great beauty, to whose voices they formed an accompaniment, began a concert which lasted till the repast was finished. The princess was delighted with it, and said she had never heard anything to equal it in the palace of her father. But she knew not that these musicians were fairies, chosen by the genie, the slave of the lamp.

When the supper was concluded, and everything had been removed, a troop of dancers of both sexes took the place of the musicians. They performed dances of various figures, as was the custom of the country, and concluded by one executed by a male and female, who danced with the most surprising activity and agility, each of whom gave the other in turn an opportunity of showing all the grace and address they were master of. It was near midnight, when, according to custom observed at that time in Cathay, Aladdin rose, and presented his hand to the princess Badroul Boudour, in order to dance together, and thus finish the ceremony of their nuptials. They both danced with so good a grace, that they were the admiration of all present. When it was over, Aladdin, who still held the princess by her hand, led her into the chamber in which the nuptial bed had been prepared. The women of the princess attended her, while the attendants of Aladdin did the same, and then every one retired. In this manner did the ceremonies and rejoicings, on account of the marriage of Aladdin and the princess Badroul Boudour, conclude.

The next morning, when Aladdin awoke, his chamberlains presented themselves to dress him. They clothed him in a different habit from that which he wore on the day of his marriage, but one equally rich and magnificent. They then brought him one of the horses that were appropriated to his use. He mounted it, and, surrounded by a large troop of slaves, rode to the palace of the sultan. The sultan received him with the same honours he had done before. He embraced him, and, after having placed him on a throne by his side, ordered breakfast to be served up. " Sire," said Aladdin to the sultan, " I beseech your majesty to dispense with conferring this honour upon me to-day ; I come for the express purpose of entreating you to partake of a repast in the palace of the princess, together with your grand vizier, and the nobles of your court." The sultan readily granted his request. He rose immediately, and as the distance was not great, he proceeded on foot, with Aladdin on his right hand, and the grand vizier on his left, followed by the nobles ; the slaves and principal officers of his palace going before them.

The nearer the sultan came to the palace of Aladdin, the more was he struck with its beauty ; yet this was but little to what he felt on entering. His expressions of surprise and pleasure continued in all the apartments through which he passed ; but when he came to the saloon with twenty-four windows, to which Aladdin had requested them to ascend—when the sultan had seen its ornaments. and had, above all things, cast his eyes on the lattices, enriched with diamonds, rubies, and emeralds, all of the finest sort and most appropriate size ; and when Aladdin had made him observe that the outside was equally rich and superb as the other— he was so much astonished that he stood absolutely motionless. After remaining some time in an ecstacy of wonder, " Vizier," he at length said to that minister, who was near him, " is it possible that there should be in my kingdom, and so near my own, so superb a palace, and yet that I should till this moment be ignorant of it ?" " Your majesty," replied the grand visier, " may remember that the day before yesterday you gave Aladdin, whom you then acknowledged for your son-in-law, permission to build a palace opposite to your own ; on the same day, when the sun went down, not the smallest part of this palace was on the spot, and yesterday I had the honour to announce to your majesty that the palace was built and finished." " I remember it," replied the sultan ; " but I never imagined that this palace would be one of the wonders of the world. Where throughout the universe will you find the walls built with alternate layers of massive gold and silver, instead of stone or marble, and the lattices studded with diamonds, rubies, and emeralds ? Never in the whole world has there been anything of the kind ever heard of."

The sultan wished to examine more closely the beauty of the twenty-four lattices ; when, in reckoning them, he only found twenty-three that were equally rich, and he was, therefore, in the greatest astonishment that the twenty-fourth should remain imperfect. " Vizier," said he, for that minister made it a point not to leave him, " I am very much surprised that such a magnificent saloon should remain unfinished in this particular." " Sire," replied the grand vizier, " Aladdin apparently was pressed for time, and therefore was unable to finish this window like the rest. But it must readily be granted that he has jewels fit for the purpose, and that it will be finished the first opportunity."

Aladdin, who had left the sultan, to give some orders, joined them during this conversation. " My son," said the sultan, " this truly is a saloon worthy the admiration of the whole world. There is, however, one thing I am astonished at—and that is, to observe this lattice unfinished. Is it through forgetfulness or neglect," added he, " or because the workmen had not time to put the finishing stroke to such a beautiful specimen of architecture ?" " Sire," answered Aladdin, " it is not for any of these reasons that this lattice remains in the state you majesty now sees it. It has been done on purpose : and it was by my orders that the workmen have not touched it. I wish that your majesty should have the glory of finishing this saloon and palace at the same time. And I entreat you to think well of my intention, that I may ever remember the favour I have thus received from you." " If you have done it with that view," replied the sultan, "I take it in good part; I will this instant give the necessary orders about it." So saying, he ordered the jewellers who were best furnished with precious stones, and the most skilful goldsmiths in his capital to be sent for.

When the sultan came down from the saloon, Aladdin conducted him into that where he had entertained the princess Badroul Boudour on the evening of their nuptials. The princess herself entered the moment after, and received the sultan her father in such a manner as made it very evident that she was quite satisfied with her marriage. In this saloon there were two tables set out with the most delicious viands, all served up in gold. The sultan sat down at the first, and ate with his daughter, Aladdin, and the grand vizier. All the nobles of the court were regaled at the second, which was of great length. The repast highly pleased the sultan's taste; and he confessed that he had never partaken of anything more excellent. He said the same of the wine, which was, in fact, very delicious. But what excited his admiration most of all, were four large sideboards, furnished and set out with a profusion of flagons, vases, and cups of solid gold, enriched throughout with precious stones. He was also delighted with the different bands of music, placed in different parts of the saloon, while the trumpets, accompanied by cymbals and drums, were heard at a distance, at proper intervals joining with the music within.

When the sultan rose from the table, he was informed that the jewellers and goldsmiths whom he had ordered to be sent for were come. He then went up to the saloon, and pointed out to the jewellers and goldsmiths the window which was imperfect. "I have ordered you to come here," said the sultan, "to finish this window, and make it perfect like the rest. Examine them, and lose no time in perfecting it."

The jewellers and goldsmiths examined all the twenty-three lattices with great attention; and after having consulted together about what they could each contribute towards its completion, they presented themselves to the sultan, and the jeweller in ordinary to the palace thus addressed him: "We are ready, sire, to employ all our care and diligence to obey your majesty, but amongst all our profession we have no jewels either sufficiently valuable or numerous to complete so great a work." "I have, then," cried the sultan, "and more than you want. Come to my palace; I will show you them, and you shall choose which you like best."

When the sultan had returned to his palace, he directed all his jewels to be brought to the jewellers, and they took a great quantity of them, particularly of those which had been presented by Aladdin. They used all these, without appearing to have made much progress. They went back for more several times, and in the course of more than a month they had not finished more than half their work. They exhausted all the sultan's jewels, with as many of the grand vizier's as he could spare, and with all these they could not do more than finish half the window.

Aladdin was well aware that the sultan's endea-vours to make the lattice of this window like the others were vain, and that he would never arrive at that honour: he went up, therefore, to the workmen, and not only made them stop working, but even undo all they had finished, and carry back the jewels to the sultan and the grand vizier.

All the work which the jewellers had been six weeks in performing was destroyed in a few hours. They then went away, and left Aladdin alone in the saloon. He took out the lamp, which he had with him and rubbed it. The genie instantly appeared. "Genie," said Aladdin to him, "I ordered you to leave one of the twenty-four lattices of this saloon imperfect, and you obeyed me. I now wish it to be made like the rest." The genie disappeared, and Aladdin went out of the saloon. He entered it again in a few moments, and found the lattice as he wished, and similar to the others.

In the meantime the jewellers and goldsmiths arrived at the palace, and were introduced to the sultan in his own apartment. The first jeweller then produced the precious stones he had brought with him, and said in the name of the rest, "Your majesty, sire, knows for what length of time and how diligently we have worked in order to finish the business your majesty employed us upon. It was already very far advanced, when Aladdin obliged us not only to leave off, but even to destroy what we had already done, and to bring back these jewels, as well as those that belonged to the grand vizier." The sultan then asked them whether Aladdin had given them any reason; and when he told the sultan that he had said nothing on the subject, the former ordered his horse to be brought, and, without any other attendants than those who happened to be about his person, and who accompanied him on foot, proceeded to Aladdin's palace. He dismounted at the flight of stairs that led to the saloon with twenty-four windows, and went up, without letting Aladdin know of his arrival; but the latter happened luckily to be in the saloon, and was just in time to receive the sultan at the door.

The sultan, without giving Aladdin time to chide him for not sending word of his intention to pay him a visit, and thus making him seem deficient in the respect he owed him, said—"I am come, my son, to ask the reason why you wished to leave this very magnificent and singular saloon in an unfinished state?"

Aladdin dissembled the true reason, which was, that the sultan was not sufficiently rich in jewels to go to so great an expense. But to let him see how the palace itself surpassed not only his, but also every other palace in the whole world, since he was unable to finish even a very small part of it, he replied, "It is true, sire, that your majesty did behold this saloon unfinished; but I entreat you to examine if at this moment there be anything wanting."

The sultan immediately went to the window where he had observed the lattice imperfect; but when he saw that it was like the rest, he thought he was mistaken. He not only examined the window on each side of it, but looked at them all one after the other; and when he was convinced that the lattice upon which his people had so long employed themselves, and had cost the jewellers and goldsmiths so many days, was finished in such an incredibly short period, he embraced Aladdin, and kissed him between the eyes. "My dear son," said he, filled with astonishment, "what man are you, who can do such wonderful things, and almost, as it were, instantaneously? There is not your equal in the world; and the more I know you, the more I find to admire in you."

Aladdin received the sultan's praises with great modesty, and replied to them in these terms: "It is, sire, my greatest glory to deserve the kindness and approbation of your majesty, and I can assure you that I will never neglect anything that will tend to make me still more worthy of your good opinion."

The sultan returned to his palace in the same way he came, and would not permit Aladdin to accompany him. When he got back, he found the grand vizier waiting his arrival. Still full of admiration at the wonders which he had seen, the sultan related everything to him in such terms that the vizier did not doubt for a moment that the matter was exactly as the sultan told it. But this still more confirmed that minister in the belief which he already entertained that the palace of Aladdin was built by enchantment; which opinion he had expressed to the sultan on the very morning that the palace was first seen. He again repeated his belief. "Vizier," said the sultan, suddenly interrupting him, "you have before said the same thing; but I very plainly perceive you have not forgotten my daughter's marriage with your son."

The grand vizier clearly saw that the sultan was prejudiced; he did not, therefore, wish to enter into any dispute with him, but suffered him to remain in his own opinion. Every morning as soon as he rose the sultan went regularly to the apartment whence he could see the palace of Aladdin: and indeed he often went during the day to contemplate and admire it.

Aladdin himself in the meantime took care to go through different parts of the city at least once every week: sometimes to attend mosques; at others to visit the grand vizier, who regularly came on stated days to pay his unwilling court: and sometimes he honoured with his presence the houses of the principal nobles, whom he frequently entertained at his own palace. Every time he went out he ordered two of the slaves who attended him as he rode to throw handfuls of gold in the streets and public places through which he passed, and where the people always collected in crowds to see him. Besides this, a poor person never presented himself before the gate of his palace, but went away well satisfied with Aladdin's liberality.

Aladdin also so arranged his different occupations, that there was not a week in which he did not once, at least, enjoy the diversion of the chase; sometimes hunting in the neighbourhood of the city, and at others going to a greater distance; and he gave proofs of the same liberality in the roads and villages through which he passed. This generous disposition made the people load him with

blessings; and it became the common custom to swear by his head. In short, without giving the least cause of displeasure to the sultan, to whom he regularly paid his court, Aladdin attracted, by the affability of his manners and the liberality of his conduct, the regard and affection of all; and generally speaking, he was even more beloved than the sultan himself. To all these good qualities he joined a great degree of valour, and an ardent zeal for the good of the state. He had an opportunity of giving the strongest proofs of it in a revolt that took place on the confines of the kingdom. He no sooner became apprised that the sultan meant to levy an army to quell it, than he requested to have the command of it. This he had no difficulty in obtaining. He instantly put himself at its head, marched against the rebels, and conducted the whole expedition with so much judgment and activity, that the sultan soon heard of their defeat and dispersion. This action, which made his name celebrated throughout the whole empire, did not in the least alter his disposition. He returned victorious, but he returned as affable and modest as ever.

CHAPTER IX.

THE AFRICAN MAGICIAN, BY A STRATAGEM, OBTAINS POSSESSION OF THE WONDERFUL LAMP.—THE DISAPPEARANCE OF THE ENCHANTED PALACE, AND ABDUCTION OF THE PRINCESS BADROUL BOUDOUR; WITH THE STEPS ALADDIN TOOK TO RECOVER HIS LOST TREASURE.

MANY years passed, and Aladdin continued to conduct himself in the way we have described; when the African magician, who had procured for him, but without intending it, the means by which he was raised to so exalted a situation, frequently thought of him while he was in Africa, whither he had returned. Although he felt persuaded that Aladdin had pined out a miserable existence in the subterraneous cavern where he had left him, he nevertheless thought he might as well learn precisely his end. As he had a perfect knowledge of the science of geomancy, he took out of a drawer a sort of square, covered box, such as he used when he made any observations in this science. He then sat down on the sofa, and placed the square instrument before him. He uncovered it, and after making the sand with which it was filled quite smooth and even, with the view of discovering whether Aladdin died in the subterraneous cave, he arranged the points, drew the figures, and formed his horoscope. When he examined it, in order to form his judgment, instead of finding Aladdin dead in his cave, he discovered that he had got out of it, that he lived in the greatest splendour, was immensely rich, highly respected and honoured, and was the husband of a princess.

No sooner had the African magician learnt by his diabolical art that Aladdin was in the enjoyment of these honours, than the blood rushed into his face. "This miserable son of a tailor," he exclaimed, in a rage, "has discovered the secret and virtues of the lamp! I thought his death certain; and now he enjoys the fruits of my long and labo-

ALADDIN DISTRIBUTING MONEY TO THE POPULACE.

rious exertions. "I will either prevent his enjoying them, or perish in the attempt." He did not deliberate long as to the method he should pursue. Early the next morning, he mounted a horse from Barbary, which he had in his stable, and began his journey. Travelling from city to city, and from province to province, without stopping anywhere longer than was necessary to rest his horse, he at last arrived in Cathay, and very soon reached the capital where the sultan lived, whose daughter Aladdin had married. He alighted at a public khan, where he ordered an apartment for himself. He remained there the rest of the day and following night, in order to recover from the fatigue of his journey.

The first thing the African magician did the next morning was to inquire what was the general opinion formed of Aladdin, and how the people

spoke of him. In walking about the city, he went into the most frequented place where people of the greatest consequence and distinction assembled, to drink a warm liquor, of a particular kind, which he recollected to have done when he was there before. He took his seat, and they poured some out into a cup, and presented it to him. As he took it, he heard, as he was listening to what was said on every side, some person speaking of Aladdin's palace. When he had finished his cup, he approached those who were conversing on this subject; and taking his opportunity, he inquired what there was in particular about this palace of which they spoke so highly. "Where do you come from?" said one of those to whom he addressed himself. "You must surely be but lately arrived in this city, if you have not seen or heard of the palace of prince Aladdin." It was thus that

5

Aladdin, since his union with the princess Badroul Boudour, was always called. "I do not say," continued the same person, "that it is one of the wonders of the world, but that it is the only wonder in the world. Nothing has ever been seen so rich, so grand, or so magnificent. You must have come from a great distance, since you seem never even to have heard of it. It fact, it ought to be spoken of everywhere since it has been erected. But see it, and you will then know if I have said anything but the truth." "Pardon my ignorance," replied the African magician, "I arrived here only yesterday, and I have come a great distance, even from the furthest part of Africa, and its fame had not reached that country when I left it. And as it was a business of great importance that brought me, and required the utmost haste, I had no other view during my journey than to get to the end of it as soon as possible. I was, therefore, quite ignorant of what you have been telling me. I shall, however, go and see it. I would this moment go and satisfy my curiosity if you would do me the favour to show me the way."

The person to whom the magician addressed himself, directed him the way to Aladdin's palace, and he immediately set out. When he had accurately examined the palace on all sides, he did not doubt but that Aladdin had availed himself of the aid of the lamp in building it: he well knew it was in the power of the genii who were the slaves of the lamp to produce such wonders. Stung to the very soul by the happiness and greatness of Aladdin, between whom and the sultan there seemed not the shadow of a difference, he returned to his khan.

The great thing to discover was whether Aladdin carried the lamp about him, or where he kept it; and this discovery he was able to make by a certain operation in geomancy. As soon, therefore, as he got back to his lodging he took his square box and his sand, which he always carried with him wherever he went. Having completed the operation, he found that the lamp was in Aladdin's palace, and his joy was so great on learning this, that he could hardly contain himself. "I shall get this lamp," he cried, "and I defy Aladdin to prevent my obtaining it; and I will compel him to sink into the obscurity and poverty from which he has taken so high a leap."

It happened most unfortunately for Aladdin that he was absent upon a hunting expedition that was to last eight days, and only three of them were yet elapsed. Of this the African magician got information in the following way. When he had finished the operation which had afforded him so much joy, he went to see the master of the khan, under the pretence of conversing with him, and he had no difficulty in finding a proper subject. He told him that he was just returned from the palace of Aladdin; and after giving him an exaggerated account of all the most remarkable and surprising things he saw, and such as generally attracted the attention of every one, "My curiosity," he added, "goes still further; and I shall not be satisfied till I have seen the master to whom so wonderful a building belongs." "That will not be at all a difficult matter," replied the keeper of

the khan, "for hardly a day passes that will not afford you an opportunity, when he is at home; but he has been gone these three days on a grand hunting party, which is to last at least eight."

The African magician did not want to know more; he took leave of the master of the khan, and returned to his own apartment. "This is the time for action," said he to himself, "nor must I let it escape." He then went to the shop of a person who made and sold lamps. "I want," said he to the master, "a dozen copper lamps; can you supply me with them?" The man replied that he had not so many finished, but that if he would wait till the next day he would have them ready for him. The magician agreed to wait; and desired him to take care to have them well polished; and, having first promised to give a good price for them, he returned to the khan.

The next morning the African magician received the twelve lamps, and paid the money asked for them. He put them into a basket which he had provided for the purpose, and went with this on his arm towards Aladdin's palace: and when he was near it, he began to cry with a loud voice, "Who will change old lamps for new?" As he went on, the children who were at play in the open square ran and collected round him, hooting, and shouting at him, as they took him for a fool or a madman. Every one who passed laughed at his folly, as they thought it. "That man," said they, "must surely have lost his senses, to offer to change new lamps for old ones."

The African magician was not at all surprised at the shouts of the children, nor at anything that was said of him; and he continued to cry, "Who will change old lamps for new?" He repeated this so often, while he walked backwards and forwards in front of the palace, that at last the princess Badroul Boudour, who was in the saloon with twenty-four windows, heard him: but as she could not distinguish what he said, on account of the shouting of the children who followed him, and whose number increased every instant, she sent one of her slaves to learn what was the reason of all the noise and bustle.

It was not long before the slave returned, and entered the saloon laughing very heartily; indeed so much so, that the princess herself, in looking at her, could not help laughing also. "Well silly one," said the princess, "why do you not tell me what it is you are laughing at?" "Princess," replied the slave, still laughing, "who can possibly help laughing at seeing that fool with a basket on his arm, full of beautiful new lamps, which he does not wish to sell, but exchange for old ones? It is the crowd of children who surround him that make all the noise we hear, in mocking him."

Hearing this account, another of the female slaves said, "Now you speak of old lamps, I know not whether the princess has taken notice of one that lies upon the cornice; whoever it belongs to, he will not be very much displeased in finding a new one instead of that old one. If the princess will give me leave, she may have the pleasure of trying whether this fellow is fool enough to give a new lamp for an old one, without asking anything for the exchange."

The lamp of which the slave spoke was the identical wonderful lamp which had been the cause of Aladdin's great success and happiness, and he had himself placed it upon the cornice before he went to the chase, from the fear of losing it. It was the usual precaution which he took every time he hunted. But neither the female slaves, the eunuchs, nor the princess herself had paid the least attention to it during his absence, till this moment. Except when he hunted, Aladdin always carried it about him.

The princess, who was ignorant of the value of this lamp, and that Aladdin, not to say herself, was so much interested in its preservation, consented to the joke, and ordered a eunuch to go and get it exchanged. The eunuch obeyed: he went down from the saloon, and close to the palace gate he perceived the African magician. He immediately called to him, and when he came, he showed him the old lamp, and said, " Give me a new lamp for this."

The magician did not doubt but that this was the lamp he was seeking; because he thought there would not, of course, be any other lamp in Aladdin's palace, where everything, that could be, was of gold and silver. He eagerly took the lamp from the eunuch, and after having thrust it into his bosom, he presented his basket, and bid him take which he liked best. The eunuch chose one, and leaving the magician, he carried the new lamp to the princess. The exchange had no sooner been effected than the children made the whole square resound with their noise, in ridiculing and mocking the folly, as they thought, of the magician.

The magician let them shout as much as they pleased, and without staying any longer near Aladdin's palace, he quickly went to a distance, and no longer invited people to change old lamps for new. He wished for no other than the one which he had got. His silence, therefore, soon induced the children to go no farther with him.

Leaving the square between the two palaces, he went along the most unfrequented streets; and as he had no further occasion either for the remainder of his lamps or his basket, he set them both down in the middle of a street where he thought no one would see him. He then turned down another street, and made all the haste he could to get to one of the gates of the city. As he continued his walk through the suburb, which was very extensive, he bought some provisions; and when he was in the open country, he turned down a bye-road, where there was no probability of seeing any person; and here he remained till he thought a good opportunity occurred to execute the design he had in coming there. He did not regret the horse he had left at the khan where he had lodged; but thought himself well recompensed by the treasure he had acquired.

The African magician continued in this retired place until the night was far advanced. He then drew the lamp from his bosom, and rubbed it. The genie instantly obeyed the summons. " What do you wish ?" cried the genie. " I am ready to obey you as your slave, and the slave of those who have the lamp in their hand; I, and the other slaves of the lamp." " I command you," replied the African magician, " instantly to take the palace which you and the other slaves of the lamp have erected in this city, exactly as it is, with everything in it both dead and alive, and transport it, with me at the same time, into the furthest part of Africa." Without making any answer, the genie, assisted by the other slaves of the lamp, took him and the whole palace, and transported it in a very short time to the spot he had pointed out.

It is now necessary to leave the African magician, the princess Badroul Boudour, and the palace in Africa, and notice the effect of this change upon the sultan.

The sultan no sooner rose the next morning than he went, as usual, to the cabinet, that thence he might have the pleasure of contemplating and admiring Aladdin's palace. He cast his eyes towards the side where he was accustomed to see it, but discovered only an open space, such as it was before the palace had been built. He thought he must be deceived; he rubbed his eyes, but still he could see nothing more than at first, though the air was so serene, the sky so clear, and the sun so near rising, that every object was distinct and plain. He looked on both sides, and out of both windows, but could not perceive what he had been accustomed to. His astonishment was so great, that he remained for some time with his eyes turned to the spot where the palace had stood, but where he could no longer see it, endeavouring to comprehend how so large a palace as that of Aladdin, which he had seen every day, since he had given permission to have it erected, and even so lately as the day before, should so suddenly and so completely vanish, that not the smallest vestige remained. " I cannot be deceived," he said to himself; " it was in this very place that I beheld it. If it had fallen down, the materials at least would appear; and if the earth had swallowed it, we should perceive some marks of it." In whatever way this had come to pass, and however satisfied he was that the palace was no longer there, he nevertheless waited some time longer, to see if in reality he was not deceived. He at length retired, after looking once more behind him, as he left the place. Returning to his apartment, he ordered his grand vizier to be instantly sent for. In the meantime he sat down, his mind agitated with so many different thoughts that he knew not how to act.

The grand vizier came in so much haste, that neither he nor his attendants observed as they passed that the palace of Aladdin was no longer in the same place. Even the porters, when they opened the gates, did not perceive the difference.

"Sire," said the grand vizier the moment he entered, " the eagerness and haste with which your majesty has sent for me lead me to suppose that something very extraordinary has happened, since your majesty is not ignorant that this is the day when the council meets, and that I should, therefore, of course, have been here on my duty in a very short time." " What has happened is indeed very extraordinary, as you have said; and you will soon agree it is so. Tell me, where is Aladdin's palace ?" " I have just now passed it, sir," replied the vizier, with the utmost surprise;

"and it seemed to me to be in the same spot. A building so solid as that is cannot easily change its situation." "Go into my cabinet," answered the sultan, "and come and tell me if you can see it."

The grand vizier went as he was ordered, and the very same thing happened to him as to the sultan. When he was quite sure that the palace of Aladdin did not stand in the place where it was, and that not the smallest part of it seemed to remain, he went back to the sultan. "Well," demanded the latter, "have you seen Aladdin's palace?" "Your majesty, may remember," replied the grand vizier, "that I had the honour to tell you that this palace, which was so much and so deservedly admired for beauty and immense riches, was the work of magic; but your majesty did not then pay any attention to what was said."

The sultan, who could not deny the former representations of the grand vizier, was in the greater rage, because he was also unable to disavow his own incredulity. "Where is this impostor," he exclaimed, "this wretch, that I may strike off his head?" "It is some days," answered the grand vizier, "since he came to take leave of your majesty: we must send to him, to inquire about his palace; he cannot be ignorant where it is." "This would be to treat him with too great indulgence," exclaimed the monarch: "go, and order thirty of my horsemen to bring him before me in chains." The grand vizier instantly gave the orders, and instructed the officer how they might take him and prevent his escape. They set out, and met Aladdin, who was returning from the chase, about six leagues from the city. The officer, when he first accosted him, said that the sultan was so impatient to see him again that he had sent them to inform him of it, and to accompany him on his return.

Aladdin had not the least suspicion of the true cause that had brought this detachment of the sultan's guard. He continued hunting on his way home; but when he was within half a league of the city the detachment surrounded him, and the officer then said, "Prince Aladdin, it is with the greatest regret, that I must inform you of the orders we have received from the sultan to arrest you, and conduct you like a state criminal. We entreat you not to take it ill in us that we do our duty, but on the contrary that you will pardon us." This declaration astonished Aladdin to the greatest degree. He felt himself innocent; and asked the officer if he knew of what crime he was accused; but he replied that neither he nor his men were acquainted with it.

As Aladdin perceived that his own attendants were much inferior to the detachment, and even that they were at some distance, he dismounted, and said to the officer, "Execute whatever orders you have received. I must, however, aver that I am guilty of no crime, either towards the person of the sultan, or the state." They immediately put a large and long chain about his neck, which they then bound round his body, so that he had not the use of his arms. When the officer had put himself at the head of the troop, one of the horsemen took hold of the end of the chain, and

going on behind the officer, he led Aladdin, who was obliged to follow on foot; and in this state he was conducted through the city.

When the guards entered the suburbs, the first person who saw Aladdin conducted in this way, like a state criminal, did not doubt but that he was going to loose his head. As he was generally beloved, some seized a sabre, others whatever arms they could, and those who had none took up stones, and in this manner followed the guards. Some of those who were in the rear wheeled about as if they wished to disperse them; but the people increased so fast, that the guards thought it better to dissemble, well satisfied if they could conduct Aladdin safe to the palace without his being rescued. In order to succeed the better, they took great care, as the streets happened to be more or less wide, to occupy the whole space, sometimes extending and at others compressing themselves. In this manner they arrived in the open square before the palace, where they all formed into one line, and faced about towards the armed multitude, while the officer and guard who led Aladdin entered the palace, and the porters shut the gates, to prevent any one from entering.

Aladdin was conducted before the sultan, who waited for him, accompanied by the grand vizier, in a balcony. He no sooner saw him, than he commanded the executioner, who was already present by his orders, to strike off his head, as he wished not to hear a word or any explanation whatever.

The executioner seized Aladdin, took off the chain, that was round his neck and body, and after laying down on the ground a large piece of leather, stained with the blood of the many criminals he had executed, he desired him to place himself on his knees, and then tied a bandage over his eyes. Having drawn his sabre, he was about to give the fatal stroke, only making the three usual flourishes in the air, and waiting for the sultan's order to separate Aladdin's head from his body; when at this very instant the grand vizier perceived that the populace, who had forced the guards, and filled the square, were in fact scaling the walls of the palace in many places, and even began to pull them down in order to open a passage. Before, therefore, the sultan could give the signal, he said to him, "I beseech your majesty to think maturely of what you are going to do: you will run the risk, sire, of having your palace forced; and if the misfortune should happen, the event cannot but be dreadful." "My palace forced!" replied the sultan; who can dare attempt it?" "If your majesty, sire, will cast your eyes towards the walls, you will acknowledge the truth of what I say."

When the sultan saw the violent commotion of the people, his fear was very great. He instantly ordered the executioner to put up his sabre, to take the bandage off Aladdin's eyes, and set him at liberty. He also commanded an officer to proclaim that he had pardoned Aladdin, and that every one might retire.

As all those who had mounted on the walls of the palace were witnesses of what passed, they gave over their design, and almost directly got down; and, highly delighted at having thus been the means of saving the life of one whom they really loved, they instantly published the news to those who were near them, thence it spread through all the populace who were in the neighbourhood of the palace; officers also ascended the terraced roof and proclaimed it publicly. The justice the sultan had thus rendered to Aladdin by pardoning him, disarmed the populace, quieted the tumult, and every one returned home.

When Aladdin found himself at liberty, he lifted up his head towards the balcony, and perceiving the sultan, he raised his voice, and addressed him in the most pathetic manner. "I entreat your majesty," he said, "to add a new favour to the pardon you have just granted me; and that is, to inform me of my crime." "What thy crime is, perfidious wretch! dost though not know it? Come up here, and I will show thee."

Aladdin ascended, and when he presented himself, "Follow me," said the sultan, walking on before, without taking any other notice of him. He led the way to the cabinet that opened towards the place where Aladdin's palace had stood. When they came to the door, "Go in," said the sultan; "you ought to know where your own palace is. Look on all sides, and tell me what is become of it." Aladdin looked, but saw nothing. He perceived the space upon which his palace had stood; but as he could not perceive how it should have disappeared, this extraordinary and wonderful event so confused and astonished him, that he could not answer the sultan a single word. "Tell me," said the latter, impatient at his silence, "where is your palace, and what is become of my daughter?" "Sire," replied Aladdin, at last breaking silence, "I plainly see, and must own, that the palace which I built is no longer in the place where it was. I see it has disappeared; but I can assure your majesty that I have no concern whatever in this event."

"I care not what has become of your palace—that gives me no pain," replied the sultan; I esteem my daughter a million times beyond it; unless, therefore, you discover and bring her again to me, no consideration shall yet prevent my taking off your head." "Sire," said Aladdin, "I entreat your majesty to grant me forty days to make the most diligent inquiries, and if I do not, during this period, succeed in my search, I give you my word that I will lay my head at the foot of your throne, that you may dispose of me according to your pleasure." "I grant your request," answered the sultan; "but do not think to abuse my favour, and endeavour to escape my resentment. In whatever part of the world you are, I will take care to discover you."

Aladdin then left the sultan's presence in the deepest humiliation, and in a state truly deserving of pity. He passed through the courts of the palace with downcast eyes, not daring to look about him, so great was his confusion; and the principal officers of the court, not one of whom he had ever disobliged, instead of coming to console him, or offer him a retreat at their homes, turned their backs upon him, both that they might not be supposed to see him, nor he be able to recognise them. But even if they had approached him in

order to console him, or offer him an asylum, they themselves would not have known him: he did not even know himself. His mind seemed deranged, of which he gave evident proofs when he was out of the palace, for, without thinking of what he did, he demanded at every door, and of all he met, if they had seen his palace, or could give him any intelligence of it.

These questions made every one think that Aladdin had lost his senses. Some even laughed at him; but the more serious, and especially those who had been on friendly terms, or even had any business with him, most sincerly compassionated him. He remained three days in the city, walking through every part, eating only what was given him in charity, without being able to form any resolution.

At length, as he could not in his wretched state remain any longer in the city, where he had hitherto lived in such splendour, he departed towards the country. He soon turned out of the high road, and after walking over a great deal of ground in the most dreadful state of mind, he arrived towards the close of the day on the bank of a river. He now gave himself up entirely to despair. "Where shall I go to seek my palace?" he exclaimed. "In what country, in what part of the world, shall I find either that, or my dear princess, whom the sultan demands of me? Never shall I be able to succeed! It is much better, then, that I at once free myself from labours which must end in nothing, and from feelings that distract me." He was then going to throw himself into the river, but being a good Mussulman, and faithful to his religion, he thought he ought not to do it without first repeating his prayers. In order to perform this ceremony, he went close to the bank to wash his face and hands, as was the custom of his country, but as this spot was rather steep, and the ground moist from the water that had washed against it, he slipped down, and would have fallen into the river if he had not been stopped by a piece of stone or rock that projected about two feet from the surface. Happy was it for him, too, that he had with him the ring which the African magician had put upon his finger, when he made him go down into the subterraneous cavern to bring away the precious lamp. In holding against the piece of rock, he rubbed the ring so stongly, that the same genie instantly appeared whom he had before seen in the subterraneous cavern. "What do you wish?" cried the genie; "I am ready to obey you as your slave, and as the slave of him who has that ring on his finger; I, and the other slaves of the ring."

Aladdin was most agreeably surprised by a sight he so little expected in the despair he was in; and directly replied, "Save my life, genie, a second time, by informing me where the palace is which I built, or again place it where it was." "What you require of me," answered the genie, "is beyond my ability: I am only the slave of the ring; you must address yourself to the slave of the lamp." "If that be the case, then," added Aladdin, "at least transport me to the spot where my palace is, in whatever part of the world it may be; and place me under the window of the princess Badroul

Boudour." He had barely said this, before the genie transported him to Africa, near a large city, and in the midst of a large meadow, in which the palace stood, and set him down directly under the windows of the apartment of the princess, and there left him. All this was the work of an instant.

Notwithstanding the obscurity, Aladdin readily recognised both his own palace and the apartment of the princess; but as the night was far advanced, and everything in the palace was quiet, he retired and seated himself at the foot of a tree. Full of hope, and reflecting on the good fortune which chance alone had procured him, he here felt himself in a much more tranquil state than since he had been arrested by the sultan's order, brought before him, and delivered from the danger of losing his head. He amused himself for some time with these agreeable thoughts; but as he had for five or six days enjoyed hardly any rest, he could not prevent himself being overcome by sleep, and he resigned himself to its influence on the spot where he was.

CHAPTER X.

THE STRATAGEM ALADDIN EMPLOYED TO DESTROY HIS ENEMY, AND OBTAIN POSSESSION OF THE WONDERFUL LAMP.—DEATH OF THE AFRICAN MAGICIAN.

THE next morning, as soon as the sun arose, Aladdin was most agreeably awakened by the notes of the birds which had perched upon the tree under which he lay, and among the other thick trees in the garden of his palace. He cast his eyes upon this beautiful building, and felt an inexpressible joy at the thought of being again master of it, and once more possessing his dear princess. He got up, and approached the apartment of the princess. He walked for some time under the window, waiting till she rose, in hopes that she might observe him. While in expectation of this, he considered within himself what could have been the cause of his misfortune; and after meditating some time, he entertained no doubt but that it arose from his having left his lamp. He accused himself of negligence and carelessness in having suffered the lamp to be out of his possession a single moment. He was, however embarrassed to discover who could be so jealous of his happiness. He would at once have comprehended it, if he had known that both he and his palace were in Africa; but of this the genie, who was the slave of the ring, had not informed him. The name alone of Africa would have brought his declared enemy, the magician, to his recollection.

The princess Badroul Boudour rose this morning much earlier than she had done since she had been transported into Africa by the artifice of the magician, whose sight she was compelled to endure once every day, as he was master of the palace: but she constantly treated him so ill, that he had never yet had the boldness to sleep there. When she was dressed, one of her women, looking through the lattice, perceived Aladdin, and ran and informed her mistress. The princess, who could scarcely believe this news, immediately went to the window, and saw him herself. She opened the lattice, the noise of which made Aladdin raise his head. He instantly recognised her, and saluted her in a manner highly expressive of his joy. "Lose not a moment," cried the princess; "they are gone to open the secret door, ascend quickly." She then shut the lattice.

This secret door was directly below the apartment of the princess. It was open, and Aladdin entered her apartment. It is impossible to express the joy they both felt in again seeing each other, after having concluded that their separation was eternal. They embraced each other with tears of joy, and gave all imaginable proofs of the tenderest affection, after so cruel and so unforseen a separation. "Before you mention anything else, my princess," said Aladdin, "tell me, in the name of God, as well for your own sake, and for that of the sultan, your ever-respected father, as for mine, what has become of that old lamp, which I placed upon the cornice of the saloon with twenty-four windows, before I went on the hunting party?" "Ah! my dear husband," replied the princess, "I doubt very much whether our mutual misfortunes have not arisen from that lamp; and what the more distresses me is, that I am myself the cause of it." "Do not, princess," resumed Aladdin, "attribute the matter to yourself; I only am to blame, for I ought to have been more careful in its preservation. But let us now only think of repairing that loss; and for this purpose inform me, I beg of you, of everything that has happened, and into whose hands this lamp has fallen."

The princess then related to Aladdin everything that had passed relative to the exchange of the old lamp for a new one, which she showed him; and how, on the morning following the night of the removal of the palace, she found herself in the unknown country where the palace now stood, and that this country was Africa, a fact she had learned from the traitor who, by his magic art, had transported her thither.

"Princess," replied Aladdin, interrupting her, "by informing me that we are in Africa, you have at once unmasked the traitor. He is the most infamous of men. But this is neither a proper time nor place to enter into a detail of his crimes. I entreat you only to tell me what he has done with the lamp, and where he has put it." "He constantly," rejoined the princess, "carries it carefully wrapped up in his bosom. I am sure of this, because he once took it out in my presence, showing it as a sort of trophy."

"Do not be offended, my princess," continued Aladdin, "at all the questions I put to you; they are of equal importance to us both. But to come at once to what most interests me; tell me, I conjure you, how you have been treated by so infamous and perfidious a wretch." "Since I have been in this place," answered the princess, "he has presented himself before me only once during the day; and I am persuaded that the little satisfaction he has derived from his visits makes him repeat them less often. All that he has ever said to me has only been for the purpose of persuading me to be faithless to you, and to take him for my husband; wishing to convince me that

I ought never to expect to see you again—that you are no longer alive, and that the sultan my father has ordered your head to be cut off. And to prove to me that you were an ungrateful wretch, he said that you owed all your good fortune to him, with a thousand other injurious expressions that I cannot repeat. And as he never received any other answer than my complaints and tears, he was obliged to retire with as little satisfaction as he came. I have, nevertheless, no doubt but that he means to suffer the more violent effects of my affliction to subside, with the hope and expectation that I shall change my mind; and if, in the end, I should persevere in my resistance, to make use of violent methods: but your presence, my dear husband, at once dissipates all my fears."

"Princess," interrupted Aladdin, "I trust you will not be deceived, as I think I have discovered the means of delivering you from our common enemy. For this purpose, however, I must go into the town; I will return about noon, and communicate to you the nature of my design, for you must yourself contribute towards its success. Let me, however, apprize you not to be astonished if you see me return in a different dress; and be sure you give orders that I may not be obliged to wait at the private door, but be admitted the instant I knock." The princess promised that somebody should be ready to open it on his arrival.

Aladdin left the apartment by the same door he had entered; and when outside of the palace he looked about on all sides, and at last discovered a peasant, who was going into the country. As this peasant had got some distance beyond the palace, Aladdin hastened to overtake him; and as soon as he joined him, he proposed to change clothes, and made him such an offer that the peasant readily agreed to it. This was effected behind a small tree; and when the exchange was completed, they separated, and Aladdin took the road that led to the town. When he got there, he turned down a street that led from the gate, and then getting into those streets which were most frequented, he came to that part where each street was occupied by a particular profession or trade. He went into that appropriated to druggists, and going to the shop which appeared the largest and best supplied, he asked the owner if he had a certain powder, the name of which he mentioned.

The merchant, who, from looking at Aladdin's dress, did not conceive that he had money enough to pay for it, replied that he had it, but that it was very dear. Aladdin readily entered into the merchant's thoughts, and therefore took out his purse, and showing him the gold, desired to have half a drachm of the powder. The merchant weighed it, wrapped it up, and giving it to Aladdin, demanded one piece of gold for it: the latter immediately paid him, and without staying in the town any longer than was necessary to take some nourishment, returned to the palace. He had no occasion to wait at the street door; it was instantly opened, and he went up to the apartment of the princess Badroul Boudour. "The aversion, my princess," said Aladdin to her as soon as he came in, "which you have expressed for your ravisher may probably

occasion you some effort in complying with the instructions I am about to give you. But permit me, in the first place, to tell you that it is necessary for you to dissemble, and even to offer some violence to your own feelings, if you wish to be delivered from his persecution, and afford to the sultan, your father and my sovereign, the satisfaction of again beholding you.

"If you will follow my advice," continued Aladdin, "you will this moment adorn yourself in one of your most elegant dresses, and when the African magician shall come, make no difficulty in receiving him with all the affability you can assume, without appearing affected, or under any constraint, in a kind of open manner; yet still with some remains of grief, which he may easily conceive will soon be entirely dissipated. In your conversation with him, give him to understand that you are making the greatest efforts to forget me; and that he may still be more convinced of your sincerity, invite him even to sup with you, and tell him that you are desirous of tasting some of the best wine this country can produce. On this he will not fail to leave you in order to procure some. While he is gone, do you go to the sideboard, which will of course be set out, and put this powder into one of the cups you usually drink out of: set the cup on one side, and tell one of your women to fill it, and bring it to you at a certain signal, which you must explain to her, warning her not to make any mistake. When the magician shall be returned, and you shall again have sat down to table, make them bring you the particular goblet in which the powder was put, and then do you make an exchange with him. He will find the flavour of that which you give him so excellent, that he will drink it up to the last drop. Scarcely shall he have emptied the cup, but you will see him fall backwards. If you should feel any repugnance at drinking out of his cup, you need only pretend to do so; and you can very easily manage this, for the effect of the powder will be so sudden, that he will not have time to pay any attention to what you do, or notice whether you drink or not."

When Aladdin had finished his instructions, the princess answered, "I confess that I shall violently shock my own feelings in agreeing to make these advances to the magician, although I am aware they are absolutely necessary. But what cannot I resolve to undertake against such a cruel enemy? I will, then, do as you direct, since your happiness depends upon it as well as mine." When these matters were all arranged with the princess, Aladdin took his leave: he passed the remainder of the day in the neighbourhood of the palace, and as the night came on he approached the secret door.

The princess Badroul Boudour, being inconsolable not only at her separation from her dear husband Aladdin, whom from the first she loved more through inclination than duty, but also at being separated from the sultan her father, between whom and herself there was an equal degree of affection, had completely neglected her person from the very moment of their distressful separation. She had even neglected the neatness so becoming to her sex, particularly since the first visit of the magician, when she had learnt from her women that he was the person who had exchanged the old lamp for a new one: after this infamous trick, therefore, she could not look upon him without horror. The opportunity, however, of taking that vengeance upon him he so justly deserved, so much sooner than she could ever hope to have the means of accomplishing, made her resolve to satisfy Aladdin.

As soon, therefore, as he was gone, she went to her toilet, and made her women dress her in the most becoming manner. She put on one of her richest habits, and that which she thought best adapted to the purpose. Her girdle was of gold, set with diamonds of the largest size, and the best chosen. She put on only a necklace of pearls; six of which on each side the centre one, which was the largest and most valuable, were so beautifully proportioned, that the proudest sultanas and greatest queens would have thought themselves happy in possessing a necklace equal to the two smallest. Her bracelets, which were formed of diamonds and rubies mixed, admirably answered to the richness of her girdle and necklace.

When the princess was completely dressed, she consulted her mirror, and asked the opinion of her women upon her appearance; and finding she was not deficient in any of those charms that might flatter the foolish passion of the African magician, she seated herself upon the sofa, in expectation of his arrival.

The magician did not fail to make his appearance at the usual hour. As soon as the princess saw him come into the saloon of the twenty-four windows, where she was waiting to receive him, she got up in all the splendour of her beauty, and pointing with her hand to the most honourable seat, remained standing till he had reached it, that she might sit down at the same time. This distinguished civility she had not shown him before.

The African magician, more dazzled by the lustre of her eyes than the brilliancy of the jewels she wore, was greatly struck. Her majestic air, the gracious manner she had put on, so opposite to the rebuffs he had hitherto met with from her, absolutely confused him. He at first wished to sit at the very end of the sofa; but as he saw that the princess declined taking her seat until he was seated where she wished, he at last obeyed.

The princess then, in order to free him from the embarassment in which she saw he was, looked at him in such a manner as to make him suppose she no longer beheld him in an odious point of view, and then said to him, "You are doubtless astonished at seeing me appear to-day quite different from what I have been hitherto; but you will no longer be surprised at it, when I tell you that I am naturally of a disposition so much the reverse of grief and melancholy, vexation, or distress, that I endeavour to drive them from me by every means in my power, as soon as the cause of them has been a short time over. I have reflected upon what you have said respecting the destiny of Aladdin, and from the disposition of the sultan my father, which I well know, I am persuaded, like yourself, that the former could not

possibly avoid the terrible effects of his rage. I concluded, therefore, that even if I were to weep and lament all the remainder of my life, that my tears would not revive him: it is then on this account, that, after having paid him, even to the tomb, every respect and duty which my affection required, I thought I ought at length to search for the means of consoling myself. These are the motives which have produced the change you see. In order, then, to drive away all sorrow, which I have now resolved to banish from my mind, and being persuaded that you will assist me in the endeavour, I have ordered a supper to be prepared; but as I have only some wine which is the produce of Cathay, and am now in Africa, I have a great desire to taste what is made here, and I thought if there were any, that you would be most likely to have the best."

The African magician, who had conceived it impossible to have so soon, and so easily, acquired the good graces of the princess Badroul Boudour, replied that he was unable sufficiently to express how sensible he was of her goodness; and, to put an end to a conversation from which he would find it difficult to disengage himself if it continued any longer, he adverted to the wine of Africa which she had mentioned, and told her that among the many advantages which that country boasted of possessing, that of producing most excellent wine was the principal, praticularly in the part where she then was; and that he had some seven years old that was yet untouched, and it was not saying too much to aver that it surpassed all other wine in the whole world. "If my princess," added he, "will permit me, I will bring two bottles, and will return in an instant." "I should be sorry to give you that trouble," replied the princess; "it would be better surely to send some one." "It is necessary for me to go myself," resumed the magician; "no one but myself has the key of the cellar; nor does any one else know the secret of opening it." "The longer you are gone, the more impatient I shall be to see you again; remember, we sit down to table on your return."

Full of the ideas of his expected happiness, the African magician not only ran, but absolutely flew to fetch the wine, and was back almost instantly. The princess did not doubt but that he would make haste, and therefore threw the powder which Aladdin had given her into a goblet, and set it aside until she should call for it. They then sat down opposite to each other, so that the magician's back was towards the sideboard. The princess, helping him to what appeared the best, said to him, "If you should prefer it, I will give you some music; but as we are only by ourselves, I think that conversation will afford us more pleasure." The magician regarded this choice as a fresh mark of her favour.

After they had eaten for some little time, the princess asked for some wine, and drank to the magician's health. "You are right," she cried, when she had drank, "in praising you wine; I have never tasted any so delicious." "Charming princess," replied he, holding the goblet they had given him in his hand, "my wine acquires additional flavour by the approbation you have

ALADDIN SLAYS THE MAGICIAN'S BROTHER.

bestowed upon it." "Drink to my health," resumed the princess; "you must confess I understand it." He did as she requested him, and in returning the goblet, he added: "I esteem myself very happy, princess, to have reserved this wine for so good an occasion; and I confess I have never in my whole life drank any in such agreeable company."

They continued eating some time, and had taken three cup each, when the princess, who had completely fascinated the African magician by her kind and obliging manners, at length gave the signal to her woman to bring some wine; at the same time desiring her to bring a goblet full, and also to fill that of the magician, which they presented to him. When they each held their goblet in their hands, "I know not," said she to the African magician, "what is your custom, when those who are fond of

each other drink together as we do. With us in Cathay each person presents his own goblet to the other, and the lovers then drink to each other's health." At the same time she presented the goblet she held, and extended her other hand to receive his. The African magician hastened to make this change, with which he was the more delighted, as he looked upon this favour as the surest mark of having made an entire conquest of the heart of the princess; and this completed his happiness. "Princess," he exclaimed before he drank, and holding the goblet in his hand, "we Africans ought to become as much refined in the art of giving a zest to love by every delightful accompaniment, as the people of Cathay; by instructing me, therefore, in a matter of which I am ignorant, I should learn how sensible I ought to be of the favour I receive. Never shall I forget, most amiable princess, that in drinking out of your goblet I have regained that life which your cruelty, had it continued, would most infallibly have destroyed."

The princess Badroul Boudour, tired of this ridiculous and troublesome discourse, cried, "Drink; you may then say what you please to me." At the same time she pretended to carry the goblet she held to her mouth, but barely suffered it to touch her lips, while the African magician did not leave a single drop in his. Wishing to drain the cup, he held his head back, but remained so long in that position that the princess, who kept the goblet to her lips, observed that his eyes were turned up; and he, in fact, fell upon his back, without the least struggle.

The princess had no occasion to order them to open the street door, and admit Aladdin. Her women, who were stationed at different parts, gave the word one to the other from the saloon to the bottom of the staircase, so that the African magician had no sooner fallen backwards than the door was opened.

Aladdin went up to the saloon, and as soon as he saw the African magician extended on the sofa, he stopped Badroul Boudour, who had risen to congratulate him on the joyful event. "My princess," he cried, "there is at this moment no time for rejoicing; me the favour to retire to your apartment, and to suffer me to be alone, while I prepare for our return to Cathay as quickly as you left it." The princess, her women, and the eunuchs, were no sooner out of the hall, than Aladdin shut the door; and then going up to the body of the African magician, which was lying lifeless on the sofa, he opened his vest, and took out the lamp, which was wrapped up exactly in the manner the princess had described. He took it out and rubbed it. The genie instantly presented himself, and made the usual speech. "Genie," said Aladdin, "I have called you, to command you, in the name of this lamp, your good mistress, immediately to transport this palace to the same spot in Cathay whence it was brought here." The genie first showed by an inclination of his head that he would obey, and vanished. The journey was instantly made, and only two slight shocks were perceptible: one, when the palace was taken up from the place where it stood in Africa, and the other, when it was set down in Cathay, opposite to the sultan's palace.

Aladdin then went down to the apartment of Badroul Boudour. "Our joy, my princess," exclaimed Aladdin, embracing her, "will be complete by to-morrow morning." As the princess had not finished her supper, and as Aladdin was much in want of food, she ordered them to bring the things from the saloon of twenty-four windows, where the supper had been served, and which had not yet been removed. The princess and Aladdin drank together, and found the old wine of the magician most excellent: and after enjoying themselves at table for some time, they retired to their apartment.

Since the removal of Aladdin's palace and the loss of the princess Badroul Boudour, his daughter, as he thought for ever, the sultan had been inconsolable. He slept neither night nor day: and instead of avoiding everything that could increase his affliction, he on the contrary cherished every thought that was likely to add to it. Thus, instead of going only every morning to the cabinet to satisfy himself, as it were, only with the recollection of what he was now unable to perceive, he went several times during the day to renew his tears, and overwhelm himself with the most painful thoughts of never again seeing what had afforded him so much delight, and for the loss of her whom he esteemed more than all the world. The sun had not yet risen when the sultan entered this cabinet, as usual, on the very morning after Aladdin's palace had been brought back to its place. When he first came in he was so much absorbed in his own feelings, and so penetrated with sorrow, that he threw his eyes over the accustomed spot in the most melancholy manner, with the expectation of beholding, as he thought, only the vacant space that had been occupied by the palace. But when he found the void filled up, he conjectured that it was only a mist. He then looked with greater attention, and could not at last doubt but it was the palace of Aladdin which he saw. Chagrin and sorrow were succeeded by the most delightful sensations of joy. He hastened back to his apartment, and instantly ordered them to saddle and bring him a horse. It was no sooner brought than he mounted it and set out, thinking he could not arrive soon enough at Aladdin's Palace.

Aladdin, who had conjectured what might be the consequence, had risen at daybreak; and as soon as he had dressed himself in one of his most magnificent robes, he went up to the saloon of twenty-four windows, from which he perceived the sultan as he was coming along. He then descended; and was exactly in time to receive him at the bottom of the grand staircase, and assist him in dismounting. "Aladdin," cried the sultan, "I cannot speak to you till I have seen and embraced my daughter."

He then conducted the sultan to the apartment of the princess Badroul Boudour, whom Aladdin had informed when he got up that she was no longer in Africa, but in Cathay, at the capital of the sultan her father, and close to his palace. She had just finished dressing. The sultan eagerly embraced her, bathing her face with his tears, while the princess on her part showed the greatest marks of delight at again beholding him. For some time the sultan could not utter a syllable, so much was he affected at finding his daughter, after having lamented her loss as inevitable, while the princess shed tears of joy at the sight of him. "My dear daughter," exclaimed the sultan, at length recovering his speech, "I would fain believe that the joy you feel at again seeing me makes you appear so little changed as though not even an unpleasant circumstance had happened to you. I am sure, however, that you must have suffered a great deal. No one can have been suddenly transported as you have been, and with a whole palace at the same time, without the greatest alarm and most dreadful feeling. Relate to me, I beg of you, everything as it happened, and do not conceal the least circumstance."

The princess felt a pleasure in giving the sultan all the satisfaction he wished. "Sir," said she, "if I appear so little altered, I beg your majesty to consider that my expectations were raised so long ago as yesterday morning by the presence cf my dear husband and liberator Aladdin, whom I had till then regarded and lamented as for ever lost to me, and that the happiness I experienced in again embracing him restored me nearly to my former self. Strictly speaking, my whole sorrow arose from finding myself torn from your majesty and my dear husband; not only out of my affection for him, but from the anxiety I suffered for fear of the dreadful effects of your majesty's rage, to which I did not doubt that he would be exposed, however innocent he might be; and no one could be more so. I have suffered less from the insolence of my ravisher, who continually held a conversation that gave me pain, but which I as often put an end to by the ascendancy I knew how to maintain over him. I was not, however, under more restraint than at present. Aladdin himself had not the least concern in my removal; I was alone the cause, although the innocent one."

In order to convince the sultan that she spoke the truth, she gave him a detailed account of how the African magician had disguised himself like a seller of lamps, and offered to change new ones for old, and of the joke she amused herself with in changing Aladdin's lamp, the important and secret qualities of which she was ignorant of; of the instant removal of the palace and herself in consequence of this exchange, and their being transported into Africa, with the magician himself, whom two of her women, and also the eunuch who had made the exchange, recollected, when he had the audacity to come and present himself before her the first time after his daring enterprise; and of the proposal he made to marry her. She then informed him of the persecution she continued to suffer until the arrival of Aladdin; of the measures which they mutually took to get the lamp, which the magician constantly carried about him; in what manner they succeeded, particularly by her having the courage to dissemble her feelings, and invite him to sup with her; with everything that passed till she presented the goblet to him in which she had privately put the powder Aladdin had given her. "With respect to what remains," added she, "I leave to Aladdin to inform you of it."

The latter had but little to add to this account. "When they opened the private door," he said, "I immediately went up to the saloon of twenty-four windows, and saw the traitor lying dead on the sofa, from the strength of the powder. As it was not proper for the princess to remain there any longer, I requested her to go to her apartment with her women and eunuchs. When I was alone, after taking the lamp out of the magician's bosom, I made use of the same secret he had done to remove the palace, and steal away the princess. I have brought the palace back to its place, and have had the happiness of restoring the princess to your majesty, as you commanded me. I have not deceived your majesty in this account; and if you will take the trouble to go up to the saloon, you will see the magician punished as he deserved."

In order to be more fully convinced, the sultan rose and went up; and when he had seen the dead body of the magician, whose face was already become livid by the strength of the poison, he embraced Aladdin with the greatest tenderness. "Do not think ill of me, my son," cried he, "for having used you in the manner I have done; paternal affection forced me to do so, and I deserve to be pardoned for the excess to which it carried me."

"Sire," replied Aladdin, "I have not the least reason to complain of your majesty's conduct; you have done only what was your duty. This magician, this infamous wretch, the most detestable of men, was the sole cause of my disgrace. When your majesty shall have leisure, I will give you an account of another piece of treachery which he was guilty of towards me, not less infamous than this, from which the peculiar providence of God has preserved me." "I will take care to find an opportunity," said the sultan, "and that very soon. But let us now only think of making ourselves happy, and having this odious object removed."

Aladdin then ordered the magician's body to be thrown away, that it might serve for the beasts and birds to prey upon. In the meantime, the sultan, after having commanded the drums, trumpets, cymbals, and other instruments to announce a public rejoicing, had a festival proclaimed of ten days' continuance, in honour of the return of the princess Badroul Boudour, of Aladdin, and his palace.

CHAPTER XI.

THE BROTHER OF THE AFRICAN MAGICIAN JOURNEYS TO CATHAY IN ORDER TO BE REVENGED ON ALADDIN. — HE DECEIVES THE PRINCESS BADROUL BOUDOUR BY DISGUISING HIMSELF; BUT IS DETECTED AND SLAIN BY ALADDIN.

IT was in this manner that Aladdin a second time escaped an almost inevitable death: but even this was not the last; he was in danger a third time; the circumstances attending which will now be related.

The African magician had a younger brother, who was not inferior to him in his knowledge of magic; and it may be said that he surpassed him in wicked intentions and diabolical machinations. As they did not always live together, nor even in the same city—one sometimes being at the eastern extremity, while the other travelled in the most western part of the world—they did not fail once every year to inform themselves, by means of their knowledge of geomancy, in what part of the world the other was, how he was going on, and whether either wanted the assistance of the other.

Some time after the African magician had failed in his attempt against Aladdin, his younger brother, who had not received any intelligence of him for a year, and who was not in Africa, wished to know where he was, whether he was well, and what he was about. Into whatever place he travelled, he never went without his square geomantic box, the same as his brother. He took, then, this box, and having arranged the sand, he cast the points, drew the figures, and formed his horoscope. In examining each part, he discovered that his brother was no longer alive, that he had been poisoned, and that his death was sudden. On searching further, he found out where this took place; and that he by whom he had been poisoned was a man of low birth, but was married to a princess, the daughter of the sultan.

When the magician was thus apprized of the melancholy fate of his brother, he did not waste his time in useless regrets, which could not again restore him to life; but he took the instant resolution to avenge his death: he mounted his horse, and directly began his journey towards Cathay. He traversed plains, rivers, mountains, and deserts; and after a long journey of almost incredible fatigue and difficulty, he at length reached Cathay, and in a short time afterwards arrived at the capital which his experiment in geomancy had pointed out. Certain of not being deceived, nor of having mistaken one kingdom for another, he took up his abode there.

The very next morning the magician went out, and in walking through the city, not so much for the purpose of seeing its beauties, which did not at all interest him, as with the intention of planning his measures in order to put his pernicious design into execution, he introduced himself into the most frequented places, and was very attentive to the conversation that passed. At a place where many people spent their time in playing a variety of games, and where, while some were playing, others entertained themselves with the news of the day, or with talking over their own private affairs, he observed that they spoke much of and highly praised the virtues and piety of a woman called Fatima, who led a retired life, and even of the miracles she performed. As he thought that this woman might perhaps be in some way useful in his business he was about, he took one of the persons aside, and begged him to give a more particular account of this holy woman, and what sort of miracles she performed.

"What," exclaimed this man, "have you never seen nor even heard of her? She is the admiration of the whole city, by her fasting and austere life, and by the good examples she sets. Except on Mondays and Fridays she never leaves her hermitage; but on these days she comes into the city, and does an infinite deal of good, for there is no one, who is afflicted even with a pain in the head, whom she does not cure by laying her hands upon them."

The magician did not want to know more on this subject; he only inquired of the same person in what quarter of the city the hermitage of this holy woman was. He informed him; upon which, after first forming the horrible design about to be mentioned, and that he might be the more sure of its success, he observed all her conduct the first time she went out after this enquiry, and did not lose sight of her the whole day, till she returned in the evening to her cell. When he had accurately remarked the spot, he returned to one of those places where, as has been said, a certain warm liquor is prepared and sold, and where if you choose, you may pass the night, particularly during the hot weather, when the inhabitants of Cathay prefer sleeping upon a mat rather than on a bed.

The magician having first paid the owner for what he had, which did not amount to much, went out about midnight, and took the road to the hermitage of Fatima, the holy woman, the name by which she was distinguished throughout the city. He had no difficulty in opening the door, as it was only fastened by a latch. As soon as he entered, he shut it again without making any noise. He then perceived Fatima, by the light of the moon, lying almost in the open air, upon a couch with a ragged mat, close to the side of her cell. He approached, and after taking out a poniard he had by his side, he awoke her.

On opening her eyes, poor Fatima was very much astonished at seeing a man on the point of plunging a poniard into her. Holding the point of the dagger against her breast, ready in an instant to plunge it into her heart, "If you cry out," said he, "or make the least noise, I will murder you. Get up, and do what I bid you." Fatima, who always slept in her clothes, got up, trembling with fear. "Fear nothing," said the magician, "I only want your habit; give it me, and take mine." When this was done, and the magician was dressed in Fatima's clothes, he said to her, "Paint my face like yours, so that I shall resemble you, and the colour will not come off. As he saw that she still trembled, he added, in order to give her courage, and that she might do what he wanted of her better, "Fear nothing, I tell you again: I swear, in the name of God, that I will spare your life." Fatima then conducted him into the interior of her cell, lighted her lamp, and taking a certain liquid in a basin, with a pencil, she rubbed it over his face; assuring him it would not change, and that there was no difference between her colour and his. She then put upon him her own head-dress, with a veil, and instructed him how she concealed her face with it when walking through the city. She finished by hanging a large necklace or chaplet round his neck, which came down nearly to his waist; she then put the stick she was accustomed to walk with into his hand, and giving him a mirror, "Look," she said, "and you will find that you cannot possibly resemble me more." The magician found everything as he wished; but he did not keep the oath he had solemnly taken in her presence. But that no one might see the blood, which would fall if he stabbed her with his poniard, he strangled her, and when he found that she was dead, he drew the body by the feet to the cistern of the hermitage, and threw it in.

The magician, thus disguised like the holy woman, passed the remainder of the night in the hermitage, after having defiled it by so detestable a murder. Very early the next morning, although it was not the usual day for Fatima's appearance in the city, he did not hesitate to go out, because he was very well aware that no one would ask him about it, or if they did, he might easily answer the question. As the first thing he did on his arrival in the city had been to inspect the palace of Aladdin, and as it was there he meant to put his scheme in execution, he took the road towards it.

As soon as the people saw the holy woman, as every one imagined him to be, the magician was surrounded by a great crowd of people. Some recommended themselves to his prayers, others kissed his hand; some, still more respectful, kissed the hem of his robe, while others, either because they had the headache, or wished to be preserved from it, bent down before him, that he might lay his hands upon them: he did so, muttering at the same time a sort of prayer. In short, he so well imitated the holy woman, that every one was deceived, and took him for her. After stopping very often to satisfy these people, who, in fact, received neither good nor harm from this imposition of hands, he at last arrived in the square before Aladdin's palace, where, as the crowd increased, the difficulty to get near him was also greater. The strongest and most zealous beat off the crowd to get a place for themselves, and hence several quarrels arose, the noise of which reached the ears of the princess Badroul Boudour, who was sitting in the saloon with twenty-four windows.

The princess demanded the occasion of the noise; and as no person could inform her, she ordered some one to go and see, and bring her an account. One of her women, however, looked through the lattice, and told her that it arose from a crowd of people, who were collected round the holy woman, to be cured of their maladies by the laying of her hands upon them.

The princess, who for some time had heard every one speak in praise of this holy woman, but who had never yet beheld her, felt a desire to see and converse with her. Having mentioned something to this effect, the chief of the eunuchs, who was present, said, that if she wished it, he was sure he could get her to come, and that she had only to give her orders. The princess consented to it, and he instantly despatched four eunuchs, with an order to bring back this pretended old woman with them.

As soon as the eunuchs were observed to issue from the gate of the palace, and make towards the holy woman, or rather the magician disguised as such, the crowd began to disperse, and when he was thus more at liberty, and saw that they were coming towards him, he went part of the way to meet them, and with the greater glee, as he saw that his cunning scheme was in a prosperous state. One of the eunuchs addressed him in these words; "Holy woman, the princess wishes to see you: follow us." "The princess honours me very much," replied the pretended Fatima. "I am ready to obey her commands:" and he then followed the eunuchs, who immediately went back to the palace.

When the magician, clothed in this sanctified dress, but with a heart the most diabolical, was introduced into the saloon with twenty-four windows, and perceived the princess, he began a prayer containing a long catalogue of exhortations to piety, and wishes for her prosperity, and the accomplishment of everything she could desire. He then displayed all his hypocritical and deceitful rhetoric, in order to insinuate himself, under the cloak of great piety, into the good opinion of the princess. And in this it was so much the easier for him to succeed, as the princess, who was naturally of the best disposition, was persuaded that all the world were at least as good as herself; particularly all those who professed to serve God in a retired life.

When the false Fatima had finished her long harangue, "My good mother," replied the princess, "I am much obliged to you for your kind prayers; I have the greatest confidence in them, and trust God will hear them. Approach, and sit down near me." The pretended Fatima sat down with the greatest appearance of modesty; and the princess continued—"My good mother, I have a request to make to you, which you must not refuse me; and that is, that you come and live with me, that I may have you constantly to converse with, and may learn from your advice and good example how I ought to serve God.

"Princess," replied the false Fatima, "I entreat you not to require my compliance in that to which I cannot agree without breaking in upon my prayers and devotions." "Do not let that give you any pain," resumed the princess: "I have many apartments which are not occupied; you shall choose that which you like best, and you may attend to your devotions with as much liberty there as if you were in your own hermitage."

The magician, who had no other object than to introduce himself into Aladdin's palace, where it would be much easier for him to execute the wicked design he meditated, by remaining under the auspices and protection of the princess, than if he were obliged to go to and fro from the palace to the hermitage, did not make much difficulty in acceding to the obliging offer of Badroul Boudour. "Princess," he replied, "whatever resolution a poor and miserable woman like myself may have made to renounce the world, its pomps and vanities, I nevertheless dare not resist either the wish or the command of so pious and charitable a princess."

Upon this answer, the princess rose, and said to the magician, "Come with me, that I may show you all the apartments that are unoccupied; you may then make your choice." He followed the princess through all the apartments she showed him, which were very large, and handsomely furnished. He chose the one which appeared to be the least so, saying at the same time that it was much too good for him, and that he only made choice of it to oblige her.

The princess wished to take this impostor back with her to the saloon with twenty-four windows, to dine with her; but as it was necessary in the act of eating to uncover his face, which he had hitherto kept concealed by the veil, and as he was afraid she might not then suppose him to be Fatima, the holy woman, he begged her so earnestly to excuse him, saying that he never ate anything but bread and dried fruits, and to permit him to take his trifling meal in his own apartment, that she readily complied with his wishes. "My good mother," she said, "you are quite at liberty; do as you would in the hermitage; I will order them to carry you in some food; but remember that I shall expect you as soon as you have finished your repast."

The princess then dined; and the false Fatima did not fail to return to her as soon as she was informed by an eunuch, whom she ordered to acquaint her when she rose from table. "My good mother," said the princess, "I am delighted at enjoying the society of such a holy woman as you are, and who will, by your presence, bring down blessings upon the whole palace. And now I mention this palace, pray tell me how you like it? But before I show you other portions, tell me how you like this saloon."

At this inquiry, the pretended Fatima, who, in order to act her part with more appearance of truth, had till now kept her head cast down towards the ground, at length raised it, and looked at everything in the saloon, from one end to the other; and when she had thoroughly examined it, she said, "Indeed, princess, this saloon is truly beautiful, and worthy of admiration. But, as far as a recluse can judge, who knows nothing of what is reckoned beautiful by the world in general, I think only one thing is wanting." "What is that, my good mother?" inquired Badroul Boudour; "I entreat you to tell it me. For my part, I thought, and had also heard it said, that nothing was wanting; but whatever may be deficient I will have supplied."

"Pardon me this liberty, princess," replied the still dissembling magician; "my opinion, if it can be of any value, is, that if the egg of a roc were suspended from the centre of the dome, this saloon would not have its equal in either of the four quarters of the globe, and your palace would be the whole wonder of the universe."

"My good mother," resumed the princess, "what kind of bird is a roc, and where could the egg of one be found?" "Princess," answered the feigned Fatima, "the roc is a bird of a prodigious size, which inhabits the summit of Mount Caucasus, and the architect who designed your palace can procure you one."

After having thanked the pretended Fatima for her information and advice, the princess Badroul Boudour continued the conversation upon various other subjects; but she by no means forgot the egg of the roc, of which she fully intended to inform Aladdin when he returned from hunting, which happened on the same evening, after the false Fatima had taken leave of the princess. As soon as Aladdin entered the palace, he went to the apartment of the princess, and saluted and embraced her: but she seemed to him to receive him with rather less affection than usual. "I do not find you, my princess," said he, "in your usual good spirits. Has anything happened to displease or vex you?" "It is a mere trifle," replied the princess; "and it gives me so little anxiety, that I did not suppose it would be so apparent in my face and manner. But since you have observed some alteration in me, which I by no means intended, I will not conceal the cause, inconsiderable as it is.

"I thought, as you did," the princess went on, "that our palace was the most superb, the most beautiful, and most ornamented of any in the whole world. I will tell you, however, what has come into my head, after having thoroughly examined the saloon with twenty-four windows. Do not you think with me, that if the egg of a roc were suspended from the dome, we should have nothing to wish for?" "It is enough,

princess," replied Aladdin, "that you think the want of a roc's egg is a defect. You shall find by my diligence, that there is nothing I will not do for love of you."

Aladdin instantly left the princess, and went up to the saloon with twenty-four windows; and then taking the lamp, which he now always carried about him since the danger he had experienced from the neglect of that precaution, out of his bosom, he rubbed it. The genie immediately appeared before him. "Genie," said Aladdin, "there requires the egg of a roc to be suspended from the centre of this dome, to make it perfect; I command you, in the name of this lamp which I hold, to get it."

Aladdin had scarcely pronounced these words before the genie uttered so loud and dreadful a scream that the very room shook, and Aladdin trembled so violently that he was ready to fall. "What, wretch!" exclaimed the genie, in a voice that would have made the most courageous tremble, "is it not enough that I and my companions have done everything thou hast chosen to command, but that thou repayest our service by an ingratitude that is unequalled, and commandest me to bring thee my master, and hang him up in the midst of this vaulted dome? Thou art deserving, for this crime, of being instantly torn to atoms, with thy wife and palace with thee. But thou art fortunate that the request did not originate with thee, and that the command is not in any way thine. Learn who is the true author. It is no other than the brother of thy enemy, the African magician, whom thou hast destroyed, as he deserved. He is in thy palace, disguised under the appearance of Fatima, the holy woman, whom he has murdered; and it is he who has suggested the idea to thy wife to make this horrible request. His design is to kill thee; therefore take care of thyself." And as the genie said this, he vanished.

Aladdin lost not a syllable of the words of the genie. He had before heard of the holy woman Fatima, and was not ignorant of the manner in which she could cure a pain in the head, at least as they pretended. He then returned to the apartment of the princess, but did not mention what had happened. He sat down, and, holding his hand to his forehead, complained of a violent pain that had suddenly seized him. The princess directly ordered the holy woman to be called, and related to Aladdin the manner in which she had induced her to come to the palace.

The pretended Fatima came; and as soon as she entered, Aladdin said to her, "I am very happy, my good mother, to see you. I am tormented with a violent headache, which has suddenly attacked me. I request your assistance; and from the reliance I place on your prayers, I hope you will not refuse me the favour which you grant to all who are thus afflicted." He then bent his head forward, and the false Fatima advanced, putting at the same time her hand upon a poniard which was concealed in her girdle under her robe. Aladdin, who watched what she did, seized her hand before she could draw it, and piercing her heart with her own weapon, threw her dead on the floor.

"What have you done!" exclaimed the princess

in alarm; "you have killed the holy woman!" "No, no, my princess," answered Aladdin, "I have not killed Fatima, but a villain, who was going to assassinate me, if I had not prevented him. It is this wretch," added he, showing his face, "who has strangled Fatima, and who has disguised himself in her clothes to murder me. To convince you still further, I must inform you that he is the brother of the African magician who carried you off." Aladdin then related to her in what manner he had learnt these particulars, and he then ordered the body to be removed.

It was in this manner that Aladdin was delivered from the persecution of the two magicians. A few years after, the sultan, being very old, died. As he left no male issue, the princess Badroul Boudour, as his legitimate heir, succeeded to the throne, and of course transferred the supreme power to Aladdin. They reigned together many years, and left an illustrious and numerous progeny.

ELMINE;

OR,

THE FLOWER THAT NEVER FADES.

In times of old, in a distant land, there lived a princess named Elmine. She was very beautiful and amiable. Youth and innocence are always so; but as innocence often passes away with childhood, so also does loveliness. The young princess was an orphan, and her education had been undertaken by a fairy of the name of Lindoriane. Elmine did not know that her governess was a fairy, but she loved Lindoriane as her friend, and revered her as a mother.

One day Lindoriane permitted her pupil to join her school-mates, who were playing in a neighbouring meadow. They amused themselves in all sorts of innocent pleasures, they ran along a brook, caught butterflies, and plucked flowers. After having collected a great many, they sat down beneath the shade of a tree and made garlands and wreaths. Amidst this occupation they conversed, sang, and told little tales, as young grown girls often do. Elmine sang the air of "the flower that never fades," which Lindoriane had taught her, and which was her favourite song.

When the wreaths of flowers were completed, they proposed to play at "run at the ring." In this game the handsomest girl is chosen queen or bride, adorned with flowers and garlands, and seated on a green turf, while the other girls dance round her. The only question was who should be deemed handsomest among them; indeed, they were all so handsome, that the best judge would have been at a loss to decide the question fairly. They at last resolved to let chance settle the point in the following way. Each girl was to choose her favourite flower, which, at a given signal, they were all to throw up, and the girl whose flower ascended highest into the air, was to be queen. They then dispersed to pluck the flowers of their respective choice.

Among the playmates of Elmine was a princess who was vain and malicious: she rushed into the field and plucked a blue-bell, which she fastened to her bonnet, but not before she had tied to its stem a small pebble to make it heavy, and cause it to fly up very high. The other girls ran to pluck their favourite flowers without any artifice whatever. One brought back a renunculus, another a primrose, a third a lily, and in short, each displayed her peculiar taste. Elmine went into a little grove to seek a wild rose, her favourite flower. She found a whole bunch of it in full blossom, but the modest Elmine plucked the smallest and lightest, with which she returned to the company. All the girls now formed themselves into a ring, and threw up their flowers at once, to see which went the highest. At that moment a little Zephyr appeared in the air, and drove the wild rose before him upwards. He was not strong enough, however, to make it go so fast as the blue-bell, which had the pebble attached to its stem, but in an instant the air grew milder, and a butterfly appeared, which caught the wild rose, and bore it upwards high above the blue-bell. The girls, quite delighted with the little miracle, congratulated Elmine on her victory, proclaimed her the handsomest, adorned her with the flowers and garlands, and after having placed her on her throne of green turf, began to dance around her.

They were interrupted in their innocent amusement by the approach of a little old woman. The girls were at first frightened, but they soon recovered their cheerfulness by the kind looks and noble countenance of the matron. She was attired in a green gown and a bonnet of rush-weed of the same colour, and adorned with a wreath of green leaves; even her gloves were green. In one hand she held a green pot, with a small green tree in it, on which account she was called Mother Evergreen. "Dear children," said she, after a pause, "I am sorry to have interrupted you in your fête, but a short time ago I heard Elmine sing the song of 'the flower that never fades.' I saw her pluck a wild rose in the grove, and conclude from her choice that she is worthy of the present I am going to make her. My child," she then said to Elmine, who looked at her with astonishment, "take this stock with four flowers and two burgeons on it. This is the stock-flower which never fades; keep it, but know that it is not by means of watering that you can preserve it fresh. Look at this flower so beautiful and red, it is the flower of modesty: it will preserve its colour as long as that which glows on your cheeks. This second flower, of the purest white, is called the flower of virtue; the moment you neglect your duty it will change its colour. This third flower, of bright yellow, is called the flower of liberality; as long as you prove charitable it will retain its freshness. This fourth flower, of a fine azure blue, is called the flower of affability; the instant you lose your temper or become discontented, it will fade. That burgeon will produce the flower of intelligence; the more you apply to your studies and progress in knowledge, the fairer and more luxuriant will be its blossoms. The other burgeon contains the flower of grace; it will open without your being aware of it, and impart a brighter hue to all the other flowers."

"Ah! my good friend," exclaimed the princess, accepting the stock, "how shall I repay you for such a gift? Pray, come home with me. Lindoriane will show you her gratitude, and I mine."—"My child," said Mother Evergreen, "the only mark of gratitude you can show me is to keep the flowers in blossom as they now are. I shall return after eight years, and if I find them then in the same state and condition they are in now, you and the flowers will always remain young, fresh, and beautiful."

Having spoken thus, she approached the other girls, and gave each of them more or less of the flowers of her enchanted tree, with similar directions to Elmine's, and then disappeared. The girls remained for some time lost in astonishment at the wonderful event that had occurred; for they no longer doubted but that the woman was a fairy who had assumed the appearance of Mother Evergreen. They left off playing, each hastening to inform her parents or relations of what had happened. Elmine hastened home with her miraculous stock, planted in a pot, and related to Lindoriane every particular concerning it. The latter seemed stricken with astonishment, but assured her pupil that the fairy meant no harm, but on the contrary would certainly prove her well-wisher, if she attended to the moral lessons imparted to her. Elmine could not close her eyes the whole night, so much did she think of the occurences of the day. At dawn she arose, and her first care was to inspect her stock, but passing by the window she was attracted by some noise in the street. She opened the window and saw a number of lazy boys mocking and making game of a poor old woman; but as they intended no mischief, she was rather amused at the joke and laughed heartily. But how great was her grief and surprise, when she soon after approached the table upon which she had placed her stock, and saw that the flower of affability was beginning to fade, and the flower of modesty to lose its beautiful red hue. She cried bitterly so as to arouse her governess, who soon entered and asked the cause of her sorrow. Elmine pointed to the flowers, and sobbed out, that she was not aware of having done anything to cause their fading. It is true that Elmine in her innocence did not know of the error she had committed, but still it was an error, she having in the first instance evinced curiosity, and then having been amused at what tormented the poor old woman. Lindoriane explained all this to her, and Elmine confessed that she was wrong, resolved never to be guilty of the like again, and had the pleasure towards evening of seeing the flowers restored to their former freshness. This small

lesson tended to render Elmine more attentive; she, however, experienced great difficulty in keeping up the brightness of the blue flower. Elmine was naturally kind and good-hearted, so that she could easily preserve the other flowers from fading by merely acting up to the spontaneous feelings of her heart; but she was also lively, and often impatient and discontented,—and whenever that was the case, the blue flower began to turn black, and Elmine repented and tried to alter her fault, which had the effect of making the flower recover its former hue. The white flower was least liable to suffer, because Elmine never strayed from the path of virtue. It is true that she observed one day a little stain upon it, but a tear which fell from the princess's eye washed it away.

It may easily be imagined that Elmine, possessing the flowers which never fade, ought to have been the most perfect and accomplished princess of her time; and so indeed she proved. The report of her excellent qualities soon spread abroad; for there is a little fairy called Fame, which wanders about in all countries, and tells all she knows of people, especially of young women, whether good or bad. All nations who heard of such a clever woman as Elmine was, felt a great wish to have her as queen. When her reputation reached Roxalan, the son of the king, he asked permission of his father to go and see her, and solicit her in marriage from Lindoriane. The king complied, and the prince departed, and arrived at the place where Elmine resided.

Lindoriane consented to the marriage, not because he was the son of a great king, but that the young prince also was in possession of the flowers that never fade, which he too had contrived by his virtues to preserve in their primitive freshness and vigour; for there are flowers of the same qualities for both sexes.

Elmine would not quit her native place without once more visiting the spot in the meadow where she had received so precious a gift—the cause of her present happiness. She hoped to meet there Mother Evergreen; for it was now eight years since she had first beheld her. Elmine put one of the never-fading flowers in her bosom and strolled out; but how great was her astonishment when she arrived at the spot to meet with Lindoriane, whom she had left at home, instead of the fairy.

"I am," said Lindoriane, "the fairy whom you seek. As Mother Evergreen I gave you the flowers, and as Lindoriane I taught you how to preserve them. My work is happily completed. The flowers will always remain fresh, and Elmine always lovely and beloved, for the virtues of the heart and the endowments of the mind are charms which are never destroyed."

The princess threw herself at the feet of Lindoriane, who most tenderly embraced her pupil, then assumed again the shape of a fairy, and vanished. Elmine, overwhelmed by grief and tenderness, stretched her arms after her, and besought her to return, but she saw her no more. She was soon consoled in the arms of the beloved prince, whom she married, and with whom she departed to his country, where they lived in love, prosperity, and perfect happiness.

THE EAGLE RESCUES SINDBAD FROM THE VALLEY OF DIAMONDS.

SINDBAD THE SAILOR.

In the reign of the caliph Haroun Alraschid there lived in Bagdad a poor porter, who was named Hindbad. One day, during the excessive heat of summer, he was carrying a heavy load from one extremity of the city to the other; and being much fatigued by the length of the way he had already come, and having still much ground to traverse, he arrived in a street where the pavement was sprinkled with rose-water, and a gentle breeze refreshed the air. Delighted with this cool and pleasant situation, he placed his load on the ground, and took his station near a large mansion. The delicious scent of aloes and frankincense issuing from the windows, and mixing with the rose-water, perfumed the air, together with a charming concert within, which was accompanied by the melody of the nightingales and other birds peculiar to the climate of Bagdad; and the smell of different sorts of viands led him to suppose that some grand feast was given there. He wished to know whose residence it was: for, not having frequent occasion to pass that way, he was unacquainted with the names of the inhabitants. To satisfy his curiosity, therefore, he approached some servants magnificently dressed, who were standing at the door, and inquired who was the master of that mansion. "What," replied the servant, "are you an inhabitant of Bagdad, and do not know that this is the residence of Sindbad the sailor, that famous voyager who has sailed over all the

7

seas under the sun?" The porter, who had heard of the immense riches of Sindbad, could not help comparing his situation, which appeared so enviable, with his own, which was so deplorable; and, distressed by the reflection, he raised his eyes to heaven, and exclaimed in a loud voice: "Almighty Creator of all things, be pleased to consider the difference between Sindbad and myself; I daily suffer a thousand ills, and find the greatest difficulty to supply my wretched family with bad barley bread, whilst the fortunate Sindbad expends his riches with profusion, and enjoys every pleasure. What has he done to obtain so happy a destiny, or I to merit one so rigorous?" Saying this, he struck the ground with his foot, as if entirely given up to despair: when, still musing on his fate, a servant came towards him from the house, and taking him by the arm, said: "Come, follow me; my master, Sindbad, wishes to speak with you."

It may easily be imagined that Hindbad was not a little surprised at the compliment that was paid him. After the words he had uttered, he began to fear that Sindbad had sent for him in order to reprimand him, and therefore he tried to excuse himself from going, saying that he could not leave his load in the middle of the street; but the servant assuring him that it should be taken care of, pressed him so much to go, that the porter could no longer refuse.

He led him into a spacious room, where a number of persons were seated round a table covered with all kinds of delicate viands. In the principal seat was a grave and venerable personage, whose long white beard hung down to his breast, behind whom were standing a crowd of officers and servants to wait on him. This person was Sindbad. The porter, quite confused by the number of the company, and the magnificence of the entertainment, made his obeisance with fear and trembling. Sindbad desired him to approach, and seating him at his right hand, helped him with his own hands to the choicest dishes, and gave him some excellent wine, with which the sideboard was plentifully stocked, to drink.

Towards the end of the repast, Sindbad, perceiving that his guest had done eating, began to speak, and addressing Hindbad by the title of brother, according to the custom amongst the Arabians when they converse familiarly, he enquired his name and profession. "My name, sir," he replied, "is Hindbad." "I am rejoiced at your presence," replied his entertainer, "and my pleasure is shared by all who are now assembled; but I sent for you hither to learn from your own lips what it was you said just now in the street:" for Sindbad, before he went to dinner, had heard from the window the complaint of the porter, and that was the reason he sent for him. At this request, Hindbad hung down his head in confusion, and replied, "Sir, I must confess that my fatigue had put me out of humour, and caused me to utter some indiscreet words, for which I entreat your pardon." "Nay, do not imagine," resumed Sindbad, "that I am so unjust as to harbour resentment, or wish to reproach you on that account. I feel for your situation, and pity you heartily; I

would undeceive you, however, on one point respecting myself, since you seem to be in error. You, no doubt, imagine that the riches and comforts I enjoy have been got without labour or trouble; this is the mistake I desire to rectify. To arrive at the state in which you see me, I have endured, for many years, much mental as well as bodily suffering. Yes, gentleman," continued he, addressing himself to the whole company, "my sufferings, I assure you, have been sufficiently great and extraordinary to deprive the most avaricious miser of his love of riches. You have heard a confused account of my adventures in the seven voyages I have made on different seas; now that an opportunity offers, I will, with your leave, relate the dangers I have encountered, which I think will not be uninteresting to you."

As it was chiefly on the porter's account that Sindbad was going to relate his history, before he began it he gave orders that his burden, which had been left in the street, should be brought in, which done, he proceeded in these words:—

THE FIRST VOYAGE OF SINDBAD THE SAILOR.

I DISSIPATED the greatest part of my paternal inheritance in youthful debaucheries; but, seeing my folly, I at length became convinced that riches, applied to such purposes as I had employed them in, were of little avail; and I reflected, moreover, that time properly husbanded was of greater value than gold; nothing being more deplorable than an old age of poverty. I remembered the words of the wise Solomon, often repeated to me by my father, that it is better to be in the grave than poor. Feeling the truth of all these reflections, I resolved to collect the fragments of my patrimony, and publicly to dispose of all my goods. I consulted those who appeared best able to give me advice; and, in short, I determined to employ as profitably as possible the small sum I had remaining. No sooner was this resolution formed, than I put it into execution. I repaired to Balsora, where I embarked with several merchants, in a vessel equipped at our joint expense.

We set sail, and steered by the Persian gulf, which washes the coast of Arabia Felix on the right, and that of Persia on the left towards the East Indies, and is commonly supposed in the widest part to be seventy leagues in breadth; beyond this gulf the Western Sea or Indian Ocean is very spacious, being bounded by the coast of Abyssinia, extending in length four thousand five hundred leagues to the island of Vakvak. I was rather incommoded at first by sea-sickness, but I soon recovered my health, and from that period the same malady has never recurred. In the course of our voyage we touched at several islands, selling and exchanging our merchandise. One day, when in full sail, we were unexpectedly becalmed before a small island, appearing just above the water, and which, from its verdure, resembled a beautiful meadow. The captain ordered the crew to lower the sails, and gave permission to all who wished it to go ashore, an opportunity which I embraced among the first. But during the time we were eating and drinking and regaling ourselves, by way of relaxation from the fatigues we had endured at sea, the island suddenly trembled, and we felt a severe shock.

Those who were in the ship, perceiving the quake of the island, called to us to re-embark as speedily as possible, for that what we supposed to be an island was the back of an enormous whale, and that unless we acted upon their injunctions we should all assuredly perish. The most active of the party at once jumped into the boat, while others threw themselves into the water to swim to the ship: as for me, I had not been able to quit the island, or, more properly speaking, the whale, ere it plunged into the sea. I seized hold of a piece of wood, which had been brought to make a fire with, and which was the only thing within my reach that offered the remotest chance of escape.

Meantime the captain, willing to avail himself of a fair breeze which had just sprung up, hoisted sail with those who had reached his vessel, and put to sea, leaving me to the mercy of the waves. In this situation I remained the whole of that day and the following night; and when daylight appeared the next morning I had neither strength nor hope left. At length, when I was beginning to sink, a breaker happily cast me upon an unknown shore, which was high and steep, and on recovering from the stupor into which I had been thrown by pain and exhaustion, I should have found great difficulty in landing, had not a branch of a tree, which fortune seemed to have placed there for my preservation, assisted me. I threw myself on the ground, where I continued more than half dead, till the sun arose.

Although extremely enfeebled, I tried to creep along in search of some herbs or fruit, to satisfy my hunger; and having found some, I had next the good luck to light upon a stream of excellent water, which contributed not a little to refresh me. I soon recovered sufficient strength to enable me to explore the island; and proceeding a short distance beyond the rocky boundary of the coast, I entered a beautiful plain, where I perceived at some distance a horse grazing. I bent my steps that way, trembling between fear and joy, for I could not yet ascertain whether I was advancing to safety or about to incur further danger. As I approached the steed, I remarked that it was a mare of exceeding beauty, and tied to a stake. Whilst I was admiring her, however, I heard the voice of a man, as if under ground, who shortly after appeared, and coming to me, asked civilly who I was. I recounted to him my adventure, when he took me by the hand and led me into a cave in which were some other persons, who appeared to be not less astonished to see me than I was to find them there.

I ate the food which they offered me; and having asked what they did in a place which appeared so barren, they replied that they were grooms to Mihrage, the sovereign of the isle; and that they came at the same period every year with some mares belonging to the king. "To-morrow," said they, "is the day fixed for our departure, and had you been one day later, you must certainly have perished; since the city where we dwell is so far off that it would have been impossible for you to reach it without a guide."

The following day they returned with the mares to the capital of the island, whither I also accompanied them. On our arrival, king Mihrage, to whom I was presented, asked me who I was, and by what chance I had reached his dominions; and when I had satisfied his curiosity, he expressed pity at my misfortune. At the same time he gave orders that I should be taken care of, and be furnished with everything I might want: which directions were executed in a manner which proved the king's generosity, as well as the obedience of his officers.

Being a merchant, I associated chiefly with persons of my own profession. I sought in particular such as were foreigners, hoping to hear some intelligence from Bagdad, and if possible to meet with a person in whose company I might return; for the capital of king Mihrage is situated on the sea-coast, and has a beautiful port, where vessels from all parts of the world daily arrive. I also sought the society of the Indian sages, in whose conversation I found great pleasure; but that did not prevent me from attending at court very regularly, nor from conversing with governors, and even with kings, who were about the person of Mihrage, being less powerful than he, and his tributaries, each of whom asked me a thousand questions about my country, which I, being scarcely less inquisitive about the laws and customs and whatever appeared to merit my curiosity in their different states, was not slow to answer.

In the dominions of king Mihrage is an island, called Cassel. I had been told that in that island was heard every night the sound of tymbals, which had given rise to the sailors' opinion that Degial had chosen that spot for his residence. I felt a great desire to witness some of the wonders of which I had heard such extraordinary rumours; and during my voyage which I undertook for that purpose I saw some fish a hundred and even two hundred cubits in length, which cause much fear to the mariners, but do no harm; they are so timid, indeed, as to be frightened away by beating on a board. I remarked also some other fish, that were not above a cubit long, and whose heads resembled those of owls.

After my return, as I was standing one day near the port, I saw a ship come towards the land; and, having cast anchor, the sailors began to unload its cargo, and the merchants to whom all the various goods belonged took them away to their warehouses. Happening to cast my eyes on some of the packages, I saw my name written, and on attentively examining them, I concluded them to be the same with which I had embarked in the ship that brought me from Balsora. I also remembered the captain, but as I was persuaded he thought me dead, I went up to him and asked him to whom those parcels belonged. "I had on board with me," replied he, "a merchant of Bagdad, named Sindbad: one day, when we were near an island, or at least what appeared to be such, though it was no other than an enormous whale which had fallen asleep on the surface of the water, he with other passengers went ashore, and kindling a fire on the back of the fish to cook the provisions they had carried with them, the supposed island began to move, and at last sank into the sea. The greater number of the persons who were on it were drowned, and along with them the unfortunate Sindbad. These parcels belonged to him, and I have resolved to sell them, that, should I meet with any of his family, I may be able to return them the profit I shall have made of the principal." "Captain," said I, when he had concluded, "I am that Sindbad whom you suppose dead: these parcels are, therefore, my merchandise."

When the captain of the vessel heard me speak thus, he exclaimed: "Great God, who shall I trust? There is no longer truth in man. I with my own eyes saw Sindbad perish; the passengers I had on board were also witnesses of it; and you have the assurance to say that you are the same Sindbad? At first sight I took you to be a man of probity and honour, and yet you assert an impious falsehood in order to possess yourself of property which cannot belong to you." "Have patience," replied I, "and listen to what I have to say." "Well," said he, "what have you to say? Speak, and I will attend." I then related in what manner I had been saved, and by what accident I had met with king Mihrage's grooms, who had brought me to his court.

He was at first rather staggered at what I told him, but soon became convinced that I was not an impostor; for some people who had just arrived from his ship knew me, and congratulated me on my fortunate escape. At last, recollecting me himself, he embraced me, and said, "Heaven be praised that you have survived so great a peril! Here are your goods, take them, and do with them what you please." I thanked him, and praising his honourable conduct, begged him, by way of recompense, to accept part of my recovered merchandise, which, however, he persisted in refusing.

I selected the most precious and valuable things in my bales, as presents for king Mihrage; who, having been informed of my misfortunes, asked me where I had gotten such rare curiosities. I related to him the manner in which my property had been restored, and he expressed his joy on the occasion: and accepting my presents, gave me others of far greater value. After that I took my leave of him and re-embarked in the same vessel, having first exchanged what merchandise remained for that of the country, consisting of aloes and sand wood, camphor, nutmegs, cloves, pepper and ginger, in order to trade with in other ports. We touched at several islands, and at last landed at Balsora, whence I came hither, having realized about a hundred thousand sequins. My return to my family was hailed by them with the joy which a true and sincere friendship inspires. I purchased slaves of both sexes, and bought a magnificent house and grounds. Having thus established myself, I determined to forget the hardships I had endured, and enjoy the pleasures of life."

Sindbad here ceased, and ordered the musicians to go on with their concert, which he had interrupted by the recital of his history. The company continued to eat and drink till night approached; and, when it was time to retire, Sindbad ordered a purse containing a hundred sequins to be

brought him, and giving it to the porter, he said, "Take this, Hindbad; return to your home, and come again to-morrow to hear the continuation of my adventures." The porter retired, quite confounded at the honour conferred on him and the present he had received. The account he gave of this occurrence to his wife and children rejoiced them very much, and they did not fail to return thanks to Providence for the bounties bestowed on them through Sindbad's means.

On the following day, Hindbad dressed himself in his best clothes and returned to the house of his patron, who again received him with smiling looks and a friendly air. As soon as all the guests were arrived, the table was served, and they sat down to eat. When the repast was finished, Sindbad thus addressed his guests: "Gentleman, I request you to listen to me while I relate the adventures of my second voyage. They are more worthy of your attention then were those of the first." The company were silent, and Sindbad began as follows:

THE SECOND VOYAGE OF SINDBAD THE SAILOR.

AFTER my first voyage I had resolved, as I told you yesterday, to pass the rest of my days in tranquillity at Bagdad. But soon growing weary of an idle life, the desire of seeing foreign countries and engaging in commerce by sea, returned. I therefore bought such merchandise as I thought most likely to succeed in the traffic I meditated, and set off a second time with some merchants whose probity I could rely on. We embarked in a good vessel, and recommending ourselves to the care of the Almighty, set out on our voyage. We went from island to island, making some very advantageous exchanges: till one day landing on one which was covered with a variety of fruit trees, we found it so deserted that we were unable to discover any habitation or trace of a human being. We walked in the meadows and along the brooks that watered them, and whilst some of my companions were amusing themselves with gathering fruit and flowers, I took out some of the wine and provisions I had brought with me, and seated myself by a little stream under some trees which afforded a delightful shade. I made a good meal of the provisions I had with me, and having satisfied my hunger, sleep gradually stole over my sences. I cannot say how long I slept, but when I awoke, I saw that the ship had quitted her anchorage. I was much surprised at this circumstance, and got up to seek my companions, but they were all gone; and I could only perceive the vessel in full sail, at a great distance; and it soon vanished entirely from my sight.

You may imagine the reflections that occurred to me in this dismal state. I thought I should have died with grief; I groaned and cried aloud, beating my head, and throwing myself on the ground, where I remained a long time, overwhelmed with conflicting thoughts, each more distressing than the other, and utterly confounded. A thousand times I reproached myself for my folly in not being contented with my first voyage, which ought to have satisfied my desire of seeking adventures; but all my regrets were unavailing, and my repentance came too late. At length I resigned myself to the will of heaven; and not knowing what would become of me, I ascended a high tree, and looked on all sides to see if I could not discover some object that might inspire me with hope. Casting my eyes toward the sea, I could discern nothing but water and sky; but perceiving something white on the land side I descended from the tree, and taking with me the remainder of my provisions, I walked towards the object, which, however, was so distant, that I could not distinguish what it was. As I approached, I perceived it to be a large white ball of prodigious size, and when I got near enough to touch it, I found it was soft. I walked round it to see if there was an opening, but could find none, and it appeared so even that it was impossible to climb it. The circumference might be about fity paces.

It was then near sunset, and the air grew suddenly dark, as if obscured by a thick cloud. I was surprised at this change, but much more so when I perceived it to be occasioned by a bird of extraordinary size, which was flying towards me. In my youth I had heard sailors speak of a bird called a roc; and I conceived that the great white ball which had drawn my attention must be the egg of this bird: nor was I mistaken; for shortly after it lighted on the spot, and assumed the attitude of a sitting-bird. When I saw it coming I drew near to the egg, so that I had one of the claws of the bird close by me: this claw was as big as the trunk of a large tree. In my despair I tied myself to the talon with the linen of my turban, in hopes that the roc, when it took its flight next morning, would carry me with it out of the desert island. My project succeeded, for at day-break the roc flew away and carried me to such a height that I could not distinguish the earth, and after some time descended with such rapidity that I almost lost my senses. When the rock had alighted I quickly untied the knot that tied me to its foot, and had scarcely loosed myself, when it darted on a serpent of immeasurable length, and seizing it in its beak, flew away.

The place in which the roc left me was a deep valley, surrounded on all sides by mountains, of such a height that the tops of them were lost in the clouds, and so steep that there was no possibility of climbing them. This embarrassed me afresh: when I compared it with the island I had left, I soon found that I had no reason to be satisfied with my change of situation.

In walking along this valley I remarked that it was strewn with diamonds, some of which were of an astonishing size. For some time I amused myself with examining them, but I soon perceived from afar some objects which converted my sensations of pleasure into fear: these were a great number of serpents, so long and large that the smallest of them would have swallowed an elephant with ease. They hid themselves in caves during the day on account of the roc, their mortal enemy, and only came out during the night. I passed the day, therefore, in walking about the valley, resting myself occasionally where an opportunity offered, and when the sun set I retired into a small cave, where I thought I should be in safety. I closed the entrance, which was low and narrow, with a stone large enough to secure me from the serpents, but which yet admitted a glimmering of light. I supped on part of my provisious, during which I heard the fearful hissings of the serpents, which now began to make their appearance. These sounds continued during the night, and, as you may suppose, struck me with great apprehensions. On the re-appearance of the day, the serpents retired; but with such awe had they inspired me that I left my cave with trembling, and though I walked upon a path of diamonds, I may truly say it was without feeling the least desire for them. At last I sat down, and, after having made another hearty meal on my provisions, notwithstanding the agitation I was in, as I had not closed my eyes during the whole night, I fell asleep. I had scarcely began to dose, when something falling, with a dull heavy sound, awoke me. It was a large piece of fresh meat, and on looking up, I saw a number of similar pieces rolling down the rocks from above.

I had always supposed the account which I had heard related by seamen and others, of the valley of diamonds, and of the means by which merchants procured them, to be fictitious; but I now knew it to be true. The method adopted is this: they go to the mountains which surround the valley, about the time that the eagles hatch their young. They cut large pieces of meat, which they throw into the valley; and to these the diamonds, on which they fall, adhere. The eagles, which are larger and stronger in that country than in any other, seize these pieces of meat to carry them to their young at the top of the rocks. The merchants then run to their nests, and by various noises oblige the eagles to retreat; they then take the diamonds that have stuck to the pieces of meat, which, as the valley is inaccessible on every side, they could not otherwise procure. I had supposed it impossible ever to leave this valley, and began to look upon it as my tomb; but this sight changed my opinion, and turned my thoughts to some device for the preservation of my life. Having conceived a project of rescue, I began to collect the largest diamonds I could find, and with them filled the leathern bag in which I carried my provisions; next I took one of the largest pieces of meat, and tied it tight round me with the linen of my turban; and in this state I laid myself on the ground, having first fastened my leathern bag around my body.

I had not lain long before the eagles began to descend, and each seizing a piece of meat, flew away with it. One of the strongest, having darted on the piece to which I had attached myself, carried me up with it to its nest; and when the merchants by their cries had frightened away the eagles, and obliged them to quit their prey, one of them approached me. On seeing me, however, he was seized with apprehension, but soon recovering from his fear, instead of inquiring by what means I came there, began to quarrel with me for trespassing on what he considered his property. "You will speak to me with pity instead of anger," said I, "when you learn by what means I reached this place. Console yourself, for I have diamonds enough for you and myself, of more value than those of all the other merchants added together; I have myself chosen a number of the finest from the bottom of the valley, and have them here in this bag." On saying this I showed him the bag, and had scarcely finished speaking, when the other merchants perceiving me, flocked round me with great astonishment, which I augmented not a little by the recital of my history. They were all no less surprised at the stratagem I had conceived to save myself, than at my courage in putting it in execution.

Having conducted me to the place where they lived together, I showed them my diamonds, upon seeing which they all expressed their admiration, and declared they had never seen any to equal them either in size or quality. I entreated the merchant to whom the nest belonged into which I had been transported, for each merchant has his own, to choose for himself as many as he pleased. He contented himself with taking only one, and that too of the smallest size. I pressed him to take more, and not be afraid of depriving me. "No," replied he, "I am perfectly satisfied with this, which is sufficiently valuable to spare me the trouble of making any more voyages to complete my little fortune."

I passed the night with these merchants, to whom I recounted my history a second time, for the satisfaction of those who had not heard it before: and when I reflected on the perils I had gone through, I could scarcely moderate my joy; it appeared to me as if the security in which I then found myself was merely a dream, and that I could not for a time believe that I had nothing more to fear.

The merchants had been for some days in that spot, and as they now appeared to be contented with the diamonds they had collected, we set off on the following day together, travelling over high mountains, where there was a great number of prodigious serpants, which, however, we had the good fortune entirely to avoid. We reached the nearest port in safety, and thence embarked for the island of Roho, which produces the camphor tree, the foliage of which is so large and thick that a hundred men may be shaded by it with ease. The gum which forms the camphor runs out at a wound made at the top of the trunk, and is received into a vase, where it acquires consistency, and assumes the form in which it is disposed of as a drug. The juice being thus extracted, the tree withers and dies.

The rhinoceros, too, which is a smaller animal than the elephant, though larger than the buffalo, is a native of this island. On its nose it has a horn about a cubit in length, and cut through the middle from one extremity to the other, on which are some white lines, which represent the figure of a man. The rhinoceros fights with the elephant, and piercing him in the belly with his horn, carries him off on his head; but as the fat and blood of the elephant run down on his eyes and blind him, he falls to the ground; and what will astonish you, the roc comes and seizes them both in his claws, and carries them both off together to feed its young.

I will pass over several other peculiarities related of this island, lest I should tire you. Exchanging, therefore, some of my diamonds for other merchandise, I went thence to more distant islands, and at last, after having touched at several ports, reached Balsora, whence I again returned to Bagdad. Afterwards I distributed much money amongst the poor, and enjoyed with credit and honour the rest of my immense riches, which I had acquired with so much labour and difficulty.

Sindbad having completed the relation of his voyage, again ordered a hundred sequins to be given to Hindbad, whom he once more invited to come on the morrow to hear the history of the third.

The guests returned home, and on the following day repaired at the same hour to the house of Sindbad, where the porter, who had almost forgotten his misery, also made his appearance. They sat down to table, and when the meal was ended Sindbad requested the company to give him their attention while he should detail the adventures of his third voyage.

THE THIRD VOYAGE OF SINDBAD THE SAILOR.

THE comfortable life into which I had settled soon obliterated the rememberence of the dangers I had experienced in my two voyages; and as I was in the prime of life, I grew tired of passing my days in slothful repose; and, banishing all thoughts of the perils I might encounter, I once more quitted Bagdad, with some rich merchandise of the country, which I conveyed to Balsora. There I embarked with other merchants bound for a long voyage, during which we touched at several ports, and transacted very advantageous commercial business.

One day, when we were in the open sea, we were overtaken by a violent tempest, which continued for several days, and drove us near an island, which the captain would gladly have been excused from touching at, but we were under the necessity of casting anchor there. When the sails were furled, the captain told us that this, as well as some of the neighbouring isles, was inhabited by savages, who would attack us, and that although they were but dwarfs, we must not attempt to make any resistance; for, as their number was inconceivable, if we should happen to kill one, they would infest us like locusts and destroy us. This account put the whole crew in terrible consternation, and we were too soon convinced that the captain had spoken the truth. We saw comeing towards us an innumerable multitude of hideous savages about two feet high, and entirely covered with red hair. Throwing themselves into the sea, they swam to the ship, which they soon encompassed, and as they approached they spoke to us, but we could not understand their language. On reaching the vessel, they clambered up the sides with so much swiftness and agility, that their feet scarcely seemed to touch them ere they were upon deck.

You may imagine the situation we were in, not daring to defend ourselves, nor even to speak to them, to endeavour to avert the impending danger. They unfurled the sails, cut the cable from the anchor, and after dragging the ship to shore, obliged us to disembark: after this, they conveyed us to another island, whence they had come. All voyagers carefully avoided this island, for the dismal reason you are going to hear; but our ill-fortune having led us there, we were obliged to submit.

Leaving the shore, and advancing farther into the island, we found some fruits and herbs, of which we ate, to prolong our lives as much as possible, for we all expected to be sacrificed. As we walked, we perceived at some distance a large edifice, towards which we bent our way. It was a large and high palace, with a folding door of ebony, which we opened. We entered the court-yard, and facing us saw a vast apartment with a vestibule, on one side of which was a heap of human bones, and on the opposite one a number of spits for roasting. We trembled at this spectacle, and, as we were fatigued with walking, our legs failed us, and we fell on the earth, where we remained a considerable time unable to move from fear.

The sun was setting, and while we were in the piteous state I have described, the door of the apartment suddenly opened with a loud noise, and a hideous black man, as tall as a palm-tree, came forward. In the middle of his forehead, one eye, red and fiery as a burning coal, stood alone; his front teeth were long and sharp, and projected from his mouth, which was as wide as that of a horse, with the under lip hanging on his breast; his ears resembled those of an elephant, and covered his shoulders; and his long and curved nails were like the talons of an immense bird. At the sight of this frightful being we all fainted, and remained a long time like dead men.

At last our senses returned, and we saw him seated under the vestibule examining us with his piercing eye. When he had viewed us well, he advanced towards us, and extending his hand to me, he took me up by the hair, and turning me round all ways to examine me, as a butcher would the head of a sheep. After having well considered the matter, he released me, finding me so meagre and little more than skin and bones. He took up each of the others in their turn, and inspected them in the same manner, and the captain being the fattest of the party, was held up in one hand, as I should hold up a sparrow, while the monster with the other ran a spit through his body. Then kindling a large fire, he roasted and ate him for his supper, in the apartment whither he retired. Having finished the repast, he returned to the vestibule, where he laid down to sleep, and snored louder than thunder. As may be readily conceived, we passed the night in the most agonising suspense; and when daylight returned, the ogre awoke and went abroad, leaving us in the palace.

When we supposed him at some distance, we gave vent to our lamentations, for the fear of disturbing the ogre had kept us silent during the night. The palace resounded with groans. Although we amounted to a considerable number, and had but one common enemy, yet the idea of delivering ourselves by his death never occurred. This enterprise, however difficult to accomplish, was nevertheless the first we ought to have attempted.

We deliberated on various methods, but could not determine upon any; and submitting ourselves to the will of God, we passed the day in walking over the island, and eating what plants and fruits we could meet with, as on the preceding one. Towards evening we sought for some sheltered place, in which to pass the night, but finding none, were obliged to return to the palace.

The ogre did not fail to return to sup on one of our companions, after which he again fell asleep and snored till daybreak, when he arose and went out as before. Our situation appeared to be so helpless that some of my comrades were on the point of throwing themselves into the sea, rather than be sacrificed in so dreadful a manner, and advised the rest to follow their example; but one of the company thus addressed them:—" We are forbidden," said he, "to kill ourselves; and even were that permitted, would it not be more rational to endeavour to destroy the barbarous monster who has destined us to such a cruel death?"

As I had already formed a project of that nature, I now communicated it to my fellow-sufferers, who approved of it. " My friends," said I, " you know that there is a great deal of wood on the sea-shore: if you will take my advice, we can make some rafts, and when they are finished we will leave them in a proper place, till we can find an opportunity to make use of them. In the meantime we can put into execution the design I proposed to you, to deliver ourselves from the ogre; if it succeeds, we may wait here with patience till some vessel passes, by means of which we may quit this fatal isle; if, on the contrary, we miss our aim, we shall have recourse to our rafts, and put to sea. I own that, in exposing ourselves to the fury of the waves on such fragile barks, we run a great hazard of losing our lives, but if we are destined to perish, is it not preferable to meet with a watery grave than to be buried in the entrails of the monster who has already devoured two of our companions?" My advice was approved by all, and we immediately built some rafts, large enough to contain three persons on each.

We returned to the palace towards evening, and the ogre arrived a short time after us. Again one of our party was sacrificed to his inhuman appetite. But we were soon revenged of his cruelty; after he had finished his horrible meal, he as usual laid himself down to sleep; and as soon as we heard him snore, nine of the most courageous of us, and myself, took each a spit, and heating the points redhot, thrust them into his eye, and blinded him.

The pain which he suffered made him groan hideously; he suddenly raised himself, and extended his arms on all sides to seize some one, and sacrifice him to his rage; but fortunately we had time to get to some distance from him, and to throw ourselves on the ground in places where he could not set his feet on us. After having sought us in vain, he at last found the door, and went out bellowing with pain.

We quitted the palace immediately after the ogre, and repaired to the shore, in that part were our rafts lay. We set them afloat, and waited till daybreak to board them, in case we should see the ogre approach with some guide to lead him on to us: but we hoped that, if he did not make his appearance by that time, and if his cries and groans, which resounded through the air, were discontinued, we might suppose him dead; and in that case we proposed remaining in the island till some safer conveyance should offer. The sun, however, had scarcely risen above the horizon, when we perceived our cruel enemy, accompanied by two ogres of nearly his own size, who conducted him, and a great number of others, walking with quick steps before him.

At this sight we ran precipitately to our rafts, and rowed away as fast as possible. The ogres seeing this, provided themselves with large stones, hastened to the shore, and even ventured up to their middles in the sea, to throw them at us, which they did so adroitly as to sink all the rafts excepting that which I was upon, so that myself and two companions were the only persons who escaped, our unfortunate brethren being all drowned.

As we rowed with all our strength, we soon got out of reach of the stones. When we were in the open sea we became the sport of wind and wave, and passing that day and night in the most cruel suspense, on the morrow we had the good fortune to be thrown on an island, where we landed with great joy. We found some excellent fruits, which served to re-establish our exhausted strength.

At night we slept on the sea-shore; but were awakened by the noise which the scales of an immense serpent, long as a palm-tree, made on the ground. It was so near to us, that it devoured one of my companions, notwithstanding the efforts he made to extricate himself; for the serpent shook him several times, and then crushing him on the earth, quickly swallowed him.

My other companion and myself immediately took to flight; and when we had gone some distance, we heard a noise which made us suppose that the serpent was vomiting the bones of the unhappy man it had destroyed. On the following day, we perceived our suspicions to have been well founded. "O God," I then exclaimed, "to what are we exposed? Yesterday we were rejoicing at our escape from the cruelty of an ogre and the fury of the waves, and to-day we have to encounter a peril not less immediate."

As we walked along, we remarked a large and high tree, on which, for safety, we proposed to pass the following night. We ate some fruit, as on the preceding day, and at the approach of night we climbed into the tree. We soon heard the serpent, which came hissing to the foot of the tree; it raised itself against the trunk, and meeting with my companion, who was lower than I was, it swallowed him and retired.

I remained on the tree till day-break, when I descended, more dead than alive; indeed, I could only expect to meet with the same fate. This idea chilled me with horror, and I advanced some paces to throw myself into the sea; but as life is desirable as long as it will last, I resisted the first impulse of my despair, and submitted to the will of the Almighty, who disposes of our lives as is best for us.

I collected a great quantity of small wood and furze, and tying it in faggots put it round the tree in a large circle, and tied some across the top to cover my head. This being done, when the evening came on I enclosed myself within the circle; having the dismal consolation that I had done all in my power to preserve my life. The serpent did not fail to return for the purpose of devouring me, but he could not succeed on account of the rampart I had formed. The whole night he was besieging me as a cat would a mouse; at last day returned, and he retired; but I did not venture out of my fortress till the sun was high in the heavens.

I was so fatigued with watching, as well as with the exertion of forming my retreat, and had suffered so much from his pestilential breath that death appeared preferable to a repetition of such horrors. I again ran to the sea, with the intention of putting an end to my existence: but Heaven pitied my condition, and at the moment that I was going to throw myself in, I perceived a vessel at a distance. I cried with all my strength, and unfolded my turban to attract the attention of those on board. This had the desired effect; I was seen by the crew, and the captain sent a boat for me.

As soon as I was on board, the merchants and seamen were eager to learn by what chance I had reached that desert island; and after I had related to them all that had happened, the eldest of them told me they had often heard of the ogres who lived there: that they were cannibals, and devoured their own kind. With regard to the serpents, they added that there were many in the island, hiding themselves in the day, and appearing at night.

After they had expressed their joy at my fortunate escape from so many perils, they pressed me to take something to eat, and the captain, observing that my dress was much torn, had the generosity to give me one of his.

We remained a considerable time at sea, and touched at several islands. At length we landed on that of Salahat, where the sandal wood is cultivated, which is much used in medicine, and where the merchants unloaded their goods. One day, the captain called me to him, and said,—"Brother, I have in my possession some goods which belonged to a merchant who was for some time on board my ship. As this merchant is dead, I am going to have them valued, that I may render an account of them to his heirs should I ever meet with them." The bales he was speaking of were allready upon deck. He showed them to me, saying; "These are the goods in question; I wish you to take charge of them, and negotiate them, receiving the usual commission for your trouble." I consented, and thanked him for the opportunity of employing myself.

The writer of the ship registered all the bales with the names of the merchants to whom they

SINDBAD'S JOY ON ESCAPING FROM THE CAVERN.

belonged; and when he asked the captain by what name he should register those destined for my charge, the captain replied, "By the name of Sindbad the Sailor." I could not hear my own name without emotion, and looking intently at the captain, I recognised him to be the very same person who, in my second voyage, had left me on the island, where I had fallen asleep by the side of a brook, and who had put to sea without waiting for me. I did not at first recollect him, so much was he changed from the time I had seen him. As he thought me dead, it is not to be wondered at, that he did not recognise me. "Captain," said I to him, "was the merchant to whom these things belonged, called Sindbad?" "Yes," returned he, "that was his name, he was from Bagdad, and embarked on board my vessel at Balsora. One day when we went ashore on an island for fresh water,

I know not by what mistake, he was left behind; none of the crew perceived it till four hours after, when the wind blew so fresh against us that it was impossible to return." "You believe him to be dead?" resumed I. "Most assuredly," replied the captain. "Well, then," said I, "open your eyes, and know that the same Sindbad whom you left in the desert island is now before you. I fell asleep on the banks of a little stream, and when I awoke I perceived the ship was gone."

At these words the captain fixed his eyes on me, and after having examined me very attentively, at last recollected me. "God be praised!" cried he, embracing me; "I am delighted that fortune has given me an opportunity of repairing my fault. Here are your goods, which I have preserved with care, and always had valued at every port I stopped at. I return them to you, with the profit I have

8

made on them." I received them with the gratitude which such an action demanded.

From the island of Salahat we went to another, where I furnished myself with cloves, cinnamon, and other spices. When we had sailed some distance from it, we perceived an immense tortoise that was twenty cubits in length and breadth. We also saw a fish that had milk like a cow; its skin is so hard, that bucklers are frequently made from it. I saw one of the make and colour of a camel. At length, after a long voyage, we arrived at Balsora, from whence I came to Bagdad with so much wealth that I did not know the amount of it. I gave a great deal to the poor, and made considerable additions to my landed estates.

Sindbad thus finished the history of his third voyage, and again gave Hindbad a hundred sequins, inviting him to the usual repast on the morrow, when he should hear the account of the fourth voyage. Hindbad and the other guests retired, and the following day returned at the same hour. After the dinner was over, Sindbad continued the relation of his adventures.

THE FOURTH VOYAGE OF SINDBAD
THE SAILOR.

THE pleasures and dissipations I entered into after my third voyage had not sufficient charms to deter me from venturing on the sea again. I gave way to my love for traffic and novelty; and having settled my affairs, and furnished myself with the merchandise suited to the places I intended to visit, I set out, and travelled towards Persia, some of the provinces of which I traversed, and at last reached a port, where I embarked. We set sail, and touched at several Oriental islands: but one day while tacking, we were surprised by a sudden squall of wind, which obliged the captain to lower the sails. All our precautions, however, were fruitless; the manœuvre did not succeed; the vessel becoming ungovernable, was driven on a sand bank and went to pieces, and a great number of the crew, as well as the cargo, perished.

I had the good fortune, with some other merchants and seaman, to get hold of a plank; on which we were all carried by the strength of the current towards an island that lay before us. We found some fruits and fresh water, which re-established our strength, and we laid down to sleep without seeking any farther; the grief we felt at our misfortunes rendering us careless of our fate. When the sun was risen, we left the shore, and advancing into the island, perceived some habitations, towards which we bent our way. When we drew near a great number of blacks came out, and seizing us, allotted us between them, and then conducted us to their houses.

Five of my companions and myself were taken to the same place. They made us sit down, and then offered us a certain herb, inviting us by signs to eat of it. My companions, without considering that they who gave it us did not eat of it, only consulted their appetites, and devoured it with avidity. I, who had a sort of presentiment that it was for no good purpose, refused even to taste it; and it was well I did, for a short time after I per-

ceived that my companions were intoxicated, and did not know what they said. They then served us with some rice dressed with the oil of the cocoa-nut, and my comrades not being sensible of what they did, ate it ravenously. I ate some also, but very little.

The blacks had presented the herb first to affect our heads, and thus banish the sorrow which our miserable situation would create, and the rice was given to fatten us. As they were cannibals, they designed to feast on us when we were in good condition. My poor companions fell victims to their barbarous custom, because they had lost their senses, and could not foresee their destiny. But for me, instead of fattening as the others had done, I grew thinner every day. The fear of death, which constantly haunted me, turned the aliments I took to poison, and I fell into a state of langour, which was in the end very beneficial; for the blacks, having eaten my comrades, were content to let me remain till I was better worth picking.

In the meantime I was allowed a great deal of liberty, and my actions were scarcely observed. This one day afforded me an opportunity of quitting the habitation of the blacks, and escaping.

An old man, who saw and guessed my intention, called on me to return, but I only quicked my pace, and soon got out of sight. The old man was the only person in the place; all the other blacks had absented themselves, and were not to return till evening, as was their frequent custom. Being therefore certain that they would be too late to come in search of me when they returned home, I continued my flight till evening, when I stopped to take a little rest, and satisfy my hunger. I soon proceeded, and walked without intermission for seven days; taking care to avoid those places which appeared inhabited, and living on cocoa-nuts, which furnished me with drink as well as food.

On the eighth day I came to the sea-shore; where I saw some white people like myself employed in gathering pepper, of which in that country was a great abundance. Such an occupation was a good omen to me, and I approached them without fear of danger. They came towards me as soon as they perceived me, and asked me in Arabic whence I came.

Delighted to hear my native language once more, I readily complied with their request, and related to them the manner in which I had been shipwrecked and got to that island, where I had fallen into the hands of the blacks. "But these blacks," said they, "eat men: by what miracle then could you escape their cruelty?" I gave them the same account which you have heard, at which they were very much surprised. I remained with them until they had collected as much pepper as they chose, when they made me embark with them, and we soon reached the island from which they had come. They presented me to their king, who was a good prince. He listened to the recital of my adventures, which astonished him; and he ordered me new clothing, and desired that I might be taken care of. The island was very populous, and abounded in all sorts of articles of commerce, a flourishing trade being carried on in the town where the king resided. This agreeable retreat began to console me for my misfortunes, and the kindness of the generous prince made me completely happy. Indeed, I appeared to be his greatest favourite; and consequently all ranks of people endeavoured to please me, so that I was considered in the light of a native rather than a stranger.

I remarked one thing which appeared to me very singular. Every person, the king not excepted, rode on horseback without either bridle or stirrups. One day I took the liberty to ask his majesty why such things were excluded, and from his replies it was quite evident that he was entirely ignorant of what I meant.

I immediately went to a workman, and gave him a model to make a saddle-tree from; which, on being finished, I covered with leather, richly embroidered in gold, and stuffed with hair. I then applied to a locksmith, who made me a bit and some stirrups, according to the patterns which I gave him.

When these things were completed, I presented them to the king, and tried them on one of his horses: the prince then mounted it, and was so pleased with the invention, that he testified his approbation by making me considerable presents. I was then obliged to make several saddles for his ministers and the principal officers of his household, who all rewarded me with very rich and handsome presents.

I also made some for the most respectable inhabitants of the town, by which I obtained great reputation and credit.

As I constantly attended at court, the king said to me one day, "Sindbad, I love you, and I know that all my subjects, who have any knowledge of you, follow my example, and entertain a high regard and esteem for you. I have one request to make, which you must not deny me." "Sire," replied I, "there is nothing that your majesty can command which I will not undertake, to prove my obedience to your orders. Your power over me is absolute." "I wish you to marry," resumed the prince, "that you may have a more tender tie to attach you to my dominions, and prevent your returning to your native country." As I did not dare to refuse the king's offer, I was shortly afterwards married to a lady of his court, who was noble, beautiful, rich, and accomplished. After the ceremony of the nuptials I took up my abode in the house of my wife, and lived with her for some time in perfect harmony. Nevertheless, I was discontented with my situation, and designed to make my escape the first convenient opportunity, in order to return to Bagdad, which the splendid establishment I was then in possession of could not obliterate from my mind.

These were my sentiments, when the wife of one of my neighbours, with whom I was very intimate, fell sick and died. I went to console him, and finding him in the deepest affliction, "May God preserve you," said I to him, "and grant you a long life." "Alas!" replied he, "how can I obtain what you wish? I have only one hour to live." "Oh," resumed I, "do not suffer such dismal ideas to take possession of your mind; I hope that will not be the case, and that I shall enjoy your friend-

ship yet for many years." "I wish with all my heart," said he, "that your life may be of long duration; but for me, the die is cast, and this day I shall be buried with my wife; such is the custom which our ancestors have established in this island, and which is still inviolably observed; the husband is interred alive with his deceased wife, or the living wife with the dead husband: nothing can save me, as all submit to this law."

Whilst he was relating to me this singular species of barbarity, which filled me with the greatest terror, his relations, friends, and neighbours arrived to be present at the funeral. They dressed the corpse of the woman in the richest attire, as on the day of her nuptials, and decorated her with all her jewels. Then they placed her uncovered on a bier, and the procession set out. The husband, dressed in mourning, followed immediately after the body of his wife, and the rest followed. They bent their course towards a high mountain, and when they were arrived, a large stone, which covered the mouth of a cavern was raised, and the body let down into it without any of the ornaments being taken off. After that, the husband took his leave of his relations and friends, and without offering the least resistance, suffered himself to be placed on a bier, with a jug of water and seven small loaves by his side, and let down as his wife had been. This mountain extended a great way, and served as a boundary to the ocean: and the cavern was very deep. When the ceremony was completed the stone was replaced, and the company retired. I need scarcely add, gentlemen, that I was greatly affected at this ceremony. None of the rest, however, who were present appeared to feel it, probably from being habituated to the repetition of the same kind of scene. So great was the detestation and horror with which I regarded the custom, that I could not forbear to express to the king my sentiments on it. "Sire," said I, "the strange custom which subsists in your dominions, of interring the living with the dead, inspires me with feelings both of astonishment and disgust; I have visited many nations, but in the whole course of my travels I never heard of so cruel and unjust a law." "What can I do, Sindbad?" replied the king, "it is a law common to all ranks, and even I must submit to its decree; I shall be interred alive with the queen, my consort, if I happen to survive her." "Sire," resumed I, "will your majesty allow me to ask if foreigners are obliged to observe this custom?" "Certainly," said the king, smiling as he guessed the motive of my question; "none are exempt from its operation who marry in the island."

I returned home perplexed in thought and sorrowful at this reply. The fear that my wife might die first, and that I should be interred with her, was a reflection of the most distressing nature. Yet how was the evil to be remedied? The only suggestions that occurred to me were to have patience, and submit to the will of God. Nevertheless, I trembled at the slightest indisposition of my wife, and alas! I soon had good reason to fear; she was taken dangerously ill, and died in a few days. Judge how my mind was disturbed at the prospect immediately before me. To be interred alive did not appear to be a more desirable end than that of being devoured by the cannibals; yet I was obliged to comply. The king, accompanied by his whole court, promised to honour the procession with his presence; and the principal inhabitants of the city, also, out of respect to me, signified their intention to be present at my interment.

When all was in readiness for the ceremony, the corpse of my wife, decorated with her jewels, and in her most magnificent dress, was placed on a bier, and the procession set out. Being the second personage in this tragedy, I followed the body of my wife, my eyes bathed in tears, and deploring my miserable destiny. Before we arrived at the mountain I wished to make trial of the compassion of the spectators: accordingly I addressed myself first to the king, then to those who were near me, and bowing to the ground to kiss the hem of their garments, I entreated them to have pity on me. "Consider," said I, "that I am a stranger, who ought not to be subjected to so rigorous a law; and that I have another wife and children in my own country." I pronounced these words in an affecting tone, but no one seemed moved; on the contrary, they hastened to lower the corpse into the cavern, and soon after I was let down on another bier, with a jug of water and seven loaves. At last, the fatal ceremony being completed, they replaced the stone over the mouth of the cave, notwithstanding the excess of my grief and piteous lamentation.

As I approached the bottom I discovered, by the little light that shone from above, the shape of this subterraneous abode. It was a vast chamber, which I judged to be about fifty cubits deep. I soon smelt an insupportable stench, arising from the carcases that were spread around. I even fancied that I heard the last sighs of some who had lately fallen victims to this inhuman law. No sooner had I reached the bottom than I left the bier, and stopping my nostrils, went to a distance from the dead bodies; where I threw myself on the ground, and remained for a long time bathed in tears; reflecting on my cruel fate. "It is true," said I, "that God disposes of us as seems best to his all-seeing providence; but, unhappy Sindbad, is it not your own fault that you are now brought to this singular death? Would to heaven I had perished in one of the dreadful wrecks from which I have been saved! I should not now have had to languish in this miserable abode of lingering death. And my accursed avarice has brought it all upon myself! Wretch that I am! I ought to have remained with my family, and enjoyed peaceably the fruits of my former labours."

Such were the useless expressions of rage and despair with which I made the cavern re-echo. I beat my head and breast, and gave way to the most violent grief. Nevertheless I confess to you, that instead of calling on death to release me from this habitation of despair, the love of life still glowed within me, and induced me to seek for the means of prolonging my days. I felt my way to the bier on which I had been placed; and notwithstanding the intense obscurity which prevailed, I found my bread and water, and ate of it.

When my eyes had become more accustomed to the gloom, I was enabled to perceive that the cave was more spacious, and contained more bodies than I had at first supposed. I subsisted for some days on my provisions, but as soon as they were exhausted, I prepared to die. I had just become resigned to my fate, when I heard the stone above raised, and a corpse and another living person, were let down. The deceased was a man. It is natural to have recourse to violent methods when reduced to the last extremity. While the woman was descending, I approached the spot where her bier was to be placed, and when I perceived the aperture above to be closed I gave the unhappy female two or three heavy blows on the head with a large bone, which stunned, or more properly speaking, killed her; but I only done this inhuman action to obtain the bread and water which had been allowed her. I had now provisions for some days; and before they were entirely expended a dead woman and her living husband were let down. I killed the man in a similar manner; and at that time there happened, fortunately for me, a mortality in the city, with every victim to which I obtained, in the way described, a fresh supply of food.

One day when I had just put an end to an unfortunate woman, I heard sounds like those of breathing, and a footstep. I advanced to the part whence the sound proceeded; and hearing a louder breathing at my approach, fancied I saw something fleeing from me. I followed the shadow, which occasionally stopped, and then again retreated, panting as I drew near. I pursued it so long, and went so far that at last I perceived a small speck of light, resembling a star. I continued to walk towards this light, sometimes losing it, as obstacles arose to preclude my vision, but always recovering it again, till I had arrived at an opening in the rock large enough to allow me to pass.

At this discovery I stopped for some time to recover from the violent emotion occasioned by my walking quick; then passing through the crevice, found myself on the sea-shore. You may imagine the excess of my joy: it was so great that I could scarcely be satisfied that my imagination did not deceive me. When I became convinced that it was a reality, and that my senses were still sound, I perceived that the thing I had heard pant, and had followed, was an animal that lived in the sea, and was in the habit of going into the cave to devour the dead bodies.

I examined the mountain, and observed that it stood between the city and the sea, without any communication between them, for it was so steep as to be inaccessible. I prostrated myself on the shore to thank God for the mercy he had shown me, and then returned to the cave to get some bread, which I brought out and ate with much better appetite than I had enjoyed since my interment in that gloomy mansion.

I returned again to collect, as well as I could, by feeling on the different biers, all the diamonds, rubies, pearls, golden bracelets, and in short everything of value that I could find, all of which I brought to the shore. I tied them up in several packets with the cords which had served to let down the biers, and of which there was a great quantity. I left them in a convenient place till a proper opportunity should offer, without fear of their being spoiled by the rain : for it was not the season for wet weather.

At the end of two or three days, I perceived a vessel just sailing out of the harbour, and passing by the spot where I was, I made signs with the linen of my turban, and cried aloud with all my strength. They heard me on board, and despatched a boat to fetch me. When the sailors inquired by what misfortune I had got into that place, I replied, that I had been wrecked two days since on that shore, with all my merchandise. Fortunately for me these people did not consider whether my story was probable but, satisfied with my answer, they took me on board with my bales.

When we had reached the vessel, the captain, happy at having been instrumental to my safety, and occupied with the management of the ship, believed, without any difficulty, the tale of the wreck, to convince him of which I offered him some precious stones, but he refused them.

We passed several islands, amongst others the island of Bells, distant about ten days' sail from that of Serindib, sailing with a fair wind, and six days' from the isle of Kela, where we landed. Here were some lead mines, some Indian canes, and excellent camphor.

The king of the isle of Kela is very rich and powerful. His authority extends over the island of Bells, which is two days' journey in extent: the inhabitants are still so uncivilised as to eat human flesh. After we had made an advantageous traffic in this island, we again set sail, and touched at several ports. At length I arrived happily at Bagdad with immense riches, of which it is needless to give you a detail. To evince my gratitude to heaven for the mercies shown to me, I spent a great deal in charity, some for the support of mosques, and some for the subsistence of the poor. I then entirely gave myself up to the society of my relations and friends, and passed my time in feasting and entertainments.

Sindbad here concluded the relation of his fourth voyage, which occasioned still more surprise in his audience than the three preceding ones had done. He repeated his present of a hundred sequins to Hindbad, whom he requested, with the rest of the company, to return the following day to dine, and hear the detail of his fifth voyage. Hindbad and the others took their leave and retired. The next day, when all were assembled, they sat down to table, and when the repast was over, Sindbad began the account of his fifth voyage, as follows :

THE FIFTH VOYAGE OF SINDBAD THE SAILOR.

The pleasures I enjoyed soon made me forget the pains I had endured ; yet they were not sufficiently attractive to prevent my forming the resolution of venturing a fifth time on the sea. I again provided myself with merchandise, packed it,

and sent it by land-carriage to the nearest seaport, where, unwilling to trust any more to a captain, and wishing to have a vessel of my own, I built and equipped one at my own expense. As soon as it was finished, I loaded it and embarked ; and as I had not sufficient cargo to fill it myself, I received several merchants of different nations with their goods.

We hoisted our sails the first fair wind, and put to sea. After sailing a considerable time, the first place we stopped at was a desert island, where we found the egg of a roc, as large as that I spoke of on a former occasion ; it contained a small roc, which was just ready to leave the shell, its beak having begun to make its appearance. The merchants who were with me broke the egg with hatchets, and cut out the young roc, bit by bit, and roasted it. I had seriously advised them not to touch the egg, but they would not attend to me.

They had scarcely finished their meal, when two immense clouds appeared in the air, at a considerable distance from us. The captain, whom I had hired to have the care of the vessel, knowing by experience what it was, cried out that it was the father and the mother of the young roc, and warned us to re-embark as quickly as possible, to avoid the danger which threatened us. We took his advice, and set sail immediately.

The two rocs approached, uttering the most frightful screams, which they redoubled on finding the state of their egg, and that the young one was no more. Designing to revenge themselves, they flew away towards the part whence they came, and disappeared for some time, during which we used all diligence to sail away, and prevent what nevertheless befel us.

They returned, and we perceived that they each had an enormous piece of rock in their claws. When they were exactly over our ship, they stopped, and suspending themselves in the air, one of them let fall the piece of rock he held. By the address of the pilot, who suddenly turned the vessel, it did not tumble on us, but fell close to us into the sea, in which it made such a chasm that we could almost see the bottom. The other bird, unfortunately for us, let his piece of rock fall so immediately on the ship that it split into a thousand pieces. The sailors and passengers were all either crushed to death or drowned. I was myself under water for some time, but rising again to the surface, I had the good fortune to seize a piece of the wreck. Thus, swimming sometimes with one hand and sometimes with the other, still holding what I had fixed myself to, and having both the wind and current in my favour, I at length reached an island, where the shore was very steep. I nevertheless overcame this difficulty and got on land.

I seated myself on the grass to rest from my fatigue, after which I arose and advanced into the island, to reconnoitre the ground. It seemed to be a delicious garden ; wherever I turned my eyes I saw beautiful trees, some loaded with green, others with ripe fruits, and transparent streams meandering between them. I ate of the fruits, which I found to be excellent, and quenched my thirst at the inviting brooks.

Night being arrived, I lay down in a convenient spot; my sleep was continually interrupted by the fear of being alone in such a desert place, so that I employed the greater part of the night in lamenting and reproaching myself for the imprudence of venturing from home when I had everything to make me comfortable there. These reflections led me so far, that I began to form a project against my life, but day returning with its cheerful light, dissipated my gloomy ideas. I arose and walked among the trees, though not without some degree of apprehension.

When I had advanced a little way in the island, I perceived an old man, who appeared much broken down. He was seated on the bank of a little rivulet; at first I supposed he might be, like myself, shipwrecked. I approached and saluted him, to which he made no other return than a slight inclination of the head. I asked him what he was doing, but instead of replying, he made signs to me to take him on my shoulders and cross the brook, making me understand that he wanted to gather some fruit.

I supposed he wished me to render him this piece of service; so taking him on my back I forded the stream. When I had reached the other side, I stopped and desired him to alight; instead of which (I cannot help laughing whenever I think of it), this old man, who appeared to me so decrepid, nimbly threw his legs, which I then saw were covered with a skin like a cow's, over my neck, and seated himself fast on my shoulders, at the same time squeezing my throat so violently that I expected to be strangled; this alarmed me so much that I fainted away.

Notwithstanding my situation, the old man kept his place on my neck; he only loosened his hold sufficiently to allow me to breathe. When I was a little recovered, he pushed one of his feet against my stomach, and kicking my side with the other, obliged me to get up. He then made me walk under some trees, and forced me to gather and eat the fruit we met with. He never quitted his hold during the day, and when I wished to rest at night, he placed himself on the ground with me, always fixed to my neck. He never failed to awaken me in the morning, which he effected by pushing me, and then he made me get up and walk, kicking me all the time. Conceive, gentlemen, the plague of bearing this burthen, without the possibility of getting read of it!

One day having found on the ground several dry gourds which had fallen from the tree that bore them, I took a pretty large one, and after having cleared it well, squeezed into it the juice of several large bunches of grapes, which the island produced in great abundance. When I had filled the gourd, I placed it in a particular spot, and some days after returned with the old man, when tasting the contents I found it to be converted into excellent wine, which for a short time made me forget the ills that oppressed me. It gave me new vigour, and raised my spirits so high, that I began to sing and dance as I went along.

The old man, perceiving the effect this draught had taken on my spirits, made signs to me to let him taste; I gave him the gourd, and the liquor pleased his palate so well that he drank it to the last drop. There was enough to inebriate him, and the fumes of the wine very soon rose into his head: he then began to sing after his manner and to stagger on my shoulders. The blows he gave himself made him return what he had on his stomach, and his legs loosened by degrees; so that finding he no longer held me tight, I threw him on the ground, where he remained motionless; I then took a large stone and crushed him to death.

Much rejoiced at having so effectually got rid of this old man, I walked to the sea-shore, where I met some people who belonged to a vessel which had anchored there to get some fresh water. They were much astonished at seeing me, and at the account of my adventure. "You have fallen," said they, "into the hands of the Old Man of the Sea, and you are the first he has not strangled; he never left those he once mastered till he had put an end to their existence; and this island is famous for the number of persons he has killed. The sailors and merchants who land here never dare approach excepting in a strong body.

Having informed me of this, they took me to their ship; and when I related what had befallen me, the captain received me with the greatest politeness. He set sail, and in a few days we landed at the port of a large city where the houses were built of stone."

One of the merchants of the ship having contracted a friendship for me, entreated me to accompany him, and conducted me to the lodging destined for foreign merchants. He gave me a large sack, and then introduced me to some people belonging to the city, who were also furnished with sacks; then having desired them to take me with them to gather cocoa: "Go," said he, "follow them, and do as they do; and stray not from them, for if you do so, your life will be in danger." He gave me provisions for the day, and I set off with them.

We arrived at a large forest of tall, straight trees, the trunks of which were so smooth that it was impossible to climb up to the branches where the fruit grew. They were all cocoa-trees, and we wanted to knock down the fruit and fill our sacks. On entering the forest, we saw an amazing number of monkeys, of all sizes, which fled at our approach, and ran up the trees with surprising agility. The merchants I was with collected some stones and threw them with great force at the monkeys, which had reached some of the highest branches. I did the same, and soon perceived that these animals were aware of our design; they gathered the cocoa-nuts and threw them down at us, with gestures that plainly showed their anger and animosity. We picked up the cocoa-nuts, and at intervals threw up stones to irritate the monkeys. By this contrivance we filled our sacks with the fruit: a thing utterly impracticable by any other method.

When we had got a sufficient quantity we returned to the city, where the merchant who had sent me to the forest gave me the value of the cocoa-nuts I had collected. "Continue to do the same every day," said he, "till you have amassed sufficient money to convey you to your own country." I thanked him for the good advice he gave me; by degrees I collected a quantity of cocoa-nuts, and sold them for a considerable sum.

The vessel in which I came had sailed with the merchants, who had loaded it with the cocoa-nuts they had purchased. I waited for the arrival of another, which shortly came into the harbour for a similiar lading. I sent on board all the cocoa-nuts which belonged to me, and when it was ready to sail, I took leave of the merchant, to whom I was under so many obligations. As he had not yet been able to settle his affairs, he could not embark with me.

We set sail, and steered towards the island where pepper grows in such abundance. From thence we made for the island of Comari, where the best species of the aloe grows, and whose inhabitants submit themselves to a law not to drink wine, or suffer any kind of debauchery. In these two islands I exchanged all my cocoa-nuts for pepper and aloe-wood; I then engaged myself with the other merchants in a pearl fishery, in which I employed many divers on my own account. By these means I collected a great number of very large and perfect ones, with which I joyfully put to sea and arrived safely at Balsora, whence I returned to Bagdad, where I sold the pepper, aloes, and pearls which I brought with me, for a large sum.

I bestowed a tenth part of my profit in charity, as I had done on my return from every former voyage, and endeavoured to recover from my fatigues by every kind of diversion.

Having concluded this narrative, Sindbad gave a hundred sequins to Hindbad, who retired with all the other guests. The same party returned to the rich Sindbad the next day; and having regaled them in the same manner as on the preceding days, he requested silence, and began the account of his sixth voyage in the following manner:

THE SIXTH VOYAGE OF SINDBAD THE SAILOR.

You are, no doubt, gentleman, surprised how I could be tempted again to expose myself to the caprice of fortune, after having undergone so many perils in my other voyages. I am astonished myself when I think of it. It was fate alone that dragged me, at the expiration of a year, to venture myself a sixth time on the unstable sea, notwithstanding the tears and entreaties of my relations and friend, who did all in their power to persuade me to stay.

Instead of taking the route of the Persian gulf, I passed again through some of the provinces of Persia and the Indies, and arrived at a sea-port, where I embarked in a good ship, with a captain who was determined to make a long voyage. Long indeed it proved; but at the same time so unfortunate, that the captain and pilot lost their way, and did not know how to steer. They at length got right again, but we had no reason to rejoice on the occasion, for the captain astonished us all by suddenly quitting his post and uttering the most lamentable cries. He threw his turban on the floor, tore his beard, and beat his head, as if his senses were distracted. We asked what occasioned these signs of affliction. "I must announce to you," said he, "that we are in the greatest peril. A rapid current carries the ship, and we shall probably all perish in less than a quarter of an hour. Pray God to deliver us from this imminent danger, for unless he takes pity on us, nothing can save us. He then gave orders for setting the sails, but the ropes broke in the attempt, and at last it became impossible to manage the ship: it was suffered to go free with the current and was dashed against the foot of a rock, where it split and went to pieces; we had, however, time to provide for our own safety, and secure part of our provisions, as well as the most valuable part of the lading.

This being effected, the captain said: "God's will be done. Here we may dig our graves, and bid each other an eternal farewell; for we are in so desolate a place that none who were ever cast upon this shore returned to their own homes." This speech increased our affliction, and with tears in our eyes we embraced each other, deploring our wretched fate.

The mountain at the foot of which we then were formed one side of a large and long island. The beach was covered with fragments of vessels which had been wrecked on the inhospitable coast, and by the infinity of bones which every where met the eye, we were convinced of the dreadful certainty that many lives had been lost in this spot. It is almost incredible what quantities of merchandise of every sort were strewn upon the shore; all of which served to increase our despair.

In every other part of the world it is common for rivers to discharge themselves into the sea; but in the island upon which we had been cast, a large river of fresh water takes its course from the sea and runs along the coast through a dark cave, the opening of which is extremely high and wide. What is most remarkable, however, is, that the mountain is composed of rubies, crystals, and other precious stones. Here too, a kind of pitch, or bitumen, distils from the rocks into the sea, and the fishes eating it, return it again in the form of ambergris, which the waves leave on the shore. The trees are principally aloes, and are equal in beauty and value to those of Comari.

To complete the description of this place, which may be termed a whirlpool, as nothing that once enters it ever returns: it is impossible that a ship can avoid being dragged thither if it comes within a certain distance. If a sea-breeze blow, it assists the current, there is no remedy; and if the wind comes from the land, the high mountain impedes its effect, and causes a calm, which allows the currents full force, and then it whirls the ship against the shore, and dashes it to pieces, as ours was. In addition to this, the mountain is so steep, that it is impossible to reach the summit, or, in fact, to escape by any means.

We remained on the shore, distracted with apprehension and expecting to die. We had divided our provision equally, so that each individual might live a longer or shorter time, according to the consumption he made of his portion.

They who died first were buried by the others. I had the office of burying my last companion; for besides managing what provisions were allowed me with more care than the rest, I had also a store which I had kept concealed from my comrades. Nevertheless, at the time I had buried the last I had so little left, that I imagined I must soon follow him; upon which I dug a grave and resolved to throw myself into it and die there, since no one remained to perform the last duties to my remains. I must confess, however, that whilst I was thus employed I could not avoid reproaching myself as the sole cause of my misfortunes, and most heartily repented of this last voyage. But I was not satisfied with reproaches only, I bit my hands in despair and was near putting an end to my existence.

But God still had compassion on me, and inspired me with the thought of going to the river which lost itself in the hollow of the cave. I examined it with great attention; and it occurred to me, that as the river ran underground, it must in its course come out to daylight again, so that if I should construct a raft and place myself upon it, the current of the water would probably bring me to some inhabited country; and even should I perish, it would be but changing the manner of my death; while on the contrary, if I got safely out of this fatal place, I should not only avoid the cruel death by which my companions perished, but might also meet with some fresh opportunity of enriching myself. "Who knows," I said to myself, "that fortune does not await me on my arrival out of this frightful cavern, to recompense me for all the losses I have sustained?"

I worked at my raft with fresh vigour after these reflections; making it of thick pieces of wood and great cables, of which there was an abundance on the beach; I tied them closely together, and formed a strong float. When it was completed, I placed on it a cargo of rubies, emeralds, ambergris, crystal, and also some gold and silver stuffs. Having placed all these things in a proper equilibrium, and fastened them to the planks, I embarked on the raft, taking with me two poles which I designed to use for oars, and trusting to the current, resigned myself to the will of God.

As soon as I was under the vault of the cavern I lost the light of day; and the current carried me on without my being able to discern its course. I rowed for some days in this obscurity, without ever perceiving the least rays of light. At one time the vault of the cavern was so low that it almost knocked my head, which rendered me very careful to avoid the danger again. During this time I consumed no more of my provisions than was absolutely necessary to sustain nature; but however frugal I might be, I consumed them all. I then fell into a sweet sleep. I cannot tell whether I slept long, but when I awoke I was surprised to find myself in an open country, near a bank of the river, to which my boat was fastened, and in the midst of a large concourse of blacks. I rose as soon as I perceived them and saluted them; they spoke to me, but I could not understand their language.

At this moment I felt so transported with joy that I could scarcely believe myself awake. Being at length convinced that it was not a dream, I exclaimed in the words of the Koran; "Invoke the Almighty, and he will come to your assistance; thou needest not care for aught besides. Close thine eye, and, while thou sleepest, God will change thy fortune from bad to good."

One of the blacks, who understood Arabic, having heard me pronounce these words, advanced towards me and spoke as follows: "Brother," said he, "be not surprised at seeing us; we live in this country, and came hither to-day to water our fields from this river which flows from the neighbouring mountain, through canals cut in the earth to admit its passage.

"We observed that the current bore something along, and we immediately ran to the bank to see what it was, and perceived this raft; one of us instantly swam to it and conducted it to shore. We fastened it as you see, and were waiting for you to awake. We entreat you to relate to us your history, which must be very extraordinary; tell us how you could venture on this river, and whence you come." I first requested him to give me some food; after which I promised to satisfy their curiosity.

They produced several kinds of meat, and when I had satisfied my hunger I related to them all that had happened to me, which they appeared to listen to with great admiration. As soon as I had finished my history, their interpreter told me that I had astonished them with my relation, and I must go myself to the king to recount my adventures: for they were of too extraordinary a nature to be repeated by any one but to whom they had happened. I replied, that I was ready to do any thing they wished. The blacks then sent for a horse, which arrived shortly after; they placed me on it, and while some walked by my side to conduct me, others who had hauled the raft out of the water, carried it on their shoulders with the bales of rubies, and followed me.

We went together to the city of Serendib, for this was the name of the island; and the blacks presented me to their king. I approached and saluted him as it is usual to accost the kings of India; that is to say, I prostrated myself at his feet, and kissed the earth. The prince made me rise, and receiving me with an affable air, he placed me by his side. He first asked me my name: I replied, that I was called Sindbad, and surnamed the Sailor from having made several voyages; and added that I was a citizen of Bagdad. "But," replied he, "how then came you into my dominions, and whence are you arrived?"

I concealed nothing from the king, and related to him what you have just heard: he was so pleased with it that he ordered the history of my adventures to be written in letters of gold, that it might be preserved amongst the archives of his kingdom. The raft was then produced, and the bales were opened in his presence. He admired the aloe-wood and ambergris, but above all the rubies and emeralds, as he had none in his treasury equal to them in value.

Perceiving that he examined the precious stones with pleasure, and that he looked repeatedly at the rarest of them, I prostrated myself before him, and

SINDBAD RECEIVED BY THE KING OF SERENDIB.

took the liberty of saying: "Sire, not only my person is at your command, but the cargo of my raft also, if your majesty will do me the honour of accepting it, and disposing of it as you think fit." He smiled, and replied that he did not desire anything which belonged to me; for as God had given it me I ought not to be deprived of it; that instead of diminishing my riches he would add to them; and that when I left his dominions, I should carry with me proofs of his liberality. I could only reply to this by praying for his prosperity, and by praising his generosity.

He ordered one of his officers to attend me, and gave me servants to wait upon me at his own expense. The officers faithfully fulfilled the charge they were intrusted with, and conveyed all the bales to the place destined for my lodging.

I went away every day at certain hours to pay my court to the king, and employed the rest of my time in seeing the city and whatever was most worthy of attention.

The island of Serendib is situated exactly under the equinoctial line, so that the days and nights are of equal length. It is eighty parasangs long, and as many in breadth. The principal town is situated at the extremity of a beautiful valley formed by a mountain, which is in the middle of the island, and which is by far the highest in the world; it is discernible at sea within three days' navigation of it. Rubies and many sorts of minerals are found in it, and most of the rocks are formed of emery, which is a sort of metallic stone used in the cutting of precious stones.

All kinds of rare and curious plants and trees, particularly the cedar and cocoa trees, grow here in great abundance, and there are pearl fisheries

9

on the coast at the mouth of the rivers; some of its valleys, too, produce diamonds. I made a devotional journey up the mountain, to the spot where Adam was placed on his banishment from Paradise, and had the curiosity to ascend to the summit.

When I came back to the city, I entreated the king to grant me permission to return to my native country, which he did in the most obliging and honourable manner. He compelled me to receive a rich present, which was taken from his treasury; and when I went to take my leave, he deposited in my care another still more considerable than the first, and at the same time gave me a letter for the Commander of the Believers, our sovereign lord, saying, "I beg you to present from me this letter and this present to the caliph Haroun Alraschid, and to assure him of my friendship." I took the present and the letter with the greatest respect, and promised his majesty to execute the orders with which he was pleased to honour me, with the greatest punctuality. Before I embarked, the king sent for the captain and the merchants with whom I was to sail, and charged them to pay me all possible attention.

The letter of the king of Serendib was written on the skin of a certain animal, highly prized in that country on account of its rareness. The colour of it approaches to yellow. The letter itself was in characters of azure, and contained the following words in the Indian language:—

"The king of the Indies—who, in his journies, is preceded by a thousand elephants, and whose residence is a palace the roof of which glitters with the lustre of a hundred thousand rubies, and who possesses in his treasury twenty thousand crowns, enriched with diamonds—to the caliph Abdallah Haroun Alraschid:

"Although the present we send you is inconsiderable, yet receive it as a brother and a friend, in consideration of the friendship we bear you in our heart: and we feel happy in having an opportunity of testifying it to you. We ask the same share in your affections; as we hope to deserve it; being of a rank equal to that you hold. We salute you as a brother. Farewell."

The present consisted of several items;—first, a vase made of one single ruby, pierced and worked into a cup of half a foot in height and an inch thick, filled with fine round pearls, all weighing half a drachm each: second, the skin of a serpent, which had scales as large as a common piece of money, the peculiar property of which was to preserve those who lay on it from all disease: third, fifty thousand drachms of the most exquisite aloe wood, with thirty grains of camphor as large as pistachio nuts: and lastly, a female slave of the most enchanting beauty, whose clothes were covered with jewels.

The ship set sail, and after a long though fortunate voyage we landed at Balsora, whence I returned to Bagdad. The first thing I did after my arrival was to execute the commision I had been entrusted with. I took the letter of the king of Serendib, and presented myself at the gate of the Commander of the Faithful, followed by the beautiful slave and some of my family, who carried the presents which had been committed to my care. I mentioned the reason of my appearance there, and was immediately conducted before the throne of the caliph. I prostrated myself at his feet, and after having made a short speech, gave him the letter and the present. When he had read the contents, he inquired of me whether it was true that the King of Serendib was as rich and powerful as he reported himself to be in his letter. I prostrated myself a second time, and when I arose: "Commander of the Faithful," said I, "I can assure your majesty that he does not exaggerate his riches and grandeur; I have been witness to it. Nothing can excite greater admiration than the magnificence of his palace. When this prince wishes to appear in public, a throne is prepared for him on the back of an elephant; on this he sits, and proceeds between two files, composed of his ministers, favourites, and others belonging to the court. Before him, on the same elephant, sits an officer with a golden lance in his hand, and behind the throne another stands with a pillar of gold, on the top of which is placed an emerald about half a foot long and an inch thick. He is preceeded by a guard of a thousand men, habited in silk and gold stuffs, and mounted on elephants richly caparisoned.

"While the king is on the march, the officer who sits before him on the elephant from time to time cries with a loud voice: 'This is the great monarch, the powerful and magnanimous sultan of the Indies, whose palace is covered with a hundred thousand rubies, and who possesses twenty thousand diamond crowns. This is the great monarch, greater than ever was Solyma or the great Mihrage.

"After he has pronounced these words, the officer who is behind the throne cries in his turn; 'This monarch, who is so great and powerful, must die, must die, must die.' The first officer then replies; 'Hail to Him who lives and dies not!'"

"The king of Serendib is so just that there are no judges in his capital, nor in any other part of his dominions; his people do not want any. They know and observe with exactness the true principles of justice, and never deviate from their duty; therefore tribunals and magistrates would be useless amongst them."

The caliph was satisfied with my discourse, and said: "The wisdom of this king appears in his letter; and after what you have told me, I must confess that such wisdom is worthy of such subjects, and such subjects worthy of it." At these words he dismissed me with a rich present.

Sindbad here finished his discourse, and his visitors retired; but Hindbad, as usual, received his hundred sequins. They returned the following day, and Sindbad began the relation of his seventh and last voyage, in these terms:

THE SEVENTH VOYAGE OF SINDBAD THE SAILOR.

On my return from my sixth voyage, I absolutely relinquished all thoughts of ever venturing again on the seas. I was now arrived at an age which required rest, and besides this, I had sworn never more to expose myself to the perils I had so often experienced; I prepared, therefore, to enjoy my life in quiet and repose.

One day, when I was regaling a number of friends, one of my servants came to tell me that an officer of the caliph wanted to speak to me. I got up from the table and went to him. "The caliph," said he, "has ordered me to acquaint you that he wishes to see you." I followed the officer to the palace, and he presented me to the prince, whom I saluted by prostrating myself at his feet. "Sindbad," said he, "I am in want of you; you must do me a service, and go at once to the king of Serendib, with my answer and presents; it is but right that I should return him the civility he has shown me."

This order of the caliph was a thunderbolt to me. "Commander of Faithful," replied I, "I am ready to execute anything your majesty may desire: but I humbly entreat you to consider that I am worn down with the unspeakable fatigues I have undergone; I have even made a vow never to leave Bagdad." I then took occasion to recount the long detail of my adventures, which he had the patience to listen to attentively. When I had done speaking: "I confess," said he, "that these are extraordinary adventures; nevertheless, they must not prevent you making the voyage I propose, for my sake; it is only to the island of Serendib; execute the commision I entrust you with, and then you will be at liberty to return. But you must go; for you must be sensible that it would be highly indecorous, as well as derogatory to my dignity, to be under obligations to the king of that island."

As I plainly saw that the caliph had resolved on my going, I signified to him that I was ready to obey his commands. He seemed much pleased, and ordered me a thousand sequins to pay the expenses of the voyage.

In a few days I was prepared for my departure; and as soon as I had received the presents of the caliph, together with a letter written with his own hand, I set off and took the route of Balsora, from whence I embarked. After a pleasant voyage I arrived at the island of Serendib. I immediately acquainted the ministers with the commission I was come upon, and begged them to procure me an audience as soon as possible. They did not fail to attend to my wishes, and conducted me to the palace. I saluted the king by prostrating myself according to the usual custom.

This prince immediately recollected me, and evinced great joy at my return. "Welcome, Sindbad," said he; "I assure you that I have often thought of you since your departure. Blessed be this day, in which I see you again." I returned the compliment, and after thanking him for his kindness, delivered the letter and present of the caliph, which he received with every mark of satisfaction and respect.

The caliph had sent him a complete bed of gold tissue, estimated at a thousand sequins; fifty robes of a very rich stuff, a hundred more of white linen, the finest that could be procured from Cairo, Suez, Cufa, and Alexandria; another bed of crimson and also a third of a different make. A vase of agate,

greater in width than in depth, of the thickness of a finger; on the sides of which was sculptured in bas-relief, a man kneeling on the ground with a bow and arrow in his haud, which he was going to let fly at a lion; and besides these, he sent him a richly ornamented table, which was supposed from tradition to have belonged to Solomon. The letter of the caliph was written in these terms:—

"Health in the name of the sovereign who directeth in the right road, to the powerful and happy sultan, from Abdallah Haroun Alraschid, whom God has placed on the seat of honour, after his ancestors of happy memory.

"We have received your letter with joy, and send you this, emanating from the council of our porte, the garden of superior minds. We hope that in casting your eyes over it, you will perceive our good intention, and think it agreeable. Adieu."

The king of Serendib was rejoiced to find that the caliph returned a testimony to his friendship. Soon after this audience I requested another to take my leave, but had some difficulty in obtaining it. At length, however, I succeeded, and the king, at my departure, ordered me a very handsome present. I re-embarked immediately, intending to return to Bagdad; but had not the good fortune to arrive as soon as I expected, for God had disposed it otherwise.

Three or four days after we had set sail we were attacked by corsairs, who easily made themselves masters of our vessel, as we were not in a state for defence. Some persons in the ship attempted to make resistance, but it cost them their lives. All who had the prudence not to oppose the intention of the corsairs, among whom my destiny was cast, were made slaves. After they had stripped us and substituted bad clothes for our own, they bent their course towards a large distant island, where, on their arrival, they sold us.

I was purchased by a rich merchant, who conducted me to his house, gave me food to eat, and clothed me as a slave. Some days after, as he had not been well informed who I was, he asked me if I knew any trade. I replied that I was not an artizan, but a merchant by profession, and that the corsairs who had sold me had taken from me all that I possessed. "But tell me," said he, "do you think you could shoot with a bow and arrow?" I informed him that it had been one of my youthful sports, and that I had not entirely forgotten it. He then gave me a bow and some arrows, and causing me to mount behind him upon an elephant, he took me to a vast forest at a distance of several hours' journey from the city. After proceeding a great way, we reached a spot where he wished to stop, when, bidding me alight, he showed me a large tree: "Ascend this tree," said he, "and shoot at the elephants that pass under it, for there are a prodigious number in this forest; if one should fall, come quickly, and acquaint me of it." Having said this, he left me some provisions and returned to the city, while I remained in the tree on the watch the whole night.

I did not perceive any during that time, but the next day, as soon as the sun had risen, a great number made their appearance. I shot many arrows at them, and at last one fell. The others immediately retired, and left me at liberty to go and inform my master of my success. To reward me for this good intelligence he regaled me with an excellent repast, and praised my address. We then returned together to the forest, where we dug a pit to bury the elephant I had killed. It was my master's intention to let it rot in the earth, and afterwards to take possession of its teeth for commerce.

I pursued this occupation for two months, and scarcely a day passed in which I did not kill an elephant. I did not, however, always place myself on the same tree; but sometimes ascended one, sometimes another; till one morning when I was waiting for a troop of elephants to pass, I perceived, to my great astonishment, that instead of traversing the forest as usual, they stopped and came towards me with a terrible noise, and in such numbers that the ground was covered with them, and trembled under their footsteps. They approached the tree in which I had stationed myself, and surrounding it, they all extended their trunks and fixed their eyes upon me. At this surprising spectacle I remained motionless, and was so agitated by fright that my bow and and arrows fell from my hands.

Nor were my fears groundless. After the elephants had viewed me for some time, one of the largest twisted his trunk round the body of the tree, and shook it with so much violence that he tore it up by the roots, and threw it on the ground. I fell with the tree; but the animal took me up with his trunk, and placing me on his shoulders, where I remained more dead than alive, he put himself at the head of his companions, who followed him in a troop, and carried me to a spot whence, having set me down, he and the rest retired.

Conceive my situation! I for a time thought it was a dream. At length, having been seated for some time, and seeing no other elephants, I arose and perceived that I was on a little hill of some breadth, entirely covered with the bones and teeth of elephants. This sight filled my mind with a variety of reflections. It occurred to me that I had been brought to this spot through the fine instinct and superior sagacity of these animals, to teach me that this was their cemetery or place of burial, and that I might safely desist from destroying them merely for the sake of possessing their teeth, as here I could obtain plenty without such necessity. I did not stay long on the hill, but turned my steps towards the city, and did not meet any elephants, they having entered farther into the forest.

As soon as my master saw me, "Ah! poor Sindbad" he exclaimed, "I was in pain to know what had become of you. I have been to the forest, and found a tree newly torn up by the roots, and a bow and arrows on the ground; after having sought you everywhere in vain, I despaired of seeing you again. Pray relate to me what has happened to you, and by what good fortune you are still alive." I satisfied his curiosity, and on the following day, having accompanied me to the hill, he was with great joy convinced of the truth of my history. We loaded the elephant on which we had come

with as many teeth as he could carry, and when we returned, he thus addressed me: "Brother, for after the discovery you have imparted to me, and which cannot fail to enrich me, I will no longer treat you as a slave, may God pour on you all sorts of blessings and prosperity! In his presence I here give you your liberty. I have hitherto concealed from you what I am now going to relate. The elephants of our forest destroy annually an infinite number of slaves, whom we send in search of ivory. Whatever advice we give them, they are sure, sooner or later, to lose their lives by the wiles of these animals. God has delivered you from their fury, and has conferred this mercy on you alone. It is a sign that he cherishes you, and that he has ordained you to remain in the world to be of use to mankind. You have procured me a surprising advantage; we have not hitherto been able to get ivory without risking the lives of our slaves, and now our whole city will be enriched by your means. Do not suppose that I think I have sufficiently recompensed you by giving you liberty, I intend to add to it considerable presents."

To this obliging discourse I replied, "Master, God preserve you; the liberty which you grant me acquits you of all obligation towards me; and the only recompense which I desire for the service which I have had the good fortune to render to you and the inhabitants of your city, is permission to return to my own country." "Well," resumed he, "the monsoon will soon bring us the vessels which trade hither for ivory. I will then send you away, with the means of paying your expenses home." I again thanked him both for the liberty he had given me and the good-will he exhibited towards me; and afterwards continued to abide with him till the season of the monsoon, in the interim making frequent excursions to the hill and filling his magazines with ivory. The other merchants in the city did not fail to do the same, for the secret soon became noised abroad.

The ships at length arrived, and my master, having chosen that in which he wished me to embark, loaded it with ivory, placing the half of it to my account. He did not omit an abundance of provisions for my voyage, and pressed me to accept some rare curiosities of that country besides. I thanked him with unfeigned gratitude for all the obligations he had conferred upon me, and embarked. We then set sail, and as the adventure which had procured me liberty was a very extraordinary one, it was always present to my mind.

We touched at several islands to procure refreshments. Our vessel having sailed from a port of the Indian continent, we went there to land; and, fearful of the dangers of the sea of Balsora, I landed the goods that belonged to me, and resolved to continue my journey by land. I sold my ivory for a large sum of money, and purchased a variety of curious things for presents: when I was equipped I joined a caravan of merchants; but from remaining a long time on the road I suffered a good deal, which, however, I bore with patience, consoling myself with the reflection that I had neither tempests, nor corsairs, nor serpents, such as I had before encountered, to fear.

All my fatigues being at last concluded, I arrived

happily at Bagdad, and went immediately to present myself to the caliph and give him an account of my embassy. This prince told me, that my long absence had occasioned him some uneasiness; but that he had always hoped God would not forsake me.

When I related the adventure of the elephants he appeared much surprised, and would have disbelieved it had not my sincerity been well known to him. He thought this, as well as the other histories I had detailed to him, so curious, that he ordered his secretary to write it in letters of gold, to be preserved in his treasury. I retired, satisfied with the presents and honours he conferred on me; and then resigned myself entirely to my family, my relations, and friends.

Sindbad thus concluded the recital of his seventh and last voyage; and addressing himself to Hindbad: "Well, my friend," said he, "have you ever heard of one who has suffered more than I have, or been in so many trying situations? Is it not just, that after so many troubles I should enjoy an agreeable and quiet life?" As he finished these words, Hindbad approached him, kissed his hand, and said: "I must confess, sir, that you have encountered frightful perils; my afflictions are not to be compared to yours. If I feel them heavily during the period of suffering I console myself with the small profit which they produce. You not only deserve a quiet life, but are worthy of all the riches you possess; since you make so good a use of them and are so generous. May you, therefore, continue to live happy till the hour of your death."

Sindbad ordered him to have another hundred sequins, admitted him to his friendship, told him to quit the profession of a porter, and continue to eat at his table, for that he should all his life have reason to remember Sindbad the Sailor.

HISTORY OF

PRINCE AHMED AND THE FAIRY PARI-BANOU.

A SULTAN who reigned in peace on the throne of India for many years, had the satisfaction of seeing in his old age that the three princes his sons, the worthy imitators of his virtues, and a princess his niece, were the ornament of his court. The eldest of the princes was called Houssain, the second Ali, the youngest Ahmed, and the princess his niece Nourounnihar.

Nourounnihar was the daughter of the younger brother of the Sultan, and on whom he had settled a very considerable fortune. He died, however, a few years after his marriage, and left her very young. The sultan, in consideration of that perfect brotherly affection which subsisted between them, and the sincere attachment the prince had always shown to his person, took charge of his daughter's education, and ordered her to come to the palace, to be brought up with the three princes. To uncommon beauty, and every personal grace and accomplishment, this princess added an excellent understanding; and her unsullied virtue distinguished her among all the princesses of her time.

Her uncle designed, when she should be of proper age, to form an alliance with some neighbouring prince by bestowing her upon him in marriage, and was very seriously thinking on the subject when he discovered that all the three princes his sons were desperately in love with her. This gave him great unhappiness; but the unhappiness arose, not so much because their attachment would prevent the alliance he had in contemplation, as from the difficulty he saw of effecting an agreement between them, and that the two younger, at least, should resign their claims to the eldest. He talked to each in private; and after remonstrating with them on the impossibility that one princess should be married to three, and on the troubles they would occasion by persisting in their passion, he used every argument to persuade them, either to submit to the declaration which the princess herself should make in favour of one of the three, or relinquish their pretensions, and look out for some other connection, in which he would allow them a free choice, and agree among themselves to consent to her marriage with some foreign prince. But as in each of them he had met with an unaccountable obstinacy, he assembled them all three before him, and thus addressing them: "My children," said he, "since, for your advantage and tranquillity, I have not succeeded in persuading you to think no more about marrying the princess your cousin, and as I am not inclined to use my authority in giving her to one of you in preference to the other two, I think I have found out a way to satisfy you, and to preserve that union which ought to subsist among you, if you will attend to me and do what I shall now recommend. I think it, then, advisable that you should separately go upon your travels, each into a different country, so that it shall be impossible for you to meet; and as you know I pay great attention to everything that is either curious, rare, or singular, I promise the princess my niece to him who shall bring me that rarity which is most extraordinary and of the most singular nature: thus, as chance will direct your judgment in the choice of the singularity of the things you shall have brought, by the comparison you will make among them, you will have no difficulty in doing one another justice, and giving the preference where it is due. To defray the expenses of travelling, and for the purchase of the rarity you are to procure, I will give you each a sum suitable to your birth, but not enough to furnish a great equipage and a numerous retinue, which, by indicating your rank, would deprive you of that freedom which will be necessary to you, not only for accomplishing the purpose of your journey, but also for giving due attention to whatever is worthy of observation ; and, in short, to derive the greatest advantage from your travels.''

As the three princes always conformed to the inclinations of their father, and as each flattered himself that he should be the person to whom fortune would give the possession of Nourounihar, they all testified their readiness to obey him without delay. The sultan immediately desired the sum he had promised to be paid them, and on that very day orders were given to make preparation for their journey ; they even took leave of the sultan, that they might be in readiness to set off very early the next morning. They went out at the same gate of the city, well mounted and equipped, dressed like merchants, each with a confidential attendant disguised like a slave, and they kept together till they arrived at the first inn, where the road separated into three, one of which each of them was to take by himself. At night, whilst they were refreshing themselves with the supper they had ordered, they agreed that they would be absent a year, and, after that time, meet again at the same place, upon this condition, that he who came first should wait for the other two, and that the two who came first should wait for the third ; so that, as they all three took leave of their father together, they should present themselves to him at the same time on their return. The next morning at daybreak, after embracing and mutually wishing one another an agreeable journey, they mounted their horses, and each took one of the three roads, without at all clashing in their choice.

Prince Houssain, the eldest of the three, who had often heard of the grandeur, riches, and splendour of the kingdom of Bisnagar, took his route towards the Indian sea ; and after a journey of three months, by occasionally joining himself to different caravans, and sometimes passing through barren deserts and mountainous tracts ; at others, travelling through a country as well peopled, more fruitful, and better cultivated than any other part of the world, at last arrived at Bisnagar, a city which gives its own name to the whole country of which it is the capital, and where the usual residence of its sovereign is fixed. He took up his lodgings in a khan appropriated for the reception of foreign merchants ; and as he had learned that there were four principal divisions, where the merchants of all descriptions had shops for their goods, in the middle of which the palace of the king, occupying a large extent of ground, was placed, forming, as it were, the centre of the city, having three enclosures, at least to leagues in length from one gate to the other, he went on the very next day to one of the three divisions.

Prince Houssian could not behold this part without astonishment. It was of considerable extent, and filled with streets intersecting each other, all arched over with guards against the heat of the sun : they were, however, very well lighted. The shops were perfectly regular, and those belonging to merchant who traded in different goods were not mixed together, but each sort collected into one street. This was also the case in those streets which were inhabited by artificers, or workmen.

After having walked through every street in this quarter, meditating upon the immense quantity of riches that he saw, prince Houssain felt himself in want of some repose. He expressed his wishes to a merchant, who very civilly invited him to come in, and rest himself in his shop. The prince accepted the offer, and had not been long sitting there before he saw a crier going about with a carpet about six feet square in his hand, which he offered to put up for sale at thirty purses. He called the crier, and desired to see this carpet, as it seemed to him to be a most exorbitant price, both on account of its size and quality. When he had thoroughly examined the carpet, he said to the crier that he could not comprehend the reason why a floor carpet, so small and so indifferently made, should be put up at so high a price.

The crier, who took prince Houssain for a merchant, replied, '' If this sum, sir, appears to you to be unreasonable, you will be more astonished when I shall inform you that I am ordered not to let it go under forty purses, and not to deliver it till the money is paid.'' '' There must, then,'' replied prince Houssain, '' be some secret quality that renders it so valuable.'' '' You have guessed it, sir,'' added the crier ; '' and you will agree to it, when you are informed that only by sitting upon this carpet you will be instantly transported, together with the carpet itself, to whatever place you wish to go ; and you will find yourself in that spot almost in a moment, without being stopped by any obstacle whatever.''

The prince of India, reflecting that the principal object of his journey was to procure some extraordinary and unknown rarity for the sultan his father, thought that he could not possibly meet with anything with which the sultan would be better pleased. '' If this carpet,'' he said to the crier, '' has the power you say it possesses, I not only do not think it dear, but I will give you the forty purses you require, and will also make you such a present as shall amply satisfy you.'' '' Sir,'' replied the crier, '' I assure you I have told you the truth ; and it will be very easy for you to be convinced of it, for, as soon as you shall have determined on the purchase at forty purses, I will show you how to make the experiment. As you probably have not the forty purses here, and as I must accompany you to the khan where, as a stranger, you have taken up your abode, in order to receive them, if the master of this shop will give us leave, we will retire into the back part of it. I will there spread out my carpet ; and when we shall both be seated upon it, and you shall have formed the wish to be transported into your apartment with me, if you are not instantly conveyed there, it is no bargain, and you shall not be obliged to complete the purchase. With respect to the present, as it is the person who sells the carpet that pays me for my trouble, I shall receive it as a favour which you wish to bestow upon me, and shall feel myself under an obligation to you for it.''

The prince accepted the conditions. He concluded the bargain according to the terms proposed : he then, having obtained the owner's leave, went into the back part of the shop. The crier spread out the carpet, and they both seated themselves upon it. The prince had no sooner formed the wish to be transported to his apartment in the khan than he found himself and the crier in the very spot. He had no need of any further proof of the virtue of the carpet; he therefore counted out the forty purses in gold, and added twenty pieces more as a present to the crier.

Prince Houssain's joy was extreme at having thus fortunately obtained, almost at the moment of his arrival at Bisnagar, possession of a carpet so rare; and he had not the least doubt but that he should obtain the princess Nourounnihar: in fact, he thought it impossible for either of his younger brothers to acquire anything, in the course of their travels, that could at all be put in competition with what he had been fortunate enough to meet with. By only sitting down on the carpet, he might, without remaining any longer at Bisnagar, have instantly returned to the spot at which they had agreed to meet; but he would then have been obliged to have waited there a long time for them; and as he was desirous of seeing the king of Bisnagar and his court, and to inform himself of the strength, laws, customs, religion, and condition of the kingdom, he resolved to employ some months in endeavouring to satisfy his curiosity.

It was the custom of the king of Bisnagar to give an audience once every week to foreign merchants. It was under this character that prince Houssain, who did not wish to discover his real rank, saw him very frequently; and as this prince, besides being handsome and well made, possessed a brilliant understanding, and was master of great address and politeness, he was very much distinguished beyond the other merchants with whom he came into the king's presence. To him, therefore, in preference to others, the king addressed his conversation when he wished to make inquiries about the sultan of India, and of the strength, riches, and government of his empire.

On the other days the prince employed himself in seeing whatever was most remarkable either in the city, or neighbouring country. Among other things most worthy of being visited, he went to the temple of idols, a building the most curious in its construction, as it was entirely formed of bronze. It was not more than ten cubits square on the inside, and about fifteen high; but that which made it the most curious was an idol of massive gold, as large as a man, the eyes of which were single rubies, and so artfully formed that, on whatever side the spectator stood, they appeared turned towards him. There was also another temple not less curious. This was situated in a village, where there was a plain of about ten acres in extent, which formed a delicious garden filled with roses and other delightful flowers, the whole of which was surrounded with a wall about four feet high, for the purpose of keeping out any animals that came near. In the middle of this plain there was a small terrace raised to about the height of a man formed of stones joined together with so much care and skill that the whole looked like one single stone. The temple, which was in the form of a dome, and erected in the middle of the terrace, was fifty cubits high, and could be seen at the distance of several leagues each way. The length

of it was thirty cubits on one side, and twenty on the other; and the marble of which it was formed was quite red, and very highly polished. The vault of the dome was ornamented with three rows of paintings brilliantly executed, and in good taste. All the other parts of the temple were also so completely filled with pictures, bas-reliefs, and idols, that there was no place from the top to the bottom where another could be put.

Every morning and evening there were some superstitious ceremonies performed here, which were followed by different games, instrumental concerts, dances, songs, and other festivities; and the ministers belonging to the temple, as well as the inhabitants of the palace, subsisted solely by the offerings which the pilgrims, who came in crowds from the most distant parts of the kingdom to fulfil their vows, brought with them.

Had prince Houssain been enabled to make a very long stay at the court of the kingdom of Bisnagar, a variety of other curious things would have agreeably amused him there until the very last day of the year, on which the princes his brothers and himself had agreed to meet. Fully satisfied, however, with what he had seen, and occupied continually with the thoughts of Nourounnihar, the dear object of his affections, the recollection of whose beauty and charms, since the acquisition he had made of the carpet, every day augmented the violence of his passion, he fancied his mind would be much more at ease, and that he should feel much more happy, when he should be at a less distance from her. Having first, therefore, satisfied the master of the khan, and told him the hour when he might come for the key of the apartment, which would be left in the door, without giving any hint by what mode he meant to travel, he went back to his room, shut the door, and left the key in it. He then spread out the carpet, and seated himself, with the attendant whom he had brought with him, upon it; and having meditated for a moment, he in the most serious manner formed the wish to be conveyed to the spot where he and his brothers had agreed to assemble; and he soon perceived that he was arrived. He took up his residence there, and, without making himself known otherwise than as a merchant, he waited for their arrival.

Prince Ali, the younger brother of Houssain, who intended to travel to Persia, set out for that country in company with a caravan which he had joined on the third day after he separated from his brothers; and after a journey of near four months, he at length arrived at Schiraz, which at that time was the capital of Persia. As he had formed a sort of intimacy during the journey with a few merchants, without letting them suppose he was anything else but a jeweller, he took up his abode at the same khan with them.

While the merchants were the next day unpacking their bales of merchandise, prince Ali, who was encumbered with nothing more than was absolutely necessary for his own comfort, having first changed his dress, desired some one to show him the quarter of the city where they sold jewels, gold and silver ornaments, brocades, silk stuffs, fine linens, and other curious and valuable merchandise. This place, very spacious and well built, was arched over, and the roof supported by large pillars, round which, as well along the walls. the shops were all ranged, and also on both sides, within and without; and this at Schiraz was called the bezestein. Prince Ali examined it in every part, and was astonished, in attempting to judge of the quantity of riches that were shut up from the profusion of rich and costly merchandise that was exposed for sale. Among the different criers who went about with specimens of various thing for sale, by way of auction, he was much surprised at seeing one who held an ivory tube in his hand, about a foot long, and not more than an inch thick, which he put up at thirty purses. He imagined the crier could not be in his senses; but, in order to be satisfied of the fact, he went up to a shop, and pointing the crier out to the merchant, he said, " Pray, sir, am I deceived in concluding that the crier who puts up the little ivory tube he has in his hand at thirty purses is insane?" " Sir," replied the merchant, " if it be so, he has lost his senses since yesterday; for I can assure you he is one of our best criers, and the most employed, as we place the greatest confidence in him whenever there is anything to be sold of greater value than common. With respect to the ivory tube which he cries at thirty purses, it certainly must be worth so much, and even more, however extraordinary it may seem from its appearance. He will pass in a moment; we will then call him, and you may inform yourself. Have the goodness in the meantime to sit down on my sofa and refresh yourself."

Prince Ali accepted the obliging offer of the merchant; and he had not been long seated before the crier passed by. The merchant immediately called him, and said, " Inform this gentleman whether you are in your senses, as, from your putting up that comparatively insignificant ivory tube at thirty purses, he has some doubts on the subject. I should myself also be much astonished at it, did I not know you to be a prudent, sensible man." " Sir," replied the crier, addressing himself to prince Ali, " you are not the only person who supposes I have lost my senses, from my conduct respecting this ivory tube; but you shall yourself judge whether it be so when I have explained its properties to you; and I hope that you, as well as the others who had an equally bad opinion of me, will then attend the sale."

" In the first place, sir," continued the crier, showing the tube to the prince, " you will have the goodness to observe that this tube is furnished with a glass at each end; and I must inform you that, by looking through one of these two glasses, whatever you may feel a wish to see you will instantly behold." " I am at this moment ready to retract my opinion," cried the prince, " if you will prove the truth of what you have advanced;" and as he held the tube in his hand, he examined it at both ends, and then added, " Show me the end through which I must look that I may be convinced." The crier immediately did so, and the prince looked through, having previously formed a wish to see the sultan his father, whom he in-

stantly beheld in perfect health, sitting on his throne in the midst of his council;—then, as nothing, after the sultan, was dearer to him than the princess Nourounnihar, he transferred his wish to her, and immediately beheld her seated at her toilet, surrounded by her women, and appearing in the most lively humour.

Prince Ali wanted nothing more to convince him that this tube was the most valuable and rare thing that existed, not only in the city of Schiraz, but throughout the whole world; and he thought that if he neglected to purchase it, he should never again meet with so extraordinary a thing, either at Schiraz or during his travels, if he spent ten years or more in the search. He then said to the crier, " I freely retract the bad opinion I had formed of your conduct; and I believe you will be fully satisfied of my sincerity, and the reparation I am ready to make you, when I inform you that I am willing to purchase your tube. As I should be sorry that any one else should possess it, tell me the exact price the owner has fixed upon it; and then, without giving you the trouble of crying it any longer, or fatiguing yourself by going about with it, you have only to accompany me, and I will count the sum out to you." The crier assured him with an oath that he was ordered not to let it go under forty purses; and if he had any doubts of the truth of what he said, he was ready to conduct him to the owner. The prince was satisfied, and carried him with him. When they had arrived at the khan where prince Ali lodged, he counted out to him forty purses of gold, and thus remained in possession of the ivory tube.

When the prince had made this acquisition, he experienced great joy, because he felt persuaded that the princes his brothers could have met with nothing so rare, and that the princess Nourounnihar would therefore be his reward for the fatigues he had undergone. He now gave himself no further trouble except to see and inform himself of what was going on at the court of Persia, but without discovering his real character; and also in seeing whatever might be curious in and about Schiraz. He had almost satisfied his curiosity, when the caravan in which he came was ready to depart. The prince immediately joined it; and without suffering any other inconvenience than the fatigue common to so long a journey, prince Ali arrived at the place where his brother Houssain already was. These two remained together, expecting the arrival of prince Ahmed.

This prince had bent his course towards Samarcand, and, on the day after his arrival there, pursued the same plan his two brothers had done, and went to the bezestein. He had hardly entered the place before he saw a crier carrying an artificial apple in his hand, which he put up at thirty-five purses. Prince Ahmed stopped the crier. " Let me see this apple," he cried; " and tell me its particular excellence, that you should put it up at the very extraordinary price of thirty-five purses." The crier gave it into his hand that he might examine it. " Sir," he said, " this apple, if you only consider its external appearance, is of very little apparent value; but if you reflect upon its properties, and the great use we can make of it for

THE THREE PRINCES TRAVEL ON THE MAGIC CARPET.

the good of mankind, you must confess it is beyond all price; and that he who possesses it possesses a true treasure; in fact, sir, there is no disease, however painful or dangerous, whether fever, pleurisy, plague, or, in short, any disorder whatever, and even if the afflicted person is at the point of death, but it will cure; and the sufferer shall return to as perfect health as if he had never been ill during his whole life. And this is effected by the easiest of all possible ways—it is simply to make the sick person smell this apple."

"If your account may be relied upon," replied prince Ahmed, "you may truly say this apple is invaluable; but can I, really wishing to make a purchase of it, be convinced that there is neither evasion nor exaggeration in what you have been relating?" "Sir," replied the crier, "the fact is known, and can be vouched for by the whole city

10

of Samarcand; and without going a step further, you have only to ask any of the merchants here, and hear what they will say on the subject. You will even find some that would not have been alive to-day, as they themselves will declare to you, if they had not made use of this excellent remedy. But to make you understand the thing better, I must inform you that it is the result of the study and long application of a very celebrated philosopher in this city, who had all his life applied himself to investigate the virtues of plants and minerals, and who had at length arrived at the knowledge of the composition you now see, by which he has performed the most surprising cures, the recollection of which will never be obliterated. An attack so sudden that he had not time to make use of this sovereign remedy caused his death a short time since; and his widow, whom he has not left in the best of circumstances, and who has several young children, is resolved to put it up for sale."

While the crier was giving this account of the virtues of the artificial apple, many people stopped and listened, and the most part of these confirmed all he said. One of them said that he had a friend who was so dangerously ill that he had given up all hopes of his life, and that this would be a favourable opportunity to try the power of the apple: prince Ahmed told the crier that he would give him forty purses if the apple cured the sick person by only smelling at it." The crier, who had orders to sell it at that price, replied, "Let us, sir, go and make the experiment, and the apple will be yours. I assert this with the greatest confidence, because I cannot suppose it will have less efficacy now than it hitherto has possessed every time it has been employed, in recovering from the very jaws of death all those who have been in that state and tried its power."

The experiment succeeded, and the prince gave the forty purses to the crier, received the apple, and waited with the greatest impatience for the departure of the first caravan. He employed the intermediate time in examining whatever was curious in Samarcand and its neighbourhood, particularly the valley of Soyda, so called from a river of that name which waters it. This valley is reckoned by the Arabs as one of the four earthly paradises, from the beauty of the country, the gardens belonging to the palace, its universal fertility, and the delightful enjoyments that are experienced in the fine season of the year.

Prince Ahmed set out, and notwithstanding all the inconveniences of so long a journey, he arrived at the place where his brothers Houssain and Ali were waiting for him, in perfect health.

Prince Ali, who had arrived some time before his brother Ahmed, asked prince Houssain, who was the first that had come there, how long he had been waiting for him. When he learned that he had been there nearly three months, he said, "You cannot, then, have been travelling very far?" "I will tell you nothing at present," replied Houssain, "respecting the place where I have been, but I assure you I was more than three months on my journey thither." "If that is the case, then," rejoined prince Ali, "you must have made a very short stay there." "You are in an error, brother," said Houssain; "my residence there was for nearly five months, and it depended only upon my own choice to have made it much longer." "Then you certainly must have flown back," resumed prince Ali; "I do not at all comprehend how you can have otherwise been here three months, as you wish to make me believe."

"I have nevertheless told you the truth," added prince Houssain; "and this is an enigma which I will not explain to you until the arrival of our brother Ahmed, when I will at the same time inform you of the success of my travels respecting the object of our pursuit. I know not how successful you may have been; perhaps it is not of any consequence, for I see your baggage is not much increased." "Well," answered Prince Ali, "with the exception of a trifling carpet which lies on your sofa, and which appears as if it belonged to you, I might return you the same compliment: but as you make a mystery of the rarity you have procured, I also shall do the same with mine."

"I esteem the extraordinary thing I have brought," replied Houssain, "so far beyond any other, whatever it may be, that I should make no difficulty in showing it to you, and making you instantly confess, without the least fear of contradiction, that it is infinitely superior to the one you may have procured; but it is proper that we should wait for prince Ahmed, and then we may discover, with the greater kindness to each other, the good fortune we have each of us met with."

When prince Ahmed rejoined the two princes his brothers, and they had mutually embraced and congratulated each other on their happy meeting, and had expressed the pleasure they received at again seeing each other, prince Houssain, being the eldest, began in these words: "We shall have time enough hereafter to amuse each other with the particulars of our different travels—we will now only speak of what is of most importance to us to become acquainted with; and as I take it for granted that you, as well as myself, remember the principal business that occupied us, we will no longer conceal from each other what we have each obtained. And when we have all shown our acquisitions, we will determine, in the first instance, for ourselves, and see to whom the sultan our father is most likely to give the preference.

"And in order to set you the example," continued prince Houssain, "I must inform you that the rarity I have procured in my travels into the kingdom of Bisnagar is the carpet upon which I am sitting. It appears a common one, and without much show, as you may observe; but when I shall have told you its qualities, you will experience the greater astonisment, as you have never yet heard of anything similar: and I am sure you will agree with me. The fact is that, notwithstanding its common appearance, whoever sits upon this carpet, as I now do, and wishes to be transported into any particular place, however distant it may be, will instantly find himself there. I convinced myself of it before I counted out the forty purses which it cost me, and which I do not in the least regret. And when I had satisfied my curiosity with seeing everything that was remarkable at court, and in the kingdom of Bisnagar, and wished to return, I made use of no other means of conveyance to bring me and my attendant hither than this wonderful carpet; and he can tell you how short a time we were on our journey. Whenever you wish it, I will give you both a proof of its power. I now wait to hear what you have brought that can be put in competition with my carpet."

Prince Ali spoke next, and addressed Houssain in these terms: "I own, brother, that your carpet is one of the most wonderful things that can be, if, as I do not at all doubt, it possesses the property you have stated. But you must, however, acknowledge that there may be other things I will not say more wonderful, but at least equally so with your carpet, although they may be of a different nature. And to convince you of it," he went on, "this ivory tube which I now show you, and which is not more valuable than your carpet in exterior, does not seem a rarity worthy of much attention : I have, nevertheless, not paid less for it than you did for your carpet, nor am I less satisfied with my purchase than you are with yours. Confident, however, as I am of your judgment and candour, you must acknowledge that I have not been mistaken, when you shall be told, and have had a convincing proof, that in looking through one end of this tube you will behold whatever object you wish to see. I do not desire you to rely upon my word," added prince Ali, in presenting the tube ; "take it, and see if I impose upon you."

Prince Houssain took the ivory tube, and as he put that end to his eye which his brother had pointed out when he gave it him with the intention of seeing the princess Nourounnihar, and of learning how she was, prince Ali and his brother Ahmed, who had their eyes fixed upon him, were extremely astonished at seeing him suddenly change countenance, as if he were not only very much surprised, but afflicted at the same time. "Princes," exclaimed Houssain, "we have in vain undertaken our painful journey through the hopes of being rewarded with the possession of the charming Nourounnihar.; in a very few moments that amiable princess will be no more. I have seen her in her bed, surrounded by her women and eunuchs, who are all in tears, and who seem to expect nothing but to see her soul take its flight. Here, look yourselves ; behold her pitiable state, and join your tears to mine."

Prince Ali took the tube from Houssain. He looked through it ; and having beheld the same object, he presented it to prince Ahmed, that he might also see the melancholy and afflicting sight, so equally distressing to each of them.

When prince Ahmed had received the ivory tube from Ali, had looked through it and seen the princess, he thus addressed the two princes his brothers : "The princess Nourounnihar, my brothers, who is equally the object of our desires, is in a condition not far removed from death ; but it seems to me that, if we lose no time, she is still to be preserved from this fatal moment."

Prince Ahmed then drew from his bosom the artificial apple that he had purchased. "This apple," added he, showing it to the two princes, "which you now behold is not less costly than the carpet and ivory tube which you have brought from your travels. The occasion that now presents itself to make you witnesses to its wonderful virtues causes me not in the least to regret the forty purses which it cost me. Not to keep you any longer in suspense, I must inform you that it possesses the virtue, only by suffering a sick person to smell it, to restore him to perfect health, although he should be in his last agony. The experience I have had of it leaves it without a doubt in my mind ; and you may now see the effect of it upon the princess Nourounnihar, if we hasten to her assistance."

"If this be true," exclaimed prince Houssain, "we can make the greatest haste, and be transported in an instant into the chamber of the princess by means of my carpet. Let us, then,

lose no time ; but come and seat yourselves by my side, for it is large enough to hold us all without much inconvenience. Let us, however, in the first place, order our attendants to return immediately to the palace, where they will find us."

When they had done this, they seated themselves upon the carpet ; and as they were all three equally interested, they all instantly formed the same wish of being transported into the apartment of Nourounnihar. Their desires were fulfilled, and they were conveyed there so quickly that they seemed at the end of their journey almost before it begun.

The sudden and unexpected presence of the three princes terrified the women and the eunuchs belonging to the princess, as they could not in the least comprehend how these men should so instantly appear in the midst of them. They did not at first recollect the princes, and the eunuchs were on the point of attacking them, as persons who had penetrated to a place they were not permitted to approach : they soon, however, discovered their error, and recognised their persons.

Prince Ahmed no sooner perceived himself in the apartment of the princess then he got up from the carpet, as did also the other two princes, and going up to the bed, he applied the wonderful apple to her nose. In a few moments the princess opened her eyes, turned her head round on one side, and looking at those who stood near her, she raised herself in bed, and desired to be dressed. She did all this with the same ease and recollection as if she had just awakened from a long sleep. Her women immediately informed her that it was to the princes her cousins, and more particularly to prince Ahmed, that she was indebted for so sudden and complete a recovery. She expressed great pleasure at seeing them again, and thanked them all, more especially prince Ahmed, for their goodness. As she had mentioned her intention of dressing herself, the princes were satisfied with only saying that they were extremely happy to have arrived at a time when they were enabled to contribute to her recovery from the imminent danger in which they had beheld her, and with expressing their most ardent wishes for the long duration of her life ; they then immediately retired.

The princes went directly to throw themselves at the feet of the sultan their father, and pay him their respects. When they came into his presence, they found that the principal eunuch of the princess had already been and informed him of their unexpected arrival, and of the manner in which the princess had been by their means perfectly cured. The sultan received and embraced them with great transport ; and he experienced the greater joy at their return, because he was at the same instant informed of the perfect and wonderful recovery of the princess his niece, whom he loved as tenderly as if she had been his own daughter, and whom all the physicians had given over. After the mutual and usual compliments and inquiries on such occasions, each of the princes presented the rarity that he had severally procured —prince Houssain, the carpet ; prince Ali, the ivory tube ; and prince Ahmed, the artificial apple. And after each had spoken in praise of his own acquisition, they delivered them into the hands of the sultan, in the order of their age, and entreated him to declare to which he gave the preference, and thus to determine on which he bestowed, according to his promise, the princess Nourounnihar in marriage.

The sultan, after having listened with great attention and kindness to everything the princes wished to say in behalf of the rarities they had brought, without giving them the least interruption, remained for some time silent, as if he were considering what answer he should make. "I would, my children," said he, "declare my opinion in favour of one of you with the greatest pleasure, if I could do so with justice; but reflect in your own minds whether I can do so. It is indeed true that the princess my niece is indebted to you, prince Ahmed, for her recovery by means of your artificial apple; but I ask you, could it have been thus employed had not the ivory tube of prince Ali afforded you the opportunity of knowing the danger in which she was, and the carpet of prince Houssain have procured you the means of instantly coming to her assistance? You, prince Ali, by means of your ivory tube, had discovered the irreparable loss that yourself and brothers were about to experience in the death of the princess your cousin; and it must, therefore, be acknowledged that she is under a very great obligation to you; but you must allow that this information would have been inadequate to produce the advantage that has taken place without the artificial apple and the carpet. Nourounnihar, too, prince Houssain, must be ungrateful if she should be deficient in gratitude to you, on account of your carpet, which proved so necessary towards the accomplishment of her cure; but you must allow that it would not have been of the smallest use if you had not become acquainted with her dangerous illness by means of prince Ali's ivory tube, and if prince Ahmed had not employed his artificial apple in the cure itself. Thus, then, as neither the carpet, the ivory tube, nor the artificial apple possess the least preference the one over the other, but each appear equally rare and excellent, and as I can bestow the princess Nourounnihar only upon one of you, you must yourselves be aware that the only advantage you have derived from your travels is the glory of having equally contributed to the re-establishment of her health.

"If this be the fact," continued the sultan, "you see that it is necessary for me to have recourse to some other method to determine me in my choice of the one on whom I ought to bestow the princess; and as I wish this affair to be settled to-day, let each of you go immediately, and procure a bow and one arrow, and repair to the great plain without the walls where the horses are exercised. I will prepare to go there myself; and I now declare that I will give the princess Nourounnihar in marriage to him who shall shoot his arrow to the greatest distance, and I thank every one of you most cordially for the present which you have each brought me. I have many rarities in my cabinet, but I possess nothing that equals in singularity or utility either the carpet, the ivory tube, or the artificial apple, with all of which I

shall now enrich my collection. They will hold the first place, and I will preserve them there most carefully, not from curiosity only, but also for the purpose of making an advantageous use of them whenever proper occasions occur."

The three princes had nothing to say in reply to the sultan's decision. They left his presence, and each furnished himself with a bow and arrow, and with their attendants, who had all assembled as soon as they heard of their arrival, repaired to the plain, followed by an innumerable crowd of people.

The sultan did not make them wait; and as soon as he was arrived, prince Houssain, being the eldest, took his bow, and made the first shot. Prince Ali then drew his, and the arrow fell at some little distance beyond that of Houssain. Prince Ahmed shot the last, but the arrow went out of sight, and no one saw it fall. They ran and searched about; but notwithstanding all the care and diligence of the surrounding people, and of prince Ahmed himself, the arrow could nowhere, either far or near, be discovered. Although it was most probable that this arrow had been shot to a greater distance, and that he in consequence deserved the hand of the princess, yet as it was necessary for the arrow to be found to render that fact quite certain, notwithstanding every remonstrance he could use with the sultan, the latter determined in favour of prince Ali. He therefore gave orders to have preparations made to celebrate the nuptials, which were solemnized in a few days with the greatest magnificence.

Prince Houssain did not honour the festivities with his presence. As his affection for the princess was very sincere and strong, he had not sufficient fortitude of mind to bear patiently the mortification of beholding the object of his love in the arms of prince Ali, who, as he thought, did not deserve her more, as his affection for her was not more perfect than his own. His displeasure and disappointment was, on the contrary, so great, that he abandoned the court, renounced his right to the throne, and assumed the habit of a dervise.

Prince Ahmed, actuated by the same motives as his brother Houssain, did not assist at the nuptials of prince Ali and the princess Nourounnihar; but he did not, like him, renounce the world. As he could not comprehend how the arrow which he had shot could have thus become, as it were, invisible, he resolved to go and search so carefully for it that he should at least have nothing to reproach himself with. He went, therefore, to the spot where the arrows of prince Houssain and Ali had been found. From this place he walked on straight forward, looking both to the right and left as he went along. Led on, however, almost in spite of himself, he kept following the same direction, till some very elevated rocks obliged him to turn on one side if he wished to proceed,

In approaching these rocks the prince observed an arrow. He took it up, examined it, and was in the utmost astonishment at discovering it to be the very same that he had shot. "It certainly is the same," he exclaimed; "but neither I, nor any other mortal, could possibly have strength to send it to such a distance." And as he had found the arrow lying flat on the ground, not stuck in it by its point, he conjectured also that it must have struck against the rock, and had thus rebounded a little way back. "There must be," he added, "something very mysterious in so extraordinary a circumstance; and this mystery may be for my advantage. Fortune, perhaps, in having afflicted me by depriving me of the possession of what I thought would have formed the happiness of my life, has some greater blessing for me."

Meditating upon the subject, he entered into a hollow part of the rocks, which by their frequent projections formed numerous excavations of this sort; and as he cast his eyes from one part to another, he observed an iron door, which had no appearance of an opening. Pushing against it, he found it opened inwards; and he saw a gentle declivity, but no steps, by which he descended with the arrow in his hand. He naturally conjectured that he should soon be in perfect darkness, but he was immediately surrounded by a light totally different from that he had left; and on entering a very spacious opening, at the distance of fifty or sixty paces he perceived a magnificent palace, which he had hardly time to admire when at that very instant a lady of incomparable beauty and majestic air, adorned with the richest stuffs and most valuable jewels, advanced to the vestibule, accompanied by a band of females, of which he could easily distinguish her as their mistress.

Prince Ahmed no sooner observed the lady than he hastened to pay his respects to her; while the lady who saw him coming, addressed him, in an elevated tone of voice, saying, "Approach, prince Ahmed; you are welcome!"

The prince was very much surprised at hearing his own name in a country which he himself had not the least knowledge of, although it was so near the capital of his father; and he could not comprehend how he could be known to a lady of whom he was entirely ignorant. He accosted her by first throwing himself at her feet; and when he arose, "Madam," he replied, "I cannot but return you many thanks, on my arrival in a place where I was afraid that my curiosity had imprudently led me to penetrate too far, for the assurance you have given me that I am welcome; but, madam, may I be permitted to ask, without being guilty of any incivility, how it has happened that I am not, as I have understood from yourself, unknown to you, while I myself have not till this moment the least knowledge of you, although you live so near?" "Prince," replied the lady, "let us first go into the saloon; I can then answer your question when we are both more at our ease."

She led the way into the saloon, which was of a most singular structure; and the vault of the dome was decorated with gold and azure, with furniture of inestimable value, forming altogether so new and grand a sight that the prince could not help exclaiming "that he had never beheld anything similar, and could conceive nothing that could at all equal it." "I nevertheless assure you," replied the lady, "that this saloon is the least worth seeing in my whole palace, as you will yourself own when I shall have shown you all the apartments. She went to the upper end, and sat

down on a sofa; and when Ahmed had taken his place by her side, at her particular request, "Prince," said she, "you say that you are surprised that I should know who you are, although you are not at all acquainted with me; but your surprise will cease when I inform you who I am. You are, doubtless, not ignorant that the world is inhabited by genii as well as mortals. I am the daughter of one of these genii, who is the most powerful and distinguished of his race, and my name is Pari-Banou. You will, therefore, lay aside your astonishment at finding me acquainted with your name, as well as that of the sultan your father, the princes your brothers, and the princess Nourounnihar. I am acquainted with your affection for her, and also of your travels, of which I can inform you of all the circumstances, since I caused the artificial apple which you bought at Samarcand to be exposed for sale, as well as the carpet of prince Houssain, at Bisnagar, and the ivory tube of prince Ali, at Schiraz. This is sufficient to inform you that I am ignorant of nothing that relates to you. Let me only add one thing more, and that is, that you seem to me to be worthy of a better fate than to be united to the princess Nourounnihar; and in order that you should pursue that plan, as I was present when you shot the arrow you now have in your hand, and as I saw that it would not go even beyond prince Houssain's, I seized it in the air, and gave it sufficient velocity to strike it against the rocks near which you found it. It will now only depend upon yourself to take advantage of the opportunity which presents itself for you to become still more happy."

As the fairy Pari-Banou pronounced these last words in a different tone of voice, and cast a tender yet modest look upon prince Ahmed, then blushed, and instantly fixed her eyes on the ground, the prince had no difficulty in comprehending the sort of happiness she meant. He reflected that the princess Nourounnihar could never be his, and that the fairy Pari-Banou infinitely surpassed her, as much in beauty and powers of attraction as in the qualities of mind and immensity of riches, at least as far as he could judge from the magnificence of the palace where he was; and he blessed the moment that the idea of going a second time to look for his arrow had struck him, and in having yielded to that inclination which seemed to draw him towards the fresh object that had inflamed his heart. "If I might, madam," he replied, "become your slave, and have the power of contemplating and admiring so many charms for the remainder of my life, I should be the happiest of mortals. Pardon my boldness in making such a request; and do not, in refusing it, disdain to receive a prince who is entirely devoted to you within the circle of your court."

"I have been, prince," answered the fairy, "for a long time mistress of my own wishes and actions, through the kind consent of my parents; but it is not as a slave that I wish to admit you into my court, but as the master of me, and everything that belongs to me; and in pledging your faith to me, and accepting me as your wife, everything will become mutually our own. I trust that you will not form a bad opinion of me from my making this offer. I have already told you that I am mistress of my actions; and I must now add, that the custom amongst fairies is not the same as with women towards men. These never make any advances, and would esteem it a disgrace to do so: but we consider that they are obliged to us."

Prince Ahmed made no answer to this speech; penetrated with gratitude, he thought he could not show it better than by attempting to kiss the hem of her robe. But the fairy did not give him time; she presented her hand, on which he impressed a fervent kiss. "Prince Ahmed," said the fairy, while he held it, "will you not now pledge your faith to me, as I do mine most firmly to you?" "Ah, madam," exclaimed he, overcome with excess of joy, "how can I do otherwise—what can delight me more? Yes, my sultana, my queen, I give up my whole heart to you without the least reserve." "Then," replied Pari-Banou, "you are my husband, and I am now wholly yours."

Some of the attendants, who had been in the saloon with her, and understood the intention of their mistress, went out, and in a short time after they brought in several dishes and some excellent wine.

When prince Ahmed had eaten and drunk as much as he wished, Pari-Banou led him through all the different apartments, where he beheld diamonds, rubies, emeralds, and every sort of precious stone, mixed with pearls, agate, jasper, porphyry, and all the varieties of the most valuable marble, besides furniture of various descriptions and of inestimable value. All these rich materials were employed in so profuse a manner, that so far from having ever seen anything that resembled it, the prince candidly acknowledged to the fairy that nothing in the whole world could equal it. "If, prince," said Pari-Banou, "you are so delighted with my palace, which I own possesses great beauties, what would you think of the palaces belonging to the chiefs of the genii, which are still more rich, spacious, and magnificent? I must also take you to admire the beauty of my garden; but that shall serve for another time. Night approaches, and it is time to sit down to table."

The hall into which the fairy and prince Ahmed went, and where the table was set out, was the last apartment that remained for him to see; and he found it not in the least inferior to all the others he had beheld. He was much struck, on entering, with an immense number of lights, all perfumed with amber, and they were arranged with so much symmetry that it was a pleasure to look at them, from the total absence of everything like confusion. He admired also the large sideboard covered with golden vases and other vessels, the workmanship of which rendered them still more valuable. Several groups of females, of great beauty, all superbly dressed, began a concert of vocal and instrumental music, the most harmonious ever heard. They sat down, and Pari-Banou was very attentive in helping prince Ahmed to the most delicate things, all of which she named to him as she requested him to taste them. He gave them all the praise they deserved, and said that the present feast surpassed all he had ever partaken of among mortals. He spoke in the same terms of the excellence of the

wines, which both he and the fairy began to drink when the dessert was served, which consisted of fruits, sweetmeats, and other things well suited to give a better flavour to the wine.

When the dessert was finished, Pari-Banou and prince Ahmed rose from the table, which was instantly removed, and seated themselves more at their ease on a sofa furnished with cushions of rich silk stuff, delicately embroidered with large flowers in various colours. At this instant a great many genii and fairies entered the hall, and began a most surprising dance, which they continued till the fairy and prince rose. The genii and fairies, still continuing to dance, then went out of the hall, and preceded the newly-married pair until they came to the door of the chamber where the nuptial bed was prepared; when they ranged themselves in two ranks, to let the prince and fairy pass on. They then retired, and left them at liberty to go to rest.

The festive rejoicings of this marriage continued for several days; and Pari-Banou found no difficulty in diversifying the entertainments by fresh preparations and fresh dishes, fresh concerts and fresh dances, with a variety of spectacles all so uncommon, that prince Ahmed would never have been able even to have thought of them while living with mortals had his life lasted a thousand years.

It was the intention of the fairy not only to give the prince the strongest proofs of the sincerity and excess of her love, but she wished him also to suppose that as there was nothing at the court of the sultan his father, nor anywhere else, that could be put into competition with what was to be found with her, not to mention her own beauty and charms, so also that he would find nothing comparable to the happiness he would enjoy with her, in order that he might attach himself entirely to her. She completely succeeded in her intentions. The affection of prince Ahmed did not diminish by the possession of the object: it increased indeed to that degree that it was no longer in his own power to control his love even if he had resolved to conquer it.

At the end of six months, the prince, who had always felt a great regard and respect for the sultan his father, conceived a strong desire to learn some intelligence of him; and as he could not satisfy his anxiety but by going in person to obtain the information he wished, he spoke to Pari-Banou on the subject, and requested her leave to put it into execution. This speech very much alarmed the fairy, who feared it might only be a pretence for abandoning her. "In what," she said to him, "have I given you cause for discontent, that you request this permission? Is it possible that you have forgotten that you have pledged your faith to me, and that you now no longer love me, who am still so passionately attached to you? You ought to be convinced of my love by the proofs I never cease from giving you."

"I am, my queen," replied prince Ahmed, "completely convinced of your affection, which I should be unworthy of did I not show my gratitude by a love equally ardent. If you are offended at my request, I beg you will pardon me; and there is no reparation I am not willing to make. Yet I have surely done nothing that ought to displease you, for I have only been guided in it from my respect for the sultan my father, whom I should wish to relieve from the pain he must feel by my long absence. And his affliction is the greater, as I have reason to believe that he supposes me dead. But since you do not acquiesce in my affording him this consolation, I will act as you wish, for there is nothing in the world I am not ready to do to oblige you."

Prince Ahmed, who loved Pari-Banou in his heart as perfectly as he had assured her by his words, ceased from urging his request, and the fairy showed how satisfied she was with his submission; nevertheless, as he could not entirely abandon the design he had formed, he affected at different times to converse about the amiable and excellent qualities the sultan of India possessed, and especially the marks of affection he had shown for himself in particular: he did this with the hope that she would at last yield to his wishes.

Prince Ahmed judged rightly of the sultan his father, for in the midst of all the rejoicings on account of the nuptials of Prince Ali and the princess Nourounnihar, he was most sensibly afflicted at the absence of his two sons. It was not long before he was informed of the resolution prince Houssain had taken to abandon the world, and of the place he had chosen for his retreat. Like a good father, who made a part of his happiness consist in the society of his own children, particularly when they were worthy of his affection, he had much rather that they had remained at court, and attached themselves to his person. As he could not, however, disapprove of the choice he had made in endeavouring to make himself better and more holy, he bore his absence with fortitude. He made also every possible enquiry after prince Ahmed. He sent courtiers into all the provinces of his dominions, with orders to the governors to detain him, and oblige him to return to his court; but he had not the success he hoped for, and his affliction, instead of lessening, daily increased. He often conversed on the subject with his grand vizier. "Vizier," he would say, "you know that of all the princes Ahmed is the one I love the most tenderly, and you are not ignorant of the means I have taken to endeavour to discover him, but without success. The misery I feel is so strong that I shall at length sink under it if you have not compassion upon me; if you have any interest in my preservation, I conjure you to assist me with your advice."

The grand vizier was not less attached to the person of his sovereign than zealous to acquit himself with honour in his administration of the public affairs of the state; and in reflecting upon the different methods by which he endeavoured to lessen the affliction of his master, he remembered to have heard some extraordinary accounts of an enchantress. He proposed, therefore, to the sultan to send for and consult her. The sultan consented; and the grand vizier, after enquiring where she was to be found, brought her with him.

The sultan addressed the enchantress as follows: "The affliction I have been in since the nuptials of my son prince Ali with the princess Nourounnihar, on account of the absence of prince Ahmed, is so public and well known that you, without doubt, are not ignorant of it. Can you, then, by your skill in magic, inform me what is become of him? —whether he be still alive?—where he is?—what he is doing?—and whether I may ever expect to see him again?" In order to answer all the questions of the sultan, the enchantress replied, "However skilful, sire, I may be in my profession, it is, nevertheless, impossible for me to satisfy your majesty immediately upon the subject of your inquiries; but if you will allow me until to-morrow, I will give your majesty an answer." The sultan granted her this delay, and dismissed her, with the promise of recompensing her very handsomely if her answer was at all adequate to his wishes.

The enchantress returned the next morning, and the grand vizier again presented her to the sultan. "Notwithstanding all the diligence I have made," said the enchantress, addressing herself to the sultan, "according to the rules of my art, in endeavouring to comply with your majesty's wishes, I have only been able to discover one thing—and that is, that prince Ahmed is not dead. Of this fact your majesty may rest assured; but I have been unable to find out in what place he is." The sultan of India was obliged to be satisfied with this answer, which left him nearly in the same distressing situation respecting the fate of his son as he was in before.

Let us now return to prince Ahmed. He so frequently turned the conversation he had with the fairy towards the sultan his father, though without again mentioning the desire he felt to see him, that this very forbearance made her comprehend his design. As she perceived, therefore, that he refrained from it through the fear he had of displeasing her, after the refusal he had before met with, she concluded that his love for her, of which he did not cease from giving her every possible mark, was very sincere; and then judging by her own feelings of the injustice she was guilty of, in thus violently opposing the natural affection of a son for his father, she resolved to grant what she could not but observe he so ardently desired.

She one day, therefore, said to him, "The permission, prince, which you requested of me to go and see your father afforded me reasonable grounds to fear that it was only a pretext to abandon me, and I had no other motive than what arose from this circumstance in refusing your request; but as I am now as fully convinced from your actions as from your protestations that I can rely upon your constancy, I have changed my opinion, and grant you the permission you formerly requested: but it must, nevertheless, be upon this condition, that you first promise me your absence shall not be long, but that you will return very soon.

Prince Ahmed wished to throw himself at the feet of the fairy, to show how much he was penetrated with gratitude, but she prevented him. "My sultana," he exclaimed, "I know the value of the favour you have granted me, but I want expressions to thank you as I wish. Supply my inability, I conjure you; and, whatever words you can use, be assured my feelings will be still stronger. You are right in supposing the promise you require of me will not pain me: I give it to you the more freely, as it is not possible that I can live without you. I will now, therefore, take my departure; and by the diligence with which I shall return, you will be convinced that I have done so, not from the fear of perjury, if I should break my promise, but because I have followed my own wishes, which extend only to pass my whole life with you; and if sometimes, with your own consent, I leave you, I will always avoid the pain of a long absence."

Pari-Banou was the more delighted with these sentiments of prince Ahmed as they entirely freed her from the suspicion she had formed, that the eagerness he expressed to see the sultan of India was merely a specious pretext to break the faith he had pledged to her. "Depart, prince," she said, "whenever you please; but do not take it ill that I first give you some advice upon the manner in which you ought to conduct yourself during your journey. In the first place, I do not think it would be proper for you to mention your marriage to the sultan, nor my rank and situation, nor the place of your residence since you saw him. Beg him to be satisfied with knowing that you are happy, and tell him that the motive for your paying him this visit is chiefly to lessen his uneasiness at being uncertain of your fate." She then gave him twenty horsemen to accompany him, all well mounted and equipped. When everything was ready, prince Ahmed took leave of Pari-Banou, embracing her, and renewing the promise he had made her of returning as soon a possible. They brought him a horse which the fairy had ordered to be prepared for him, and which, besides being most richly caparisoned, was also much more beautiful, and of greater value, than any in the sultan's stables. He mounted it very gracefully, and after bidding the fairy farewell, he set out.

As soon as prince Ahmed entered the city, the people were delighted to see him, and received him with acclamations of joy. The most part of them left their business, and accompanied him in crowds till he arrived at the sultan's apartment. His father received and embraced him with the greatest joy, complaining, nevertheless, in a manner which denoted his paternal affection, of the affliction into which his long absence had thrown him; "and this absence," added the sultan, "has been the cause of so much the more pain as, after fate had determined to your disadvantage in favour of your brother prince Ali, I was afraid that your despair had caused you to commit some rash action."

"Sire," replied prince Ahmed, "I will leave it to your majesty to reflect whether, after having lost the princess Nourounnihar, who had been the sole object of my wishes, I could resolve to be a witness to the happiness of prince Ali. If I had been capable of an indignity of this nature, what would the court and the whole city have thought of my love?—what would even your majesty have thought of it? Love is a passion which will not abandon us at our pleasure: it completely subjects us—it tyrannizes; and a true lover has no longer the use of reason.

"Your majesty may remember," continued the prince, "that in drawing my bow, the most extraordinary thing happened to me that was ever known, for it was impossible, even in a plain so large, so level, and so unincumbered as that in which the horses are exercised, to find the arrow I had shot; in consequence of which I lost the acquisition of an object that was not in justice less due to my affection than to that of the princes my brothers. Conquered, as it were, by the caprice of fate, I did not pass my time in useless complaints; but to satisfy my restless and uneasy mind, without being perceived, I returned by myself to the place, in order to look for my arrow. I searched for it in every spot I could think of, to the right and to the left of the places where those of the princes Houssain and Ali had been found, and where I thought it most likely that mine had fallen also; but all my endeavours were useless. I did not, however, give over, but pursued my inquiries, continuing to proceed straight forward in the line in which I thought it was likely to fall. I had already proceeded more than a league, looking on both sides as I went along, and sometimes even going out of the road, if anything at all appeared like an arrow, to examine it, when I began to reflect that it was not possible for mine to have gone so far. I stopped and asked myself whether I was not insane to think that I could have strength enough to shoot an arrow to so great a distance, when not one of the most ancient heroes who had been famous for their strength had ever done so. I thus reasoned with myself, and was about to abandon my enterprise; but when I was going to put my resolution into execution, I felt myself led on, as it were, against my will; and after walking four leagues, and till the plain was terminated by some steep rocks, I perceived an arrow. I ran and took it up, and knew it to be the very same I had shot, but which had not been found either within the space or at the time it was necessary.

"Far, however, from thinking," continued prince Ahmed, "that your majesty had been guilty of an injustice in determining in favour of prince Ali, I interpreted what had happened quite differently; and I did not doubt but there was some mystery attached to this circumstance which was for my advantage, and that I ought not to neglect anything that would tend to this development: and, in fact, I had no need to seek further. But this is a mystery concerning which I entreat your majesty not to take it ill if I remain silent; and I request you to be satisfied with knowing from my own lips that I am happy and contented with my lot. In the midst of my happiness, there was one thing only that troubled me, or was capable of affording me uneasiness, and that was the distress I had no doubt you experienced from your ignorance of what had become of me after I thus disappeared from your court. I thought it, therefore, my duty to come and free you from this unpleasant state, as I have now done. This was my only motive for coming: and the only favour I ask of your majesty in return is, to permit me to come, from time to time, to pay my respects to you, and inform myself of the state of your health."

"My son," replied the sultan, "I cannot

possibly refuse the permission you request; I should, nevertheless, have preferred that you had determined to come and live near me. Tell me, at least, by what means I can learn any intelligence of you, whenever you should fail to come here yourself, or whenever your presence might be necessary."

"Sire," replied prince Ahmed, "what your majesty demands of me forms a part of the mystery I have mentioned; I entreat you, then, to suffer me to be silent on this point. I will so frequently return to pay my respects that I only fear you will think me too importunate, rather than accuse me of negligence in not coming when my presence might be necessary."

The sultan, notwithstanding this explanation, continued to express a desire that the prince would inform him more fully concerning the mystery of his long absence.

"Sire," said Ahmed—"if I have made any mystery to your majesty of what has happened to me, and of the plan I pursued after having found my arrow, it was from circumstances over which I have no control, and I very much wish you would excuse me from telling you further, and suffer me to enjoy the happiness of our mutual affection, without my appearing to possess any interested motive. But the request of a father is a command to a son who, like me, makes it his duty to obey him in everything. I cannot however, express how much against my inclination, and how repugnant to my feelings, this request is. If I cease from coming to pay my respects to you, you may consider it as a consequence of your curiosity. I therefore now ask you to pardon me, and to consider that it is yourself who will reduce me to this extremity."

The sultan did not press prince Ahmed any more upon this subject. "My son," said he, "I do not wish to penetrate any further into your secret; I leave it entirely to yourself: but I must say, that your presence affords me the greatest pleasure you can bestow upon me; that I have not received so much happiness for a long time past as you now afford me; and that you will be truly welcome whenever your own affairs, or your inclination, may induce you to come."

Prince Ahmed remained only three days at the court of the sultan his father. He set out very early on the fourth morning, and Pari-Banou saw him return with the greater joy as she did not expect to see him so soon; and the haste he made urged her to condemn herself for having suspected him of being guilty of infidelity towards her, so contrary to his most solemn promise. She did not dissemble her position, but frankly confessed her weakness, and requested his pardon.

The union of these two lovers was hereafter so perfect that the one did not breathe a wish unfelt by the other.

About a month after the return of prince Ahmed, the fairy observed that, after having given her an account of his visit, and mentioned the conversation he had had with his father, and that he should get permission to come and pay his respects to him very often, this prince did not speak of the sultan

any more than if no such person existed, although he had formerly constantly turned the conversation to him; and she concluded that he abstained from it on her account. She, therefore, one day took an opportunity of speaking upon the subject.

"Tell me, my prince," she said, "have you forgotten the sultan your father, and do you not remember the promise you made him that you would frequently go and see him? I have not forgotten what you said to me on your return, and I now put you in mind of it that you may not wait any longer before you perform your promise for the first time."

"Madam," replied prince Ahmed, in the same cheerful tone of voice in which the fairy had spoken, "I do not feel myself culpable for the negligence and forgetfulness with which you accuse me, because I would rather suffer the reproach which you now make, without deserving it, than be exposed to the chance of a refusal, by showing too much haste to obtain what it might give you pain to grant." "Prince," replied the fairy, "I do not wish you to retain this circumspect conduct on my account; and that the same thing may not happen again, as it is now a month since you have seen the sultan your father, I think you never ought to let a longer time than this elapse between your visits to him. Begin, then, to-morrow, and continue to visit him every month, without having either to speak to me on the subject, or wait till I mention it. I consent very willingly to this plan."

Prince Ahmed set out the next day, with the same attendants, but better equipped; while he himself was still more magnificently mounted and dressed than he had been the first time. He was received by the sultan with the same joy and satisfaction as before. He continued in that way for many months regularly to go and pay his respects, but always in a richer and more magnificent style.

At length some viziers who were favourites of the sultan, and who judged of the grandeur and power of prince Ahmed by the different proofs he thus gave of it, abused the liberty the sultan allowed them of speaking to him, in order to excite some emotions of anger in the sultan's breast against his son. They represented to him that it was no more than common prudence in him to wish to know where the prince's place of retreat was; whence he derived the means of living at so vast an expense, as he himself had assigned him no establishment or fixed revenue that could enable him to come to court, which he did only as a sort of boast, and to let him see that he had no occasion for the sultan's liberality to enable him to live like a prince; and that, in short, they were afraid that he intended to excite a rebellion against his person, and dethrone him.

"You mean to amuse me," replied the sultan. "My son loves me; and I am the more convinced of his affection and fidelity, because I have not given him the least cause to be dissatisfied with me."

Upon this, one of the favourites said, "Although,

11

sire, in the opinion of every sensible person, your majesty could not have taken a better plan than that which you followed in directing your choice respecting the marriage of the princess Nourounnihar with one of the princes your sons, yet who can tell whether prince Ahmed has submitted to the decision of chance with the same resignation as prince Houssain. May not he think that he himself was alone worthy of her, and that your majesty, in bestowing her upon one of his elder brothers in preference to him, and in suffering the matter to be decided by chance, has been guilty of an injustice towards him.

"Your majesty may perhaps say," continued this malicious favourite, "that prince Ahmed has not shown the least mark of discontent, that our fears are vain, and that we are wrong in suggesting any suspicion of this nature, and which may not have the least foundation against a prince of his rank; but, sire, it is possible that these suspicions are well founded. Your majesty is not ignorant that, in so delicate and important an affair, it is necessary to be very careful. You should consider that dissimulation on the part of the prince may be only for the purpose of deceiving you; and that the danger is also the more to be dreaded, as prince Ahmed seems to reside at no great distance from your capital. If your majesty, also, had paid the same attention to everything as we have done, you might have observed that every time the prince comes to visit you, both he and his attendants are quite fresh; even their horses are not the least fatigued, and appear as if they merely came from their exercise. These are evident marks that prince Ahmed resides in the neighbourhood, and for your own preservation, as well as for the good of the state, it belongs to you to take such steps as you judge most proper."

When the favourite had concluded, the sultan put an end to the conversation by saying, "However all this may be, I do not believe that my son Ahmed can be so wicked as you wish to persuade me; I am, nevertheless, obliged to you for your advice, and do not doubt that you have said nothing but with the best intentions."

The sultan spoke in this manner to conceal the impression their discourse had made upon his mind. He could not help, however, being greatly alarmed; and he resolved to observe the conduct of prince Ahmed, without even informing his grand vizier. He ordered the enchantress to be sent for privately, and had her introduced secretly, and conducted to his apartment. "You told me the truth," said the sultan to her, on her entrance, "when you assured me that my son Ahmed was not dead; but you must now afford me a further satisfaction. Although I have since discovered him, and he now comes every month to pay me a visit, yet I have not been able to learn from him in what spot he has fixed his residence; and I do not wish to put such a restraint upon him as to compel him to tell me against his inclination. You know that he is here; and as he is accustomed to depart without taking leave either of me or any one else, you must lose no time. Go to-day, and place yourself on the road he takes, and observe

him so well that you may know to what place he retires; and then bring me the information."

After leaving the palace, the enchantress having learned the spot where prince Ahmed had shot his arrow, she instantly went and concealed herself so carefully among the rocks that no one could perceive her.

Prince Ahmed set off the next morning as usual at daybreak, without taking leave of his father or any of the courtiers. The enchantress saw him, and followed him with her eyes till she lost sight both of him and his attendants.

As these rocks formed an insurmountable barrier to mortals either on foot or horseback, on account of their being so steep, the enchantress thought that one of these two things must be the fact: either that the prince retired into a cave, or into some subterraneous place where genii and fairies took up their abode. As soon as she supposed that the prince and his attendants had disappeared, and had gone into the cavern which she conjectured to be there, she came out of the place in which she had concealed herself; and going into all the recesses as far as she could, she looked about on all sides of her, walking backwards and forwards several times. But notwithstanding all the care she took, she could not perceive any entrance, nor even the iron door, which had not escaped the sight of prince Ahmed: in fact, this door was incapable of being seen but by men, and only by such of those as the fairy Pari-Banou wished to see it, and not at all by women.

The enchantress, after much useless trouble, was obliged to be satisfied with the discovery she had already made. She returned, therefore, to give an account of her proceedings to the sultan; and having related the several steps she had taken, she added: "Your majesty may easily conjecture, after what I have the honour of informing you, that it will not be a very difficult matter for me to afford you all the satisfaction you can wish respecting the conduct of prince Ahmed. I will not say what I think at present, because I would rather make it known to your majesty in a way that can leave no doubt on your mind. In order to accomplish it, I only request time and patience, and full permission to follow my own plans, without being obliged to inform you of the means I make use of."

"You shall do as you please," said the sultan:—"go—you are mistress of your actions; and I will wait with patience to see the effect of your promises."

In order to give her some encouragement, he presented her with a very valuable diamond, telling her at the same time that it was only the beginning of a greater reward, when she should complete the important service she had undertaken.

The enchantress waited till the next month had elapsed; and a day or two before it was quite over, she did not fail to go on foot to the rocks, and wait at the very same spot in which she had lost sight of prince Ahmed and his attendants, for the purpose of putting the scheme she had formed into execution.

The next morning, when the prince, as usual, came out of the iron door, with the same attendants as always accompanied him, he passed close to the enchantress, whom he did not know to be one; and observing that she was lying down, with her head resting against a piece of the rock, and that she complained like one in great pain, compassion induced him to go nearer and enquire what was the matter with her, to see whether he could afford her any assistance. The cunning enchantress, without lifting up her head, but looking at the prince so as still more to excite his compassion, replied in broken and interrupted words, as if she had great difficulty in breathing, that she had left her house in the city, and upon the road was seized with a most violent fever, so that her strength quite failed her; and she was obliged to stop, and remain in the state they then saw her, in a place very distant from any house, and without the hopes of being relieved. "My good woman," said prince Ahmed, "you are not so far from assistance as you may suppose. I will have you conveyed to a place very near this, where you shall not only have every attention paid you, but will very soon be cured. You have, therefore, only to rise and suffer one of my people to take you behind him."

At hearing this, the cunning enchantress did not refuse the kind offer he so generously made her; and in order to show rather by her actions than her words that she accepted of it, she made several efforts to rise, pretending all the time that her illness prevented her. On this, two of the attendants dismounted, assisted her in getting up, and placed her on horseback behind another. While they were remounting, the prince turned back, and went first towards the iron door, which was opened by one of the horsemen. He went in; and when he arrived at the court of Pari-Banou's palace, without dismounting, he sent one of the attendants to say he wished to speak to her.

The fairy made the greater haste, as she could not conceive the motive that induced the prince to return so suddenly; who, without giving her time to enquire the reason, said, "I entreat you, my princess," pointing towards the enchantress, whom two of the attendants had taken from the horse, and then supported by holding her arms, "to have compassion on this poor woman. I found her in the state you see, and have promised her all the assistance she may require; and I recommend her to you, as I am well satisfied you will not have her neglected, either from your own kind consideration, or because it is my request."

Pari-Banou, who had not taken her eyes off the pretended sick woman during the whole of prince Ahmed's speech, ordered two of her women to take her into an apartment of the palace, and also to take as much care of her as they would of her own person.

Prince Ahmed then took leave of the fairy, and again pursued his journey, and soon arrived, with his attendants, at the court of his father, who received him in his usual manner, endeavouring to appear as if nothing had happened, and that the conversation which his favourites had held had excited no suspicion in his breast.

In the meantime, the two females conducted the enchantress into a very beautiful apartment richly furnished. They at first made her sit down on a sofa, where, while she supported her head against a cushion of gold brocade, they prepared a bed near her on the same sofa, the mattresses of which were made of satin richly embroidered, the sheets were of the finest linen, and the counterpane of cloth of gold. When they had assisted her in getting into bed—for the enchantress still continued to pretend that the fever fit with which she had been attacked tormented her so much that she could not assist herself—one of them went out of the room, and came back very soon with a basin of the finest porcelain containing a liquor which she presented to the enchantress, while the other female assisted her in setting up. "Take this liquor," said she who brought it; "it is water from the fountain of lions, and is a sovereign remedy for fevers of any kind. You will find the good effects of it in less than an hour."

To act her part the better, the enchantress suffered them to entreat her for a long time, as if she had an insurmountable dislike to drink this liquor. She at last took the basin, and swallowed its contents, shaking her head at the same time as if she did the greatest violence to her feelings. When she had again laid down, the two females covered her all over. "Remain as you are," said she who had brought the basin, "and even go to sleep if the desire should come upon you. We will now leave you, and hope to find you quite cured when we return an hour."

The attendants came back at the time mentioned, and found the enchantress risen, dressed, and sitting on the sofa, from which she got up the moment she saw them come in. "O admirable draught!" she exclaimed; "it has produced its effect much sooner than you told me; and I have been a long time impatiently waiting for you, to entreat you to conduct me to your charitable and excellent mistress, that I may thank her for her great goodness."

These two females, who were of the fairy race as well as their mistress, after making known how much they rejoiced in her speedy cure, walked on before to show her the way; and they conducted her through many apartments, all of which were more superb than that she had been in, until they came to the most magnificent and richly-furnished saloon of any in the whole palace.

Pari-Banou was seated in this, on a throne of massive gold enriched with diamonds, rubies, and pearls of an extraordinary size; and on each side of her there were a great number of fairies, all extremely handsome, and superbly dressed. The enchantress was quite dazzled at the sight of so much magnificence: she could not utter a word, even to thank the fairy as she intended, but remained, after prostrating herself at the foot of the throne, like a person struck motionless. Pari-Banou spared her the trouble of addressing her, by immediately saying, "I am very happy, my good woman, that I now find you in a fit state to pursue your journey. I do not wish to detain you, but perhaps you would have no objection to see my palace? Go with my women; they will show you things worth seeing."

The enchantress continued in her state of astonishment, and again prostrated herself before the throne till her face touched the carpet which covered the foot of it. She then took her leave, without having the courage to utter a single word, and was conducted by the two fairies who before accompanied her. She was shown all the apartments, one after the other, through which Pari-Banou herself had carried prince Ahmed, the first time he presented himself before her, as has already been mentioned; but what most surprised her, after having observed the whole palace, was what the two fairies told her respecting her mistress; that all this was but a small part of her grandeur and power; that in different parts of her dominions she had other palaces, even more than they could tell, all on different plans and of different styles of architecture, and not less magnificent. While conversing with her, they conducted her to the iron door through which prince Ahmed had brought her; they opened it, and wished her a good journey. She then took her leave, and thanked them for the trouble they had been at on her account.

After proceeding a few steps, the enchantress turned round to observe the door that she might know it again: but she looked in vain. It was now invisible with respect to her, as well as to every other female, as has been before remarked. She now went back to the sultan well satisfied, except as to this one circumstance, of the success of her plan; and with having so happily executed the commission she had been charged with. As soon as she got back to the city, she went along the most private streets, and was introduced by the same secret door as before into the palace. The sultan, being informed of her arrival, ordered her into his presence; and as he observed that she had rather a gloomy cast on her countenance, he thought she had not succeeded, and immediately said, "I conjecture from your looks that your journey has been unsuccessful, and that you can give me no information concerning the business I entrusted to your care." "Sire," she replied, "your majesty will give me leave to say, that it is not from my appearance that you ought to judge whether I have succeeded in the commission you have honoured me with, but from the faithful report I shall make of what I have done, and of everything that has happened to me, by which you will find that I have neither forgotten nor neglected anything that could render me worthy of your majesty's approbation."

The enchantress then related the particulars of her journey, giving a glowing account of the riches and splendour of Pari-Banou; and having finished this account of the success of her commission, went on with her discourse in these terms: "What does your majesty think of these unheard-of riches? Perhaps you will say that you are in the greatest admiration at them, and that you rejoice at the great fortune to which prince Ahmed is arrived, by thus partaking of them in conjunction with the fairy. With respect to myself, sire, I entreat your majesty to pardon me if I take the liberty of saying that I am of a different opinion, and that I am even greatly alarmed when I think of the misfortunes that may in consequence

happen to him. This was the cause of that uneasiness which your majesty remarked in my countenance, and which I was unable entirely to conceal from you. I am sure that prince Ahmed is naturally of too good a disposition to undertake anything that is hostile to your majesty's interest; but who can be sure that the fairy will not, through her attractions, her caresses, and the influence she has by these means acquired over the mind of her husband, inspire him with the horrid wish of supplanting you, and seizing the crown? It is, therefore, your majesty's business to pay every attention that so important an affair deserves."

However satisfied the sultan of India was of the excellence of prince Ahmed's natural disposition, he could not help being affected at her speech. "I am much obliged to you," he said, "both for the trouble you have given yourself, and for your good advice: I am aware of its importance, and I shall take the opinion of others on the subject."

At the very moment when they had come to announce the arrival of the enchantress to the sultan, he was conversing with the same favourites who had excited those suspicions in his breast against prince Ahmed. These were still further increased by the enchantress. He then returned to his favourites, and took her with him. He partly informed them of what he had learned; and having communicated to them the reason why he was fearful the fairy would alter the disposition of the prince, he asked them by what means they thought he might be enabled to prevent so great an evil.

One of the favourites then spoke in the name of the rest: "In order, sire, to counteract this evil, as your majesty knows the person who is the author of it, as he is now in the midst of your court, and as you have the full power to do it, you ought not to hesitate, but instantly to arrest him; and, I do not say to take away his life—that perhaps would be going too far—but, at least to imprison him very closely for the rest of his life." All the other favourites were unanimous in applauding his advice.

The enchantress, however, who thought this mode of proceeding too violent, requested the sultan's leave to say a few words; and when she had obtained it, she said, "I am persuaded, sire, that it is from the zealous interest which these counsellors have in your majesty's welfare that they are induced to propose to you the arrest and imprisonment of prince Ahmed; but if by some other less violent method the sultan can secure himself from the wicked designs that prince Ahmed may form against him, without the least danger of sullying his majesty's glory, or of any person suspecting that he has any ill design, would it not be right to pursue that method? If his majesty has any confidence in my advice, he will induce prince Ahmed, from a point of honour, to procure him certain advantages through the power of his fairy, under the pretence of deriving a considerable benefit from them, as genii and fairies can easily accomplish things that are far above the power of mortals. For instance, every time your majesty wishes to take the field, you are obliged to be at a considerable expense, not only for pavilions and tents for yourself and army, but also for camels, mules, and other beasts of burthen, only to carry all this apparatus. Now, could you not prevail upon him, through the influence he has over the fairy, to procure a pavilion so small that it might be carried in the hand, and yet so large that your whole army might encamp under it? I need not say any more to your majesty. If the prince should procure this pavilion, there are many other requests of a similar nature which you can make, till at last he will be obliged to sink under either the difficulty or the impossibility of executing them."

The sultan asked the favourites if they had anything better to propose; and as he observed that they were quite silent, he determined to follow the advice of the enchantress, as it seemed to him to be the most rational and best suited to the mildness of his disposition.

The next day, when prince Ahmed presented himself before the sultan, who was conversing with his favourites, and when he had taken his seat by his side, as his presence did not cause any restraint, the conversation continued for some time to turn upon different topics. At last the sultan, addressing himself to prince Ahmed, said, "When you first appeared and relieved me from the misery in which the great length of your absence had plunged me, you made a mystery of the place you had chosen for your retreat. Satisfied with seeing you, and being told by yourself that you were contented with your situation, I did not desire to penetrate into your secret when I found you did not wish it. I know not what reason you may have had to pursue this conduct towards a father who, like me, has always shown that he took the most lively interest in your happiness. I now know, indeed, in what that happiness consists, and I sincerely rejoice in it with you. I heartily approve the steps you have taken in marrying a fairy so worthy of being beloved, so rich and so powerful, as my information, which is very good, points out. In the high rank to which you are elevated, I ask you not only to continue upon the good terms with me that you have hitherto done, but that you will employ your influence with the fairy to obtain her assistance in anything I may have occasion for; and I shall at this moment put your influence to the test. If you will consider the pleasure you can afford me, I am sure you will not make any difficulty in requesting the fairy to give you a pavilion so small that you can hold it in your hand, and yet sufficiently large to contain my whole army—particularly when you inform her it is for me. The difficulty of the thing will not cause you to be refused, for all the world knows that fairies can do most extraordinary things."

Prince Ahmed was not in the least prepared to expect that his father would make such a request of him, as it appeared to him not only very difficult, but absolutely impossible; for, although he was not entirely ignorant of the great power of genii and fairies, he, nevertheless, very much doubted whether that power was able to produce such a pavilion as he requested. Besides, he

would much rather that he should have required anything else of him than to expose him to the risk of displeasing Pari-Banou, who was so dear to him; and on account of the vexation he felt from what had passed, he left the court two days sooner than his usual time. As soon as he arrived, the fairy, before whom he had hitherto constantly presented himself with an open and contented countenance, inquired of him the cause of the change she observed. For a long time the prince resisted her importunity, but at length was obliged to satisfy her.

"You may have observed," he said, "that I have till now been satisfied with your affection for me, and have never requested any favour of you but to continue your regard. After possessing, indeed, so amiable a wife, what could I wish for more! I am not, however, ignorant of the greatness of your power; but I had made it a point not to put it to the proof. Consider then, I entreat you, that it is not I, but the sultan my father who makes a request which seems to me very foolish and indiscreet; it is, that you would procure a pavilion which may secure from the injuries of the weather, when he takes the field, himself, his court, and all his army, and yet so small that you may hold it in your hand. Once more let me say, that I do not make the request, but the sultan my father by means of me."

"Prince," replied Pari-Banou with a smile, "I am really sorry that such a trifle should have afforded you the least embarrassment, or have disturbed your mind as it has done, do not let this vex you any more; be assured that, so far from your being importunate, I shall always have a great pleasure in granting, through my affection for you, everything you can wish."

Having said this, the fairy ordered her female treasurer to appear. When she came, Pari-Banou said to her, "Nourgihan, bring me the largest pavilion that is in the treasury." Nourgihan went out, and almost instantly returned with a pavilion that she could hold in her hand, but which might be quite hidden if she closed it. She presented it to her mistress, who took it, and then gave it to prince Ahmed that he might examine it.

When the prince saw what the fairy called a pavilion, and the largest, as she said, that was in her treasury, he thought that she meant to joke with him, and his countenance expressed evident proofs of his surprise. Pari-Banou, who had conjectured what he thought, burst into a fit of laughter. "And do you think, my prince," she exclaimed, "that I mean to ridicule you? You shall instantly see whether that is my intention. Nourgihan," she said, addressing herself to the treasuress, and taking the pavilion at the same time from the hands of prince Ahmed, "go and erect it, that the prince may judge whether the sultan his father will find it smaller than what he wishes."

The treasuress left the palace, and went far enough to erect the pavilion, one end of which, when it was finished, reached up to the palace. As soon as it was extended, prince Ahmed found it, not indeed too small, but so large that even two armies, both as numerous as that of the sultan's could easily be covered by it. "I ask you my princess," exclaimed the prince. "a thousand pardons for my incredulity. After what I now see, I do not doubt but that you can readily execute whatever you may wish to undertake." "You think, then," replied the fairy, " that this pavilion is larger than he will ever have occasion for; but you must observe also, that it has the property either of extending or contracting itself to the exact size of what it is wanted to cover of its own accord."

The treasuress took down the pavilion, reduced it to its original form, brought it, and presented it to the prince. He immediately took it, and set out the next morning on horseback, accompanied by his usual attendants.

The sultan, who was persuaded that such a pavilion as he had demanded was an impossibility, was very much astonished at the diligence of the prince his son. He received the pavilion, and after having admired its small size, he was in the greatest surprise, from which he was certainly not relieved by seeing it erected in the great plain, and that two armies, quite as large as his own, could be very conveniently encamped under it. For fear he might regard this as superfluous, and even incommodious, prince Ahmed did not forget to inform him that its size would always be proportionate to that of his army.

The sultan, in appearance, gave his son the strongest proofs how much he was obliged to him for so magnificent a present, and to prove the great value he set upon it, he ordered it to be kept very carefully in his treasury. But in reality he felt still more jealous than when the enchantress and his flatterers first excited that hateful passion in his breast.

When the sultan had, as usual, assembled his courtiers in the evening, where prince Ahmed also was present, he addressed him in these terms: "I have already shown you, my son, how much I feel myself obliged to you for procuring the pavilion for me, which I esteem as the most valuable thing in my treasury; but you must also, from your regard for me, do another thing which will not afford me less pleasure. I understand that the fairy, your wife, has a certain water from the fountain of lions which cures all sorts, even the most dangerous, of fevers. Now, as I am well assured that my health is very dear to you, I do not suppose that you will be unwilling to request some of it and bring it to me, as a sovereign remedy that I may make use of whenever I have occasion."

When prince Ahmed returned to the fairy the next morning, he gave her a sincere and faithful account of everything that he had done, and of what had happened at the court of the sultan when he presented the pavilion, for which he acknowledged himself much obliged to her. Nor did he also omit to mention the fresh request that the sultan had charged him to make; and in conclusion, he said, " I mention this to you, my princess, because I would faithfully tell you all that passed between the sultan and myself. You, however, are mistress, either to comply with or reject it, as if I had no interest in it. I wish exactly what you do."

"No, no," replied the fairy; "I am very well pleased that the sultan of India is aware that you are not indifferent to me. I wish to satisfy him, and whatever advice the enchantress may give him —for I know very well that he attends to what she says—he shall find no deficiency either in you or me. There is great malice in what he demands, as you will be convinced of from the account I am going to give you. The fountain of lions is in the middle of the court of a large castle, the entrance to which is guarded by four very powerful and fierce lions, two of which sleep alternately, while the other two watch. But let not this alarm you; I will afford you the means of passing them without danger."

Pari-Banou was at this moment employed with her needle, and she had several balls of thread by her; she took one and gave it to the prince. " In the first place," said she, " take this ball; I will tell you presently what use you are to make of it. Secondly, order two horses to be got ready; one for you to ride, and the other for you to lead, which is to be loaded with a sheep divided into four quarters, and which you must have killed to-day. Thirdly, you must provide yourself with, or rather I will give you, a vessel to get the water in to-morrow. Early in the morning you must mount one horse and lead the other; and when you have got beyond the iron door, throw this ball of thread before you. Do you follow it there; and when it stops, as the gate will be open, you will see the four lions. Those two that are watching will awaken the others that are asleep with their roaring. Do not, however, be alarmed, but throw to each of them a quarter of the sheep, without dismounting, Having done this, lose no time, but spur your horse, and go with the utmost speed to the fountain; fill your vessel while on horseback, and return with the same celerity. The lions will be still employed in eating, and will suffer you to come out."

Prince Ahmed set out the next morning at the time the fairy had told him, and he performed every part of his expedition in the manner she had pointed out. He arrived at the gate of the castle, distributed the four quarters of the sheep to the four lions, and after passing intrepidly through without disturbing them, he came to the fountain and got the water. Having filled his vessel, he went back, and left the castle in as perfect safety as he entered. When he had got to a little distance, he turned round, and perceived two of the lions following him. Without being at all alarmed, he drew his sabre, and prepared to defend himself; but as he observed, while he kept going on, that one of them turned out of the road on one side at a little distance from him, and made signs with his head and tail, that he was not come for the purpose of doing him any injury, but only to go on before him, while the other followed behind, he put his sabre again into its sheath, and in this manner pursued his journey to the capital of India, which he entered, accompanied by the two lions, who did not leave him till he arrived at the gate of the sultan's palace. They then suffered him to enter, after which they took the same road back again by which they had come.

Many officers who presented themselves to assist the prince in dismounting accompanied him to the sultan's apartment, where he was in conversation with his favourites. Prince Ahmed then approached the throne, and setting the vessel of water at the feet of the sultan, he kissed the rich carpet that covered the footstool; and when he got up, he said, "Here, sire, is the salutary water which your majesty wished for, to put among the richest and most valuable contained in your treasury. I can only pray that your health may be so perfect that you may never have occasion to make use of it."

When prince Ahmed had finished, the sultan, who had attended to him with evident marks of pleasure, but who, nevertheless, internally felt his envy and jealousy increase instead of diminishing, got up and retired to the interior of his palace, where he waited quite alone for the enchantress, whom he had sent for.

On her arrival, she spared the sultan the trouble of mentioning the prince, or the success of his expedition, for the report of it was spread over the city, and she said that she was now prepared with the most infallible method. She informed the sultan what this method was; and the next day, in the assembly of the courtiers, the sultan declared it to prince Ahmed, who was present, in these words: "I have now, my son, but one more partition to urge, after which I will require nothing further either from you or the fairy your wife: and this is, to procure a man for me who is not more than a foot and a half high, but whose beard is thirty feet long, who carries a bar of iron on his shoulders that weighs five hundred pounds, which he makes use of as a quarter-staff, and who can speak."

The following day, when prince Ahmed returned to the subterraneous kingdom of Pari-Banou, and had acquainted her with the fresh request of the sultan his father, which he looked upon, he said, as a still more impossible thing than he had conceived the two former, he added, "I cannot possibly imagine in what part of the universe there can be a man of this kind. If, then, there be any means to extricate me with honour from this dilemma, I beg you will explain them to me."

"Do not, my prince, alarm yourself," replied the fairy: "you ran a considerable risk in procuring the water from the fountain of lions for the sultan your father, but there is no danger in discovering such a man as he requires. In fact, my brother Schaibar is just such a man, who is so far from resembling me, although we have the same father, that he is of the most violent disposition, of which nothing can prevent him from giving the most sanguinary proofs whenever his passions are excited, or he is in the least displeased or offended. Except in this one point he is the best creature in the world, and he is always ready to oblige me in whatever may be required of him. He is made exactly as the sultan has described, and he carries no other weapon than a bar of iron that weighs five hundred pounds, without which he never stirs; and this serves to make him respected. I will cause him to make his appearance, and you shall judge whether I have not spoken the truth; but, above all things, mind and prepare yourself against

being alarmed at his extraordinary figure when he presents himself." "My queen," replied prince Ahmed, "do you not say that Schaibar is your brother? However ill-made and deformed he may be, I shall be so far from being frightened at him that this circumstance alone will make me love, honour, and look upon him as one of my nearest kinsmen."

The fairy then ordered a golden vessel, in which perfumes are burned, to be brought into the vestibule of the palace, full of fire, and also a box of the same metal; both of which were immediately presented to her. She opened the box and took out a perfume that was kept there, and as she threw it upon the fire a thick and dense smoke arose.

A few moments after this ceremony, "My prince," said Pari-Banou, "my brother is come; do you not see him?" The prince looked and perceived Schaibar, who was only a foot and a half high, and who approached in a grave and sedate manner, with the iron bar of five hundred pounds' weight upon his shoulder, and his thick and well-grown beard of thirty feet long, which projected forwards, and did not touch the ground. His mustachios, which were in proportion, went quite back to his ears, and almost covered his whole face; his little pig's eyes were buried in his head, which was of enormous size, and was covered with a pointed cap: added to all which, he had a projecting hump both before and behind.

Schaibar, who, as he advanced, looked at prince Ahmed with an eye that would have chilled his very soul, demanded of Pari-Banou, as he first addressed her, who that man was. "Brother," she replied, "he is my husband; his name is Ahmed, and he is son to the sultan of India. The reason that I did not invite you to my nuptials was, that I was unwilling to take you off from the expedition in which you were then engaged, and from which I have learned, with the greatest pleasure, that you are returned victorious: and it is on his account that I have now taken the liberty of sending for you."

On hearing this speech, Schaibar cast a most gracious look on prince Ahmed, which, however, did not in the least lessen his savage and haughty appearance. "Sister," he said, "is there anything in which I can be of any service to him?—he has only to mention it. It is enough for me to know that he is your husband, to induce me to gratify him in anything that he may wish." "The sultan, his father," replied Pari-Banou, "has expressed himself curious to see you; I beg you will have the goodness to let him be your conductor." "He has only to precede," added Schaibar; "I am ready to follow him." "It is too late, brother," said Pari-Banou, "to begin the journey to-day; you had better, therefore, wait till to-morrow morning. In the meantime, as it is but proper that you should be informed of what has passed between the sultan of India and prince Ahmed since our marriage, I will give you an account of everything this evening."

The next morning Schaibar began his journey very early, accompanied by prince Ahmed, who was to present him to the sultan. They arrived at the capital, and Schaibar had no sooner appeared at the gate than all who saw him were seized with fright at the appearance of so hideous a figure, and ran and hid themselves in their shops or houses, the doors of which they instantly shut; others took to flight, and communicated the same alarm to those they met, who instantly turned back, without once looking behind them. In this manner, as Schaibar and prince Ahmed advanced in a regular pace, they found the greatest solitude in all the streets and public places through which they passed in their way to the palace. When they arrived there, the porters, instead of trying, at least, to prevent Schaibar from going in, endeavoured to save themselves on all sides, and left the entrance quite free. The prince and Schaibar, therefore, advanced without the least obstruction to the council hall, where the sultan was seated upon his throne giving audience; and as all the officers and attendants had abandoned their posts as soon as Schaibar made his appearance, they entered without the least hindrance.

Schaibar, with his head erect, haughtily approached the throne, and without waiting for prince Ahmed to present him thus addressed the sultan: "Thou hast demanded my presence; see, here I am. What dost thou want with me?"

The sultan, however, instead of answering, put his hands before his eyes, and turned them away, in order to avoid the sight of so dreadful an object. Schaibar was enraged at this uncivil and offensive reception, after he had taken the trouble of coming. He lifted up, therefore, his bar of iron, and exclaiming, "Wilt thou not speak?" let it fall directly on his head, and crushed him to the earth. He did this before prince Ahmed had the power of requesting his patience. It was now as much as he was able to do to prevent him from destroying the grand vizier, who was close to the sultan's right hand; and he prevailed upon him only by representing that the advice he always gave the sultan his father was very equitable and excellent. "Where then are they," exclaimed Schaibar, "who have given him such execrable advice?" And saying this, he destroyed all the other viziers, who were on both sides of the throne, and all the favourites and parasites of the sultan, who were the enemies of prince Ahmed: in short, death followed every blow, and none escaped except those whose fear was so powerful as to fix them to the very spot, and thus prevent them from saving their lives by flight.

Having completed this dreadful execution, Schaibar left the hall of audience, and went into the middle of the court, with the bar of iron on his shoulder. "I know there is," he cried, looking at the grand vizier, who accompanied prince Ahmed, to whom he owed his life, "a certain enchantress, who is even more an enemy to the prince my brother-in-law than these infamous favourites whom I have punished: let her be brought before me." The grand vizier immediately sent for her, and had her conducted there, when Schaibar, as he crushed her with his bar of iron, said, "Learn the consequence of giving wicked advice, and pretending sickness." The enchantress was instantly annihilated on the spot.

"This is not sufficient," exclaimed Schaibar; "I will destroy the whole city, if prince Ahmed, my brother-in-law, is not instantly acknowledged sultan of India." All those who were present, and who heard the determination, immediately the air resound with "Long live sultan Ahmed and in a short time the whole city echoed with same sound. Schaibar next made the prince clothed in the robes of the sultan, and had him stantly installed; and after having himself him homage, and taken an oath of fideli allegiance, he went for his sister Pari-Ban ducted her to the city in great pomp, and   d her to be acknowledged sultana.

With respect to prince Ali and the pr   ss Nouronnihar, as they had taken no part   the conspiracy against prince Ahmed, and, inde   , as they were even ignorant of its existence, prince Ahmed gave them a very considerable province, with its capital, for their establishment, where they went and passed the remainder of their days. He sent also an officer to prince Houssain, his eldest brother, to announce the change that had taken place, and offered him the claim of any province in his kingdom in full sovereignty; but this prince was so happy in his retirement that he requested the officer to return his sincerest thanks to the sultan for his good and kind intentions, to assure him of his entire submission to his interests, and to say that the only favour that he requested was to be permitted to pass the remainder of his life in the retreat he had chosen.